MY TOTALLY ELFED CHRISTMAS

AUDREY FURNAS

I dedicate this one to my mama.
She spoiled me with endless holiday spirit
at a very young age.
She also helped me plot this book.
And she thinks I'm amazing
despite any evidence to the contrary.

Love you, Mom.

ONE

W hen I find my way home, my stepbrother better be prepared to get stuffed inside the turkey. I mean, I love Drew, but this? *Not acceptable.* I close my laptop—on which he just texted me a slap in the face—and slip it into my bag. I check for an exit, but I'm sandwiched. At least ten of my classmates are blocking me in on either side.

Since I'm not about to stand up and call attention to myself in the middle of this four-hundred-person lecture, I'm stuck for the next twenty minutes.

A row ahead, Charlie Drake's douchey face snags my eye. The only thing helping me handle his proximity is the promise of homemade pie, which is now in jeopardy. Douche Face smirks as he reaches his arm over the shoulders of a blond in a tight blouse. His fingers graze her bare neck. A shudder reaches the depths of my spine.

I put my head down. Guys were supposed to make college more fun, not ruin it.

Ten a.m. creeps closer and closer.

"For anyone who needs extra help on the Krebs cycle," says Professor Armstrong, "I'll be holding a study group this evening. Bring your questions and a notepad. This will be a thorough review of most of the material I plan to include on the final exam."

My professor looks at her watch for about the fifteenth time this lecture. We can both taste freedom.

I take hold of my belongings.

"For those of you I don't see tonight, enjoy the break. Class dismissed." She slips her materials into her bag and hurries toward the auditorium's front exit.

Storming the student exit, I beat her to the quad, but not to speak to her. I *should* speak to her. I'm not exactly acing this course. The most I could tell you about the Krebs cycle is that it has something to do with exercise. Dentists don't really need to know about exercise-related biologic processes. Right?

Anyway, I've got bigger concerns, namely figuring out a way home for Thanksgiving now that my stepbrother has bailed on me. Before Avery University took over my life, I had a family that needed me around. They'd be devastated if I missed any of our holiday traditions. I'm talking pre- through post-Thanksgiving Day merriment. We Italians like to drag things out. I have to get there before all the fun.

Who could I ask for a ride?

Think, Adia.

Other than Douche Face, I know about five people on campus, and most of them aren't from Greensboro. How can I find someone who is? Would a hitchhiking sign be weird?

Having some friends would be super handy right about now.

I run through the list of people from my high school who I know go to this college. Doesn't Molly's older brother? I shoot her a text requesting his number. She doesn't reply right away, probably because she's in class. Dang.

There's always Gil.

I don't want to ask Gil. He's so awkward.

I better get to linguistics, my final class before break. It's a seminar with only thirty or so students, and the professor takes attendance very seriously. All along the quad, maple trees burst with marigold and ginger leaves. This campus is beautiful in late fall, I'll give it that. It showcases most of the vibrant foliage North Carolina has to offer.

The orange hues make me want pumpkin bread. Or, at least,

pumpkin something. As I approach the student union, I slow my march. Do I have time to stop for a hot beverage?

My phone clock discourages it. No worries. Mom will have plenty of goodies prepared.

I can't wait to see her. We've never been apart this long, and phone calls just aren't the same. I want to watch her eyes squint while she talks and hear the rustle of her busywork in the background of my day. I want to do things alongside her where we don't even bother talking but just exist together as part of the same fabric. I want to be where I belong.

"Are you going to that study group?" Heather McCoy says loudly from behind me.

My feet falter. I met Heather the first day of chem class. She's striking and athletic and gritty and, in summary, amazing. I usually let her leave class first to avoid that awkward encounter where we pretend she doesn't know me.

"Oh, sorry," I say. "I'm headed home to see my family."

She wrinkles her brow, looking past me.

I turn, tracking her bemused gaze.

Oh. Her pal walks around my other side and says to Heather, "Definitely. Let's meet at my place and walk together."

"My bad," I laugh. "I thought you were talking to…"

They're not paying attention to me anymore.

I don't get it. I never struggled to bond with people back home, but here on campus, it's been different. I don't fit. This newfound freedom doesn't feel like the opportunity it was sold as. It feels like ripping off a thousand band-aids all at once.

Maybe I *should* get coffee. I swivel on my heel and hurry away.

Waiting for my order, I dial Mom. I know she had plans this afternoon, but I'm in a bind here.

Voicemail. Typical.

I dial Jemma.

"Hey, chicklet," she answers in her perpetually chipper accent.

"Tell me you changed your mind about coming home."

"It's too expensive to fly from California for a long weekend."

"I will sell my body to buy you the ticket, okay? Just come."

"It's not about the money. It's the practicality..."

Cradling my phone with my shoulder, I grab my to-go cup. My fingers savor its warmth. Armed with liquid pleasure, I return to my best friend making excuses not to see me.

"...waste like four hundred dollars traveling like a crazy person back and forth, or I could stay here, which a bunch of my friends are doing, and use the extra time to study. I've got, like, so much to do."

I whine. Thanksgiving will be less sweet without her around for all our little rituals. Who will talk me down from my fifth set of door-buster Christmas pj's?

"Who do we know at Avery that went to our high school?"

"Bad-breath Gil does."

"Besides him."

"Um, Molly's older brother Jordan goes there, I think. Why?"

"Drew backed out on picking me up because he's staying at Clemson until tonight so he can bring *Claudia*, his new girlfriend, home to meet us. She's got a Pilates class she can't miss, apparently."

"Drew's bringing a girl home?"

"Crazy, right?"

"Totally."

"Well," I sigh, "I guess I need to let you go so I can arrange a ride with Gil."

"Seriously? You must be desperate to go home."

"We'll be in a car, so there's built-in personal space."

"Yeah, and a limited amount of circulating air."

I stop walking at the top of the steps to Parley Hall. "Unlike some of us, I'm willing to make sacrifices to see my loved ones."

"I have FaceTime. Plus, you know Thanksgiving's not a big deal for us anyway."

"Fine. I just hate you."

"I know. Talk to you tomorrow, okay?"

"Yeah, okay."

I miss her face so much.

∾

My phone vibrates in my pocket.

I know the linguistics professor's rules, but in this one instance, I must break them. We're talking about family time here. I shift in my desk and slide the edge of the screen into view to skim the notification.

Gil Stoddemeyer: No problem. I'm leaving at noon from my dorm, which is Henson. Can you meet me there?

Class ends at 11:30. I can make this work if I pack quick.

Which means I can no longer avoid my roommate Adrienne's yoga party. Or her friends' way of making me feel like a fourth wheel in my own living space.

How essential are toiletries?

Professor Frume is still writing on the whiteboard. I unleash my phone entirely. I'm about to type a response when a text from Mom pops up. A ghost freak-out face. I send her the good news that I no longer need a ride. She starts to text a response. I look back up and quickly conceal my phone under a notebook as my professor turns toward the classroom. The vibration from Mom's reply makes a faint buzz against the plastic desktop.

Professor Frume's eyes darken.

I pull my hand back out into the open, but he isn't fooled. He marches over to me. "Miss Bell, was that a device I just heard?"

I suck in a large breath and nod. *Don't take my phone. Don't take my phone.*

"And what is our class policy about disruptive cell phones during lecture?"

"They are to be removed from class," I recite.

"May I have the device, Miss Bell?"

He thrusts his old wrinkly palm into my face. I droop.

"The phone, Miss Bell."

"Okay, can I just…" I pull out the offending object and tap on the text from Mom. All I get is some sort of address before he snatches it. I wonder what she has planned!

"Take this to the administration office," Professor Frume says to the teaching assistant. "Miss Bell can retrieve it on her own time."

He swings back around and resumes his discussion of indigenous speech patterns. The TA disappears with my lifeline.

I nurse my pumpkin latte, plotting how I'm going to recover my phone, get back to my dorm to pack, and reach Gil before he leaves me behind. One stress gulp goes down the wrong pipe. I hawk it up.

A neighboring classmate glares. Poor me.

I don't even know where the administration office is located.

"It's on the other side of Bezley Hall," my classmate says as we walk out of the language arts building. The sun shines brighter now that I'm done with lectures for the long weekend. The air is easier to breathe.

"Where is that exactly?"

She points to North Campus.

Nuts.

First of all, I have never heard of Bezley Hall. Secondly, that is the exact wrong direction I need to be going. So...?

I go without a phone for a few days.

That won't be so bad, right?

As long as I make it to the getaway car in time, I won't need a phone. I'll be too immersed in family activities to care about the outside world.

I turn toward South Campus and sprint. Okay, it's more of a trot. Boots are heavy.

TWO

Gil turns into Meadowdale, my long-lost neighborhood, and I start bouncing. Bring on the good cheer. Bring on the relaxation. Bring on the triangular slices of happiness. At least, I assume pie's where we'll start.

But I'd also be fine with a pastry.

The car stops in front of our house.

"So, Adia..."

Gil sucks in a sizable breath. Before he can release it, I jump out and turn for my bags. It's not that I have zero desire to continue our chitchat. I really miss my mom.

"Do you need a ride back on Sunday?"

I hope not. "Can I text you, er—email you about that? I'm not sure what my family's plans are just yet."

"Sure. Yeah. Just let me know before Sunday. I like to plan out my schedule the night before."

"Cool, cool. Thanks for bringing me home. Enjoy your Thanksgiving."

"I hope you get to eat a lot of gravy. It's the best."

"Um...thanks? Bye."

I wave him away for fear he might watch me walk all the way into my house, or something just as weird.

Once his taillights disappear, I spin around triumphantly. I made it!

My smile dies as I inspect home base. The grass reaches above my ankles and is mostly composed of weeds. Also, the grown-ups must have forgotten to let out the greeting committee, because I receive zero wet kisses on the lawn.

One sad pumpkin hails me up the entryway steps. It's all crooked and dirty, like it was too burdened to be a pumpkin today. Where are Mom's adorable painted gourds and her fall wreath? She has little excuse for the lackluster entryway, considering she's been out of work for almost three months now.

This tragedy must be remedied ASAP. The pumpkin comes with me into the house. I inhale deeply to determine the exact brand of baked love Mom intends to shower upon me, and I get...

Fish?

Dear lord, tell me she's not dieting.

"Mom, we're going to need to talk about your lack of preparation for the holiday while we're taking our power walk."

No one responds, not even Wizard, who normally would have knocked me down by now and turned my face into a puddle.

Upon taking one step down the hallway, I hear the most terrifying sound known to man.

A meow.

A full-grown cat's menacing green eyes narrow in on me. *Stay calm.* Maybe this feline isn't filled with darkness and spite. I take one step toward the living room.

That's a fang. *Retreat!*

I wall myself off upstairs in my parents' bedroom. At least I think it's their bedroom. The furniture and bedding are new.

And poorly chosen. Mom must be in a phase.

"Why on earth would you get a cat? You know I can't live with a cat!" I say.

"Madelyn?" The reply comes from an unrecognizable male voice in the master bathroom. Something that's buzzing clicks off.

Who's Madelyn?

"Mom?" My voice is the highest octave it can go. First a cat. Now a secret liaison. Do I need to get weapons involved here?

The mystery man leans out of the bathroom. His light brown hair is thinning, which he might be trying to make up for with the patch growing under his lower lip. Besides a towel, his only covering is shaving cream smeared all over his chest. In the middle of the cream are two baby-bottom smooth lines running from sternum to waist, right through a set of baggy pecs. The shave lines look like suspenders, skin-spenders. Couple the chest with the white stickers over his nose and under his eyes, and he looks like a sunscreen experiment gone wrong.

"Hey, man," he drawls. "What's the deal here?"

This guy is the complete opposite of my stepdad, Cal, who is bulky and tan and *not* into primping. "What are you doing in my mom's bedroom?"

"What are *you* doing in *my* bedroom, and who's your mom?" He pulls the towel tighter around his waist.

My eyes move from his fleshy body to the bed, and that's when it hits me. I'm enclosed in the room of a mostly naked male stranger, a *strange* male stranger.

"I think…"

I don't know what to think. I think I'm losing my mind, so I can't be trusted to think.

"I…"

The creep's tongue emerges from his mouth. My pumpkin flies toward his head. He shrieks and bats it away. It busts on the edge of a TV stand, and pumpkin guts glop down the side.

"Hey!" His eyes turn fierce—as fierce as eyes with Bioré strips beneath them can be.

"You've got something on your face!" I yell and run from the room. I'm doing more running today than I'm used to.

"What the hell! Get back here!"

A hiss on the stairs brings me to a halt. My cat friend drags its paw across the wood. Judging by its impenetrable stare, I'm almost positive it wants to dig its claws into my throat. *Nice kitty.* I move to the opposite side of the steps. The pet moves with me. Skin-spenders flies into the hall with a second towel twisted up in his hands. Is that meant for me?

I look between my two opponents. Who do I have the best shot against?

The banister creaks at my back. Hold on a minute. I may be living in some sort of alternate reality here, but this is, or used to be, my turf. I know my way around. My hands grip the railing, and I swing my legs over it. I'm quite high up, but this jump is the best option I've got. The landing jars my pelvis. It's well worth the advantage. I bound toward the front door and slam it in the cat-monster's face.

On the far side of the Reagans' house, I take a moment, huffing and puffing into my knees. I'm about to reach for my phone when I remember it's far, far away.

Just perfect.

The Reagans aren't likely to be home since their carport is empty. I double-check with a knock, to no avail.

I cruise toward the playground since I don't feel like explaining this to any of my other neighbors. How would that go down? *What's that? Sure! I'm totally good. Totally sane. Also, do you know if I still live in this neighborhood?*

I wish I had a car right about now. And didn't dread driving.

In the distance, a middle-school-aged kid is walking her dog. *Please have a phone.*

"Here you go," she says, passing me a brand-new iPhone.

I dial Mom.

Voicemail.

I fire off a text.

555-0043: It's Adia. PICK UP YOUR PHONE

Waiting for a response, I roll through the possible explanations in my head. *I'm dreaming....* Except I don't usually feel the windy chill of fall in my dreams. So...

My mom and stepdad have redecorated and taken in a bum? But that doesn't explain what he was doing in their bedroom.

The phone rings and I move a few paces away from my audience before taking the call. "Mom! What the heck!?"

"What's going on, hun?" she asks softly.

Oh, no you don't. This is not going to be a gentle exchange. "Um, the saggy soft-rock wannabe living in our house, for starters."

"Honey, where are you?"

"At home. Or at least I was, until I got scared off by the cat and the stranger."

She squeaks.

"Did we move? There's no way, right? I know I would have gotten a phone call to relay such life-altering news."

"Well, it happened so fast...."

I have no words. Zero.

"We're still getting everything worked out. It's only temporary, until I find a new job."

"You're serious. This is *for real?*"

Mom mumbles incoherently.

I plop down onto the curb. "Oh, my god."

"I'm sorry, honey. I did send you a text with our new address."

"I thought that was the address of a restaurant or something!"

"Why would I tell you we're living at a restaurant?"

"I didn't read the whole thing. Jeez, Mom. This is insane! I just walked in on an old man shaving his chest. But he wasn't, like, old, old. He was creepy, middle-aged, I-should-not-have-been-in-his-bedroom old. You should've called."

"Oh, dear! I'm so sorry. Leave the house. I'm on my way to get you."

"I'm not still there! I'm not crazy, unlike some people, who leave their daughters at the mercy of sexual deviants. I'll be on the swings, remembering a time when my life was acceptable."

"See you in ten."

In typical Samantha Bell fashion, she shows up in thirty-three.

Mom passes me a bag of pastries when I climb into the car.

"Hey, baby girl," she says, reaching for my cheek.

"Hey." I'm still upset. I sniff the apple fritters. They aren't home-made, but they are my favorite ones from Fresh Market, at least.

She wraps her hand around mine. "I know this is a lot. I am so sorry about the mix-up."

I shrug, watching my neighborhood disappear.

"You ready to see our fancy new place?"

I assume her forced smile isn't any easier than mine.

Mom looks different. I can't put my finger on how, but she does. "Have you changed your hairstyle?"

"A friend of mine put a few highlights in it."

Since when does she have friends? Did her and Mrs. Karen upgrade their neighborly relationship after I left? "You mean the orangish lines?" I see some subtle streaks.

"Adia." She swats at me.

"I like your hair chocolatey dark. It's our color."

"I was just having some fun. It won't last, since it's from a box. How's school?"

"Great." Far away. I roll my eyes and look out the window.

We pull into a round parking lot. This isn't the array of charming yards I'm used to from Meadowdale, but it does have a terrace filled with wooden reindeer. They're cute, I'll give 'em that.

The apartments are accessible from outside walkways. A few residents have taken the time to personalize their stoops, but most remain blah.

"We're on floor three," Mom says. "Makes for great exercise."

I get plenty of exercise traversing campus, so this is not a win.

On floor two, we cross paths with a delivery boy. He doesn't see us; he's too busy paying attention to whatever's playing in his earbuds. A long package sways atop each of his shoulders. No way he'll get either one on a doorstep without breaking something. He's going to need help.

I keep an eye on him.

He strides along the walkway with his head down. He's medium height, probably half a head taller than me, but slim, like he doesn't know the beauty of a home-cooked meal. The bomber jacket layered over his brown tee is worn-out and totally unsuitable for this cold weather. Should I go find him a coat? With how outdated his clothes are, I can't help but wonder if he's trying to look oblivious, or if he's some sort of stray.

He stops in front of his destination and squats, tipping his shoulder so that one package rolls smoothly down into his elbow. Using his forearm to set it on the doormat, he frees himself up to ease the other package down damage-free too. Okay, UPS.

He pops back up to his feet—with pure thigh power—and holsters his scanner. He's swift. Before I can play it cool, he spots me. His eyes narrow.

I jump behind the stairway enclosure and catch up to my mom.

She leads me halfway down the third floor to one of the nondescript doorways. The UPS truck is visible from our balcony.

"Things are a tad cramped in here, but we don't plan to stay long." Mom wiggles the key into the doorknob.

"When did all this happen?"

"About three weeks ago. One of the neighbors knew of a guy looking to buy in Meadowdale, so we jumped on it."

I bite my tongue and watch UPS. He opens up the back of his truck to remove more packages, stacking five in his arms. It must be a pain to deliver packages in an apartment building, all that back-and-forth. With how rampant online shopping is now, he'll probably be gracing the halls of this complex every day.

He doesn't seem bothered by the work, though. Just focused, like a delivery robot.

Maybe the earbuds help. He's probably lost in...well, I can't even guess what he listens to while he works. Heavy metal?

A white Mustang pulls into the lot. The moment UPS sees it, he ducks behind the side of the truck.

This move is less robotic.

He peeks over to where the car parks and doesn't move until a slinky young strawberry blonde with at least one tattoo, which is displayed along the entirety of her forearm, emerges from the car. She looks much cooler than I'll ever be, one of those magnetic types who usually draws an entourage.

Do they have a history?

Once she disappears to the other side of the building, he does too, without delivering any of the other packages.

The classic hide-and-flee move.

Been there.

Maybe apartment living will be more interesting than I first suspected.

THREE

I find Mom in a cramped bedroom.

"This one's yours. And Claudia's, while she's here with Drew. Make yourself at home."

So now there's no place in my life where I can avoid sharing a room with a stranger?

I drop my bags on the desk crammed between the wall and the rickety old bunkbed I last saw when I was eight. "Where are all my things? Mr. Boo?"

"Mr. Boo's in that drawer." She points to the dresser. "The rest is packed away in storage."

I pull my stuffed bunny out and hug it to my chest. "You didn't give away any of my stuff, right?"

"Certainly not. I know how you are." She swats my butt.

I do a three-hundred-and-sixty-degree scan of our new home, and the visual insult of all the clutter overwhelms my senses. "Are there greenways around here? I need some fresh air."

"We're surrounded by busy roads, I'm afraid."

"How will we do our pre-prep power walk?"

"About that..." She drops her eyes.

It's her makeup. That's what's different. Clumps of mascara dot her lashes, and wide black lines are penciled across her lids. When was the last time she washed a layer off?

"I think Thanksgiving is going to look a little different this year."

"Different how?"

"Less people. Less food. I've actually signed us up for a charity event with my new church."

"By 'new church,' do you mean the one you visited once, like, two months ago?"

"Yes. I've been attending regularly, with my friend Linda and some other ladies. You'll love them. We're organizing a big event tomorrow at the homeless shelter."

"On Thanksgiving? What time?"

"Lunchtime. We'll still have plenty of time for a nice meal together afterwards, just a little simpler maybe."

"But we normally cook all day. How will we make stuffing? And what about having Auntie Kay's family and Papa over for pre-dinner football and snacking? If you're gone half the day, we can't do any of our normal stuff."

"We don't have much space for a big gathering. Plus, Drew's bringing Claudia to the shelter to help."

I slump against the desk.

"Why don't you come?" she says. "My friends would love to meet you."

Honest answer? Old people intimidate me a little bit. I know not all homeless people are old, but they seem that way. Like, aged by the stress of their lives. And what do you say to someone like that? I feel so guilty just thinking about what they're dealing with. I have no idea how I'd face one in person knowing I'm not doing anything to help.

Maybe I can make an extra-large canned food donation at Meadowdale's Light It Up party this year—if they'll let us come now that we're no longer members of the neighborhood.

"I dunno, Mom. I'll probably stay here and cook. Did you at least get the stuff to make charlotte and pie? We might as well cancel the whole holiday without that."

She looks beyond the bedroom door to the messy kitchen and

blows out a breath. "All right, hun. We can run out and get the stuff to make dessert."

"Great." I jump up and clap, which would normally rile up our dog. "Hey, where's Wizard?"

"Oh, honey." Mom squeezes my hand.

My eyes grasp for answers.

She shakes her head.

"The dog's gone too? I need to lie down." I have to take off three packing boxes, a tool bag, some towels, and a half-eaten Pop-Tart before I can collapse onto the dumpy mattress of the bottom bunk.

"Adia." My mom squeezes my leg.

"Maybe don't talk to me for a few hours."

A little retail therapy puts me in a better mood. I sweep several kitchen gadgets and some mail aside and set our shopping bags down. Unpacking groceries makes me feel normal. While pulling out ingredients, I almost forget that I'll never glimpse our fireplace from the kitchen doorway again. Or sit in Mom's bay window and talk about my day.

I place the final item, heavy whipping cream, beside the rest. "Let's get cooking."

Mom pats the edge of the counter.

I ponder this odd movement for a moment. "Mom?"

"Hmm?" She looks up and pastes on a smile. "Let's cook."

I extract the necessary tools from various drawers and cabinets while my mom gathers the remaining ingredients from the pantry.

I get a comfortable lean going on the counter. We're going to be here awhile, which is half the fun of charlotte. The slow monotony of the process lends itself beautifully to reflection and conversation.

We run through the usual family updates while we stir. Aunt Stella and her partner, Opal, bought a ranch about thirty minutes outside of town. My nonna has started a diet regimen for prediabetes. Aunt Tina just got a promotion, but she wants Uncle Lou to stay home and educate their two boys; she's worried about school violence.

"Elementary school's harmless. What we need is homeschool for higher education," I say. "Those suckers can be brutal."

The further we get into our creation the more relaxed my mom's posture becomes.

We introduce the vanilla and egg yolks into the bowl of warm sugar goo.

"Tell me more about school," Mom says.

"It's fine, I guess. Hard."

"Do you have any inspirational professors?"

"My professors are all interesting in their own ways, but I'm not going to be following any of them on social media." I change from a spatula to a whisk and resume the stirring. "Actually, we had this one guest lecturer when my public speaking professor had to miss, and she was incredible. She said all this stuff about human nature and finding your voice. It really made me think about what I'm putting out into the world, like online and stuff. I've never really thought about that before."

"What does she do when she's not guest lecturing?"

"She's a PR professor in the business school."

"You should take one of her classes."

"I doubt I'll have time for all that."

"College doesn't have to be all about work, you know. It can be a little about fun. Discovering new things."

"Not when you're predental. There's no room for personal interests."

I set my beaters into a bowl containing room temperature egg whites and fire up the motor. Our conversation halts with the noise. Mom places the custard base on the counter to cool and starts on dish duty. The smell of powdered sugar mingles with the scent of vanilla bean. I close my eyes and soak in all the memories this familiar smell evokes. I'm in my nonna's kitchen, standing on a stool, Mom's hand guiding mine over the beaters. This is everything to me. This is life.

The eggs stiffen into fluffy white mountains. I slip them into the custard and gently fold the two mixtures together. The charlotte turns airy and soft. Tomorrow we will have a vanilla mousse to complement our pies.

"When's Cal getting back in town?" I ask.

Mom's shoulders droop. "He had to go deal with an issue up in Montana last minute, but he's hoping to get on the road tonight to be here by tomorrow morning. He has to turn around and go right back to the site this weekend, though."

"They don't have any machinist work closer?"

"He's had to do some overtime lately to help us get by, so he's taken some of the reject machine repairs. It means more travel and farther away."

"Oh, dang. How often is he gone?"

"About every other week." She frowns at my frown. "It's not that bad."

Being apart half the month? It's not that good either.

I scoot the finished topping toward her. "Do we have a glass container to put this in?"

She pulls open a cabinet and searches. Her arms drop, resting against the counter for a moment. Then she opens another cabinet. She looks tired. Worn. The Cal situation and the job loss must be weighing on her more than she's admitting. Poor Mom.

"Can I help?" I ask, opening another cabinet.

"Here's one." She starts to pull it out, but it clatters against the shelf. She huffs. "It's right there, Adia. I need to lie down. My head is splitting."

After sealing the charlotte up airtight, I stick it in the fridge.

Then I move on to pie. I dig around for the dishes.

"Did we leave the pie plates in storage?" I yell to Mom.

No response.

I search some more until I'm convinced they're not here.

I'm sorry, but we have to have pie.

Amazon to the rescue. I order two dishes with next-day delivery. Enjoying homemade pie together will be worth the extra shipping fee. Mom needs the pick-me-up.

I look around this empty, unfamiliar apartment, unsure what to do next. Homework?

I grab my book bag and squeeze into the table between the couch and china cabinet, quickly overwhelming the surface with my books and laptop. The brightness of the screen glares at me.

Drew bursts through the front door with an armful of bags. Thank god.

A thin, graceful-looking girl walks in behind him. Her hair is silky and almost black. I immediately want her bronzy-brown skin and her gorgeous almond-shaped eyes. Go, stepbro.

She smiles and greets me in a delicate voice.

Drew beams from beside her. His face looks much thinner and smoother than the last time I saw him. In fact, he's cut. Has everyone changed in the three months since I left?

"It seems we're going to be getting cozy," he says, looking around the new digs.

"Did you know Mom gave Wizard away?"

"Yeah, I heard. It makes sense. The boy loves to run."

"He also loves *me*, and I didn't even get to say goodbye."

"Poor sis. Do you need a hug?" He tackles me to the floor and holds me down for a noogie. I scream for mercy, kicking and flailing. My already wild hair kinks around my face. Drew's way more built than I remember.

"Don't think you're getting away with bailing on me today," I say from my pinned position. He tickles more giggles out of me. "No fair! I'm mad. Claudia, what kind of dirt do you want on my brother? I will tell you anything."

I spend the rest of the evening getting to know the perfection that is Claudia. Mom never comes back out of her room, but it's fine. Tomorrow promises great things for us Bells.

FOUR

I wake up to the sound of persistent slurping. The top bunk jostles above me, and a beefy man foot is hanging off one side. *Not cool, Drew.* I've been ousted from my childhood bedroom and thrown into a hostage situation.

Should I blow my cover or wait this out?

Please don't hear me.

My hand stretches toward its target, my computer. My body teeters over the edge of the bunk as my fingers nudge the distraction closer. Just another inch.

But that inch shifts me beyond the tipping point. At the thunk of my drowsy carcass against the laminate floor, Claudia squeaks.

"Your sister's awake," she whispers.

"Good morning," I say. Might as well roll with it.

Claudia squeaks again and the bed shakes. This is no better than dorm life.

"I'll give you two a minute."

I take my computer into the bathroom and pop a squat.

Three messages await. Jemma's text is a twerking turkey meme, which draws a chuckle out of me. Then a whimper. I could really use her shoulder right about now.

The remaining two messages are from my other high school besties, Hailey and Viv. Hailey's text says she can't join our annual Black Friday shopping adventure because her family's driving to Asheville. Viv says she can't make it because of a boy.

Those tramps.

Zero homemade baked goods await me in the kitchen. Luckily, the Fresh Market apple fritters come back to life with a quick nuke. I take my plate and perch myself by the front window to see what kind of activity is going on beyond these walls. The parking lot is idle.

Bored of watching nothing, I grab my computer to check email. It's weird and kind of exciting to see all the bolded, unread notes. I guess that's what happens when you only check your inbox once a day.

The first message says my pie plates are in transit. *UPS saves the day!* School wants to bother me in several other emails, which can wait until Sunday. I land on a Black Friday ad and transform into a bargain huntress.

Now that I'm a shopping-deprived college student, I'm itching to be set loose on some stores. I form a five-part plan: Target, Best Buy, Belk, Old Navy, Bath & Body Works. I make my gift list. Then I make my "other people" gift list. Since my friends all flaked, Mom can join me for shopping. It'll be better this way. She has more buying power.

I do a quick scroll of Instagram and then stretch and check the clock.

Eight forty-five. Macy's Thanksgiving Day Parade time!

I throw some water on my face and enter the living room. With remote in hand, I plop down on a recliner. "Parade's on!"

Not a single person responds. Stinkers.

By ten thirty, I lose patience and start knocking on doors.

"Get your butts up. I need some help with food before y'all go to that charity headache."

My stepdad pokes his head out. "Welcome home, baby."

I squinch my face at him.

"I'm grabbing a quick shower, and then I'll be out. Your mom told me to tell you she's ordered stuff for the meal today, so we don't have to cook anything."

"Doesn't that kind of defeat the purpose of the occasion?"

"Uh, nope. As long as there's food on the table, I think we've met the minimum criteria."

The two lovebirds pass through the hall, still tangled together. Zero embarrassment registers on their faces. There isn't room for it between longing gazes. I follow them into the kitchen.

"We need a plan of attack. What time are people getting here?"

"People?" my brother replies.

"Papa. Auntie Kay's gang. Anyone we associate with on a regular basis."

"Why would they be coming?"

"Because it's Thanksgiving!" Has everyone forgotten how this day works?

"We have a space issue. Remember?"

"Excuses." I point to the love seat, recliner, and two couches filling out the living room. "We've got like a thousand cushions jammed into this place. Call our people."

"I don't think Sammy wants to invite anyone. Besides, with my charming personality, do we even need others?" He bats his eyes.

Only Claudia falls for it.

"Just five people to feed? Don't you care that Claudia isn't going to experience the true Bell tradition?"

He dodges as I charge past him.

"Mom!"

I bust into her room. She dips her mascara brush down so she can see me.

"Did you make plans with any family for today?"

She groans.

"Why not? It's Thanksgiving! If you don't spend it with family, what's the point?"

"Can you keep it down, Adia? There are other people around here."

"I need your help in the kitchen, and you're in here primping?"

"There is nothing we need to do. Harris Teeter has us covered, honey."

"Yeah. I heard. Did you ever think about the fact that maybe I like the cooking part more than the eating part?"

"Adia, I'm going to remind you again, this is temporary. How about, instead of fussing, you try something new? Come with us to the soup kitchen."

I grunt. "Can we at least make ginger beer before you go?"

She turns back to the mirror. "Go look for the bottles. I'll be out in a minute."

No luck on the bottles. Go figure. I expedite another Amazon order so we have a chance to fit in this tradition before I return to school.

Half an hour later, a peppy knock on the front door lures my mom from her room.

"Sausage meatballs for the Banquet O' Plenty coming at you," a middle-aged woman sings. She has caramel-colored hair curled just to the top of a bulky sweater. Her white teeth are framed by very red lips. She looks like one of those wind-up toys they sell at Cracker Barrel.

"Smells amazing, Linda," says Mom. "What'd you put in there?"

"It's my special recipe, adapted from years of trial and error. My boys are tough critics. The secret is rosemary and extra sharp, top-of-the-line cheddar cheese."

"These are definitely going to be a hit. Come meet my daughter, if you've got a minute. Adia, this is my good friend Linda."

I brace for impact as two arms come for me.

"I've heard so much about you." Linda feels the need to rub my back. "Your mother tells me you're in your first year at Avery University. And you want to be a dentist?"

I nod. I want a dreamy career where I can do something noble and make good money but still have time for my family. Dentist fits the bill.

"What fun. How are you liking college?"

"I really like the breaks."

"I bet you do. You get to come visit this lovely lady."

Oh, please. They can't like each other that much. They've only been friends for like two minutes.

"You guys ready?" Mom asks the room.

Linda scurries off with all of my family members.

I collapse onto a barstool to sulk. What a Thanksgiving. I'm spending it alone, not cooking. I might as well have stayed at my dorm.

I tear a strip of cardboard off a box. *To take a nap.* And another. *To take a nap not...*

At the sound of a truck engine outside, I jump up and spot UPS.

"My package!" I cry. To no one.

I sprint out to the landing to check. Sure enough, headed up a flight of stairs is the delivery boy. He's got on a tight hoodie today, and his mess of dark hair is covered by a beanie. He's manhandling another large box.

It doesn't look like a set of pie dishes.

He turns away from me.

I might as well make his job easier and go with him to get my stuff. I could use the fresh air and the high of a good deed. 'Tis the season.

"Hello," I say cheerily.

No response.

"Excuse me."

His earbuds must be up to an unsafe volume. I tap his shoulder.

He jumps at least a foot in the air and elbows me on his way. I crumple. He tries to catch me and only further accentuates my descent. The package crunches.

Sprawled over it, I look up to find icy eyes on me, sea-glass green eyes. Gorgeous eyes. In fact, his whole face is stunning. It's pale with dark outlines where there's hair, as if an artist carefully sketched him and only embellished the most important parts with color.

"Sorry," I squeak.

He groans and not so much helps me up as tosses me off of the cargo. "Why would you just sneak up on a stranger like that?"

"I tried talking first."

"Next time, try harder."

"Sorry." I do my best to smooth the crunched cardboard.

He examines it and mumbles something about how this is "just great."

I apologize again while he scans the bar code, then walks away at a fast clip.

"Hey, wait!" I run after him down the stairwell. "Are all UPS carriers as zippy as you?"

"Job's not done until the truck's empty."

"Maybe I can help you then. I'm expecting a package that I have reason to believe is on your truck."

"Nope."

"Um, are you arguing with GPS? Because my tracking info says it is."

"Well, I don't have any other packages for this building, and my loader never makes a mistake."

"Can you double-check for me? It's really important."

"They're all important."

We arrive at his truck. A LEGO character dangles from the rearview mirror. Other than a sudoku book and an aluminum lunch box stacked neatly on the passenger seat, the driver's cabin is spotless.

I push past him. "Mind if I take a quick look?"

He steps in front of me, finally finding the decency to face me while we talk. He goes stiff, except for his eyebrows, which disappear behind his scraggly bangs.

I muster up the biggest puppy dog eyes I can produce.

He reaches for the side of his vehicle. I think he's going to lean against it to recover whatever senses he just lost, but he swings up into the seat instead. "You're slowing me down."

"You don't understand. I need that package today!"

"This isn't open-heart surgery."

"Excuse me if my problems aren't important enough to merit your help...Miller," I say, eyeing his name tag.

He turns the key. "I'm sorry you don't have enough decency to keep from harassing the hourly laborers trying to stay sane during the holidays."

"Well, *I'm* sorry someone took your joy and turned it into a turd." With that, I twist on my foot to make my grand exit. The grunt of an engine disrupts me.

Dang it. *I'm* supposed to be the one vindicated here. I growl at the back of his vehicle. Meanie.

He's basically Santa's helper. The least he could do is smile.

I would be way better at his job.

I stomp back up the apartment stairs. Now what am I supposed to do about the pie?

FIVE

By the time the gang returns, I've addressed our crisis. A nearly round pumpkin pie graces the bottom of a Corningware dish. I slide it into the oven, next to the apple crisp with the perfect crumble topping—which I nailed on my first try. We may have to eat store-made turkey, but we will not eat store-made dessert. I'm also tackling a stuffing since we have all the ingredients. Looking up from my cutting board, I grin.

Mom pats my back and excuses herself to her bedroom.

"Smells good," Drew says.

Cal sets a brown bag full of imposter food on the counter. I assess. Mom got turkey, gravy, baked potatoes, corn, and green bean casserole. Everything besides the turkey is cold. We need to get these sides warming.

I pull the uncooked desserts out of the oven. They'll have to wait their turn.

Claudia washes her hands. "What can we do?"

I'll keep her.

While politely listening to a recap of their volunteering event, I dole out tasks and throw a stick of butter into the microwave to pour over the stuffing.

"Hey, Ads. Can we leave out the butter and other animal products? Claudia's vegan."

I will *not* keep her!

All animal products! That's basically like saying, "Can you leave out the flavor?"

"How long have you been practicing?" I ask.

She giggles. "It's not like a religion or anything. I just don't feel right about how animals are treated by the food industry. I used to spend my summers in Mexico, helping my grandpa on his cattle ranch. The steers became like family to me. I couldn't stand to see them sold for slaughter."

"So you couldn't just give up meat?"

"Dairy cows in many places experience terrible treatment. Standing all day getting milked. Infections. Poor diet."

I think over the menu. The store probably already put butter all over the sides, and my desserts are riddled with it. "This whole dinner's a vegan nightmare."

"I'm used to it. I don't need much. Potatoes are really filling. Plus, we brought this." She goes to the fridge and pulls out a big beige lump.

"Is that edible?"

She chuckles. "It is. It's a lentil tofu loaf. Basically, my version of tofurky. It's actually pretty tasty."

"That's...fun." I push it back toward her. The smell alone is ruining my appetite. "I'll let you handle getting it heated. What is Mom doing?"

"Resting?" says Drew.

"This is not a time for rest. This is a time for gathering. I need her to figure out how to make vegan stuffing taste good."

Mom graces us with her company an hour later. She looks wobbly. What was she doing in there?

I pour her a cup of coffee and decide to nix the stuffing, throwing some carrots into a saucepan as a replacement. "If you could be so kind as to set our, er, countertop," I tell her, "I would be so appreciative. When you're ready, of course."

She doesn't even attempt to give it back to me.

When the herb smells consume the kitchen, I know the time to eat is near. I steal a few minutes to snap pictures. Mom stirring gravy. Cal slicing the golden goose. Claudia with her fake meat thingy.

By six o'clock we squeeze around the kitchen island to attack our heaping plates. The famished feeling I have right now might be my favorite part of this whole day. I earned this gluttony.

"Look at this feast," Mom says. "And I hardly had to lift a finger. I could get used to this."

"But don't," I say.

Cal rubs his hands together. "Let's get this jam started. I'll take one of everything. Except that brown lump with spots on it. That don't look right."

Drew goes pale.

"Honey!" Mom flashes her eyes at him.

"If your turkey is so good, why'd you get out ketchup, Mr. Bell?" Claudia grins.

"Yeah, Pops, talk to us when you can save livestock, reduce cholesterol, and scare away small children with one dish."

"All right, you got me. Put some of that mush on my plate. I can get it down with some rolls. Where are those?"

"Sorry, hun. No bread."

"What?"

Mom shakes her head at Cal's goofy expression. "Claudia, tell us about yourself. Drew tells us you're an English major."

"Yes, ma'am. I hear it looks good on law school applications."

"A lawyer, eh?" Cal remarks. "That's a fine career. How about you, Drew? You flip-flop again yet?"

"Sticking with engineering, for now. Just have to pick out which type."

"Good for you, son. Good for you."

I'm halfway through my plate by the time Claudia takes her second bite. Must be a taste issue. I slow my fork a little on the store-bought green bean casserole. It isn't half bad. Okay, it's tasty.

But the turkey is nothing without cranberry sauce.

No matter. Dessert has always been the highlight.

Wait.

"The pie!"

With all the veganizing, I forgot to set a timer. *Please be okay.*

Char smell hits me before I open the oven. I toss the stinky dishes onto the stovetop and inspect. I haven't totally murdered the desserts, but they're in serious condition. The crumbles on the apple crisp look beetle-infested, and the beautiful sheen of the pumpkin filling has scabbed. Not the Bell standard.

"No," I growl.

Thanksgiving with no pie might as well be Lent.

Claudia's not one of us yet, so all the anger inside of me gets contained between my fists and teeth.

"Adia, honey," Mom says.

Claudia approaches the dishes and starts picking away at the damage. "I think we can salvage some of it if we just—"

I don't wait for her to finish. Armed with a container full of charlotte, I storm to my room to lick my wounds in private.

There's only one thing I can count on right now: the Hallmark Channel.

SIX

Halfway through the movie, a stomachache emerges. I valiantly finish the entire dish of mousse, the last bite ending in tears as a dying grandma encourages the hero not to give up on his heart.

Some food might be on my cheek. I can't be bothered to verify.

The combination of stomach cramps and sad movie vibes is not a good one. Should I get closer to a toilet?

Yes.

The bedroom door creaks open to darkness. I hear slurping coming from the common area. This time, I can't fault them. I appreciate being left alone, so who am I to judge what happens on the other side of the wall?

On tiptoes, I sneak into the bathroom.

My bowels may need some time. I wish I had a phone.

Nothing escalates. Clearly, my overstuffed body needs to move. It's around eleven, so there's still a little time to join the first wave of the Black Friday hunt.

I put on the only acceptable footwear for this time of night, UGGs, and enter Mom's room.

Cal's already asleep. Mom's reading a book.

"Hey," I whisper. "Let's go Black Friday shopping, kay?"

She grunts.

"I want to hit the sales. Can you take me?"

"Go to bed, honey. It's late."

"Come on, Mom. Let's have some fun. We can grab lattes at Starbucks and then work our way through the main stores."

She shakes her head and turns back to her book.

"Please. Pretty, pretty please."

"Don't you have friends you do this insanity with?"

"They're all busy, but thanks for rubbing it in."

"I'm already in my nightgown."

"Mom, I'll be all alone if you don't take me. And I don't have a ride."

"There's a Kohl's and a Home Depot across the street." She mumbles something unintelligible and rubs her hand over her face. I wait long enough to realize she's reading.

"Mom!"

"Hmm?"

"Shopping."

"Mm mm."

I snatch the book.

"Adia May, stop being such a pest. I don't want to subject myself to the torture of Black Friday shopping, especially not at this hour. Now, either leave me alone or I'll have to punish you."

There's only one way to proceed. I snatch her blankets.

She screeches.

Cal pops up with crazy hair. "What is it?"

I giggle.

"Give me that," Cal says, reaching for the blanket.

"Not until Mom agrees to come with me."

"Fine," she grumbles. "Go start a pot of coffee and come get me when it's done."

Success!

At least that's what I think it is, until I come back, travel mug brimming with caramel energy in hand, and find a locked door. It's a dirty move. A low-down, dirty move.

I'm fit to yell. But I can't right now, due to the hundreds of strangers living just beyond these walls.

"I guess I'll go out into the darkness with all the creepers and walk across a treacherous highway by myself. Let's all hope I don't die."

"Good luck," Mom calls from the other side of her barred door.

Perfect. I'm going this alone.

I suit up in a jolly hat and blanket scarf in lieu of an obstructive coat and arm myself with coffee—an espresso for me, since my stomach is hardly interested in more sugar, and Mom's caramel mocha with the lid off, ready to get thrown on any scuzzballs.

It only takes half a mile outdoors to make me regret my choices. My nose feels like it might crack off if I touch it, and my fingers are burning. One particularly bone-chilling animal noise causes me to slip. Hot liquid blisters the back of my hand. But I won't turn back. If I have any hope of redeeming my holiday, this must be done.

My entire body is chattering by the time I pass through the Kohl's entrance. I toss the emptied espresso mug into my cart and hover over the other mini-heat source, enjoying the caramel caress. Now, let's see...

Where are my fellow comrades who appreciate a good deal? I was ready to bob and weave. I was ready to tangle. Have Americans forsaken all notion of patriotism? At this rate, I may not even get to wait in line. When will I decide which of my conquests I mean to keep?

I pass a little girl being tugged along by her dad. Her hand slips from a stuffed animal with giant eyes. I pick it up for my cousin, who's about her age.

I don't know this store like I know my usuals, which doesn't bode well. My cart wanders into the belly of a clothing section. These snoopy pajamas need to be had. In goes a set for me and one for Jemma...and one for Mom...and an extra pair in case Claudia's around come Santa Day. Then I notice a coat I've been coveting. And a super cute dress.

I'm elbow-deep in a clearance rack when the loudspeaker announces the store closing in thirty minutes.

I reroute, seeing how terribly off-plan I've gone. I usually follow a strict EHF strategy: electronics, housewares, fashion. It saves time and puts the priority on my "other people" gifts.

Let's regroup. What's my primary goal?

Scoring the most impressive gifts a college budget can buy.

I grab a frantic store clerk. "Electronics?"

He points to the escalator.

Fat chance with this cart.

I'm pleased to discover an elevator before I try to tilt the cart up and hope for the best.

The elevator opens up to the second floor like a curtain on *The Price Is Right*—there's a doorbuster Samsung TV standing tall in the middle of the aisle, still here five hours after the Black Friday kickoff. Holy elf bells. Am I going to become a Christmas-morning hero? Will that moment get talked about for years to come?

The fire ignites. I wrangle the last big screen into my cart. What other unthinkable deals await me in this underappreciated gift haven?

WoodWick candles going for five dollars apiece! A whole case slides into my cart's undercarriage to satisfy my rule of twos—as in, always include two things in the gift bag or else you basically look like you don't even care.

In housewares territory, I snatch up adorable Christmas mugs going for practically nothing. These BOGO knickknacks are ideal for the holiday wreath I want to construct, and The Home Depot next door should have fresh pine bases. A fragrant, gold-adorned beauty hanging from our doorway is sure to leave a positive impression on the neighbors. Yay!

The entertainment-themed ornaments catch my attention. Cal will love the Philadelphia Eagles player. But would he appreciate the *Game of Thrones* stuff? I decide to decide later and toss them aboard the sleigh.

A voice over the loudspeaker encourages all shoppers to head to the checkout lanes. The store will be closing in five minutes.

I trip a man in my frenzied route to the accessories.

"Sorry!" I yell. I definitely sound a little crazed, but that's what you get when you mix lots of caffeine, emerging delirium, and some mad deals. People get it.

I find an adorable winter accessory set: mittens, a scarf, and a hat, all in red plaid. It makes me want to burst into Christmas flames. Plus, the mittens will make the walk home tolerable. I buy two extra sets, for my mom and…someone.

Other last-minute items with yellow deal stickers go into the cart: fuzzy socks, oven mitts, Christmas UNO, a reindeer toothbrush… These should cover lots of people on my list. They're versatile.

It's kind of good my friends bailed on me this year. I've gotten a ton more accomplished, and I didn't even need five stops to do it. Someone might as well promote me to Santa Claus and give me a reindeer.

Good thing I waited until the last minute to check out. I step into the sizable Black Friday line to which I'm accustomed and pore over my selections. An old lady, surrounded by a group of similarly wrinkled friends, takes the slippers I cast out onto a nearby shelf. She winks. It's teamwork at its finest.

I complete my journey with a few final scores near the checkout lanes, including peppermint Christmas Peeps—who knew! The young cashier smiles at me from under her peppy Santa hat. A jolly soul.

"Nice sheets!" she remarks.

I'd forgotten about those. They'll be the cutest pop of holiday for my dorm room. I beam, right up until my Christmas mascot calls out the purchase total. One thousand four hundred and seventy-eight dollars and eighty cents.

Come again? Wasn't this stuff discounted?

I try to look natural as my heart stops beating. My card slices through the machine. She hands it back, somehow still cheerful even though she's just murdered my future.

While she passes me my last bag and receipt, she delivers the final blow, a "Merry Christmas!"

Those two glorious words are the official proclamation of the Christmas season. I'd normally receive them with sheer glee. But, instead, my shaky hands scan over the receipt. I'm trying to make sense of it all. There must be something she rang up wrong.

The ornaments. They're supposed to be two-for-one!

I head over to the customer service line, hoping to find some other glaring mishaps.

"The two-for-one is taken off here on the bottom," the cashier explains, pointing.

"I missed that. Um..." I'm paralyzed in place. I've just spent my entire college savings. At this point, I may not even be able to pay for the gas back to school, much less room and board. "I need to return this."

"Return what?"

"All of this." The gifts have turned on me.

"Your whole purchase?"

"Yes."

She turns pale as she looks from my loaded cart to the growing line of customers behind me.

"We...I... Can you just bring the stuff back a different day? We've opened up this line to check people out, and it's kind of crazy right now."

I peek behind me to see at least a dozen people waiting in various states of impatience. A middle-aged lady smiles one of those do-the-right-thing smiles. A baby cry seals my fate.

"Fine, but I'm going to need to take home this cart."

She waves me away like I'm some kind of psycho.

Heaving a loaded, rickety shopping cart through landscaping and up a high embankment is not for the faint of heart. Luckily, I have gobs of heart.

No foliage or terrain can hold me back. These ugly shrubs can kiss it. I push my belongings over them with a monster shoulder heave.

Prickly leaves claw at my legs. My feet slide. The mugs try to topple over. I trap those rascals down and make it to the top, baby.

Now on to crossing a main road vagrant style. I wait until the coast is clear and then haul tushy. The cart's wheels threaten to misbehave, but I womanhandle them—I high-pitch scream and demand they cooperate. We fly, skidding and screeching, toward the opposite end of the road.

While contemplating how to best get the cart down the next embankment without it capsizing and destroying all the precious, needing-to-remain-in-pristine-condition goods, I remember, I need a wreath!

I can't go home without that. What will I do tomorrow? And I'm not taking this walk again. It wouldn't be good for my Krebs cycle.

Swinging my cart around, I contemplate bringing it back with me....

Heck no. We barely made it out of the parking lot the first time. Plus, bruises. How badly do I care about maintaining this post-Thanksgiving tradition?

Well, someone has to care. Mom and I always have a wreath for Christmas. We can't let a change in life circumstances ruin everything for us. As long as we have a door, we can still have this sense of normalcy.

I need to go back.

I walk up the road, toward a copse of trees where I suspect I can hide my purchases for at least a little while. If I pray no criminals pass by in the fifteen minutes I'm away, it will probably be fine. *Please, God?*

Just as I reach the trees, an ear-piercing horn sounds out of nowhere, along with a hyena howl. I jump away on instinct, and my foot hits a pothole. My ankle twists, forcing my legs to collide. My feet stumble. I grab for my cart, but instead of helping me, it makes a run for the other side of the road.

The blur of spinning wheels passes across my vision as the world rolls around me. An UGG dislodges. The chilly wind gropes unexpected sections of my skin, and then a tree smacks me in the shoulder.

While I'm fumbling over myself, I'm treated to another honk—this one the much deeper, more commanding octave of a big rig. Tires squeal, followed by a booming clap.

Um. What was that?

Flailing reindeer sheets shoot over the embankment, loosening themselves from their plastic packaging and sinking to my feet.

The angry wail of the horn drifts away. A couple sets of tires skid to a halt. Doors slam. Voices grumble and curse over whatever devastation was significant enough to impede their journey.

I cover myself like the dead person I am.

Until I hear a police siren. At that point, I hide-and-flee. I can't succumb to destitution and criminality on the same night.

SEVEN

I walk over to the embankment Friday afternoon, in the daylight, to see if I can recover any items. Only a small sprinkle of ornament glass on the curb proves there was ever any wreckage. I'm not getting back a single penny.

I spend the rest of the morning coming up with a strategy for how to tell Mom without her killing me. Confessing tomorrow at the end of the annual Meadowdale Christmas party, among lots of eyewitnesses, seems best. That way I don't ruin the whole weekend.

I avoid everyone with the help of Netflix.

Saturday morning begins with a familiar simplicity. I wake to a quiet house and start the coffeepot. Mom emerges next and fills up a mug. She pulls a baggie of muffins from the freezer.

"What flavor you got there?"

"They're my butterscotch pumpkin ones."

"Yes please."

She adds an extra to the plate and then tries a few times to open the microwave before huffing and slamming the dish on the counter.

"Here." I hop up and turn on the toaster oven. "These are best toasted anyway. Let me at them."

Coffee in hand, she drifts over to the couch.

"Is everything okay, Mom?"

"Oh, everything's fine. My mind's just elsewhere."

When Cal comes out a few minutes later, a clunky brown suitcase rolling behind him, I get it. He's leaving again. I'm about to go tuck myself into her side when she pops up, pastes a large smile on her face, and kisses Cal's cheek.

"Adia's toasting some muffins for you to take on the road."

I slip three muffins into a brown bag and hand it to him.

He squeezes my shoulders. "Thank you, baby. You guys don't have too much fun without me, okay?" He disappears out the door.

Mom gets up without a word and shuts herself in her room.

It's for the best. This is not the time to accidentally get pushed into a confession.

By Saturday afternoon, though, I'm getting nauseous. How am I going to tell my mom what I've done? She's going to be so mad, and she doesn't need my problems right now. I can't even enjoy *Queer Eye* I'm so nervous.

My stepbrother knocks on my door and pops his head through the opening. "Claudia and I are leaving. We didn't want to go without saying goodbye."

"Already? What about the Light It Up party?"

"Are we still invited to that?"

"I sure hope so, 'cause I'm going."

"We have some plans at school that we want to get back for."

Who's going to be my mom buffer now?

I look away. "Bye then."

"Don't be like that. Come give your big bro a squeeze."

While I do it, I try to display enough agony to change his mind and get him to stay through tomorrow. I want it to be like old times. Not Cal gone. Not Drew either making out with some invader or straight-up ditching us for her. Not Mom bummed out.

"Take care, you. And take Sammy to that party. She seems like she could use some fresh air."

"I will if she'll let me."

Claudia pokes her head into the room. "Thanks for putting up with me in your space."

"Sure."

Though I'm happy for them, it stings watching her slip her hand in my brother's and take him away.

I hear mom give them a warm send-off and then exhale heavily as she closes the front door.

Nothing good can come from two mopey females stuck in a small space. We both need a pick-me-up.

I brush my teeth, pull on a vintage snowman t-shirt and my black jeans, and slap on a smile.

"I need you to drive me somewhere," I say, entering the living room.

"You can take my car."

"Mom." I give her a look. She knows how I feel about driving. "I want you to come with me."

"Adia, I don't really feel like going out."

"The Light It Up party is tonight, and we've never missed it. Please, Mom. You already turned me down for shopping. I could really use this."

She twists her mouth as she studies me.

I give her my best chin quiver.

She hangs her head.

I put on my antlers, pocket two pairs of rubber gloves, and tune us into the Christmas radio station as we cruise toward our former neighborhood. My stomach distress eases. This could be a great night!

Mom sighs and turns the carols down. "Adia, there's something I need to talk to you about."

Does she have access to my bank account? I don't want to be murdered before I get to make a Christmas light ball. How else will I decorate my dorm room? "What is it?"

"Well." She clears her throat. "As you may have guessed, Cal and I are in a bit of a financial slump."

"I could tell a little."

"Without tightening things even more, we won't be able to keep making ends meet."

"What do you mean?"

"We can't afford to help you with school anymore, honey. I'm so sorry to put this on you, but whatever your loans don't cover, we need you to find the money for on your own."

Boy, would this conversation have been great two days ago. I had no idea things were this bad. How much did she make at her old job? Did she and Cal not put any money into savings? Did they not make money selling our house?

"I don't have that kind of money! I just spent—"

A tear trickles down Mom's cheek. I can't remember the last time I saw her cry. Not since Dad died.

That was a dark period. My parents both picked me up from kindergarten one day and drove to the lake. While we fed the ducks, they threw out phrases like "Daddy's got a yucky tummy" and "the doctors don't have medicine for this kind of sickness." The next thing I knew, Dad was gone and Mom stopped getting out of bed. My nonna had to come take me away for a while after a neighbor got concerned that I was spending too much time outside by myself. I didn't see Mom again for three months. But when we reunited, she was back to normal. Better than normal. She turned into this supermom who planned amazing trips and holidays and Saturdays and Tuesday afternoons. She filled *all* the space there was to miss my dad. And ever since, Mom and I have an unspoken agreement. We don't let each other get sad.

I shut my jaw up tight.

"A lot of people take over financial responsibility at your age." Another tear drops from her face. "Having a job can be a great experience, and it will definitely look great on your résumé."

I squeeze her hand. "It's fine, Mom. I'll figure something out."

I better live it up tonight. I'm going to be adding a job search to my list of responsibilities, effective immediately.

EIGHT

Mom refuses to get out of the car when we pull up to the party. "I know this is a huge letdown, but I can't do this right now. I don't want to have to explain our situation to everyone. I just can't."

I get it. I really do.

And I hate it.

But I get it more.

"Pick me up later, I guess."

"What time?"

"Not sure. I'll try to text you from Mrs. Karen's phone."

"Sounds like a plan. Thank you, sweet girl." She grabs my cheek and squeezes it.

I feel a lot heavier getting out of the car than I did getting in.

But when I steel my breath, the smell of cinnamon apples and chili greets me with cheer. All of my longtime neighbors are littered across the lawn and into the street. The Reagans spot me and come over, but not before my mom escapes.

"Hi, darling," Mrs. Karen says, hugging me. "How have you been, you pretty little thing?"

She calls everyone a pretty little thing. I think she's fairly near-sighted, so her opinion can hardly be trusted.

"I'm good. Missing this place, for sure." I pass along the bag of canned green beans and yams I brought for the food bank collection.

"And we miss you. I hate that y'all had to move so quickly. I didn't even get to make your mom a meal before they were up and gone."

"Yeah. I didn't even know it happened until I got home for break."

"Your poor mom's been through it this year. I know how much she put into that job she lost."

"Yeah, such a shame Dr. Spitz retired and couldn't find someone to take over the practice."

"He retired? I hadn't heard that."

Mrs. Karen is a patient there. How irresponsible of the practice to wait so long to inform their clientele.

"Is she reemployed?"

I shake my head. Mrs. Karen shakes hers too.

"I'll keep my ear out for any opportunities. She'll find something soon, I'm sure."

"Hope so."

"Come to make a light?" Mr. Bob asks.

"I've come for it all."

The air gets brisk as the sun begins its descent. Everyone has bundled themselves up tight in scarves and hats. Rubber gloves pose for mittens and make the task of wire twisting much more bearable. Like every year, tons of new faces have come, string lights in hand, to learn the secret art of the Lighted Christmas Ball. When these beauties are fully constructed, they become twinkling globes of joy that get launched high up into the neighborhood's towering poplars and oaks. Then hundreds, maybe thousands, of people drive through these streets to marvel at them all.

Mrs. Karen tucks a cup of steamy cider into my hands. The sweet spice expands in my chest as we admire the merriment. Dads smoking meat. Neighbors sharing stories. Newcomers struggling with wires. Teenagers pointing potato guns at the treetops. Friends laughing together...making memories. It truly is the most wonderful time of the year.

After I devour a bowl of chili, I join Mr. Bob at the project table. He passes me some wire clippers. I measure out enough chicken wire for miniature ball lights that can hang inside our apartment. They might bring Mom a little cheer. I snip my sheets of wire to size. Then I fold one piece into a cylinder, fastening the clipped edges together with my rubber gloves. After pressing down the top and bottom of the cylinder to form a sphere, I string on some spare colored lights from Mrs. Karen.

"Those blink. You'll love them."

I beam as I admire my finished product. I could do this in my sleep after years of showing new neighbors and visitors the ropes. I can't imagine a world where I don't do this at Christmas.

"Have you met any nice boys up at school?" Mrs. Karen loves to ask me about boys. I think she's from a time when men were gentlemen and courtship looked like getting to know someone, not using them.

"Not so much. Guys my age are stupid."

"That's what we're here for, darling. We catch their eye and then show them how to act right. It's the whole point of feminine charm."

If only it were that simple. I sway to the holiday music, letting a facet of my feminine charm loose. What other charms do I have? Baking? Enthusiasm?

Do any of those help?

Mrs. Karen dances alongside me to "Jingle Bell Rock." My heart gets bouncy.

"Is the Twinkle Dash happening this year?" I ask.

The Twinkle Dash, the neighborhood's Christmas Eve 5K fundraiser, is quite possibly my favorite activity of the whole holiday season. Hundreds of people show up before daybreak to run under the lighted balls. Taking part is like existing in a voluntary dream.

"Sure is, and we could use some help organizing it, if you're interested."

"I totally am."

"Wonderful. Meetings start this week. They're every Monday evening. Come after your Christmas break starts, and we'll get you plugged in."

Eek! I have Christmas business to conduct. My feet do a happy dance.

~

When I ask Mr. Bob if I can use his phone to call my mom, he insists on giving me a ride home. Neighbors are the best. The Reagans were the best of the best.

I'm floating on a wave of twinkle lights and cider by the time I reach the apartment. The holidays are good for the soul. They are little landmarks of joy along the winding, unpredictable road of life. I want to rest in this space for a while. Forget about school and money and loneliness and bask in the season. And I want Mom to bask with me.

As I'm running up the steps to make a plan of attack, I see UPS pulling into the lot. Perfect!

"Mom," I call, "the glass bottles are here. Let's put on *It's a Wonderful Life* and make a night of it. Maybe try again on the pie. What do you think?"

I figured she wouldn't respond right away, but a good elf never gives up.

I poke my head inside her bedroom.

She's slumped against the bed with a pile of vomit in her lap. Her skin is pale in a kind of way that isn't synonymous with health, a bluish-white. My heart almost stops.

"Oh my god, Mom. What did you do?"

I don't see pills anywhere. Or booze. Just a single glass of water sitting on her nightstand.

She flops over in my arms, eyes rolling into her head. I hold her face, willing her to wake up.

To my immense relief, she does.

I'm on my feet and urging her to walk. She guards her right arm when I try to grab it. Hooking her by the waist, I take a big swing and lift her off the floor. We make it a few steps before her foot catches mine. We lurch forward. Her head bangs against the wall, but I keep her on her feet. Her eyes roll back. I need a doctor before this gets any worse.

I invite my muscles to join in and drag Mom toward the couch.

"Sit here," I say, letting go. "I'm calling an ambulance."

"No," she slurs. "No money."

Crap. We lost our health insurance when she got laid off. I had to apply for some special school aid. Panic builds in my chest.

Something thunks outside our apartment.

UPS doesn't give the courtesy knock, but it's got to be him. I wrench open the door.

"I need help! My mom's in trouble, and I don't know what to do!"

Since I'm yelling loud enough to reach the shoppers across the highway, he hears me and pulls out his earbuds.

"I need help," I repeat.

He closes his eyes for a moment. Then he asks, "What's wrong?"

"My mom's acting super out of it. I think she might have taken some pills. I'm not sure."

He follows me inside. We find her passed out on the couch, cradling her arm.

"She doesn't have insurance right now, and I'm not sure what to do." No matter how many extra times I breathe, I can't get my voice down to a normal pitch.

He kneels beside her. "What's her name?"

"Samantha."

"Samantha, can you hear me?"

She moans.

He checks her pupils...her pulse...

"Her heart's racing. We need to call nine-one-one. Where's your phone?"

"I don't have it!"

"Where's any phone?"

"We can't afford an ambulance!"

"Too bad. Your mom could die here."

I burst into tears. This is not my life. Not at all. My life is back at the Light It Up party, socializing with neighbors and sipping cider. My mom should be teasing me about Bad-breath Gil, not drooling on herself.

Miller scoops her into his arms. "I'll take her to your car as long as you promise you'll go right to the ER."

My sobs get louder. "I don't drive."

His head drops. After a moment, he walks toward the front door. "Come on. I'm giving you a ride."

I'm too sensitive to handle a crisis. Why the adults of the world even trust me to live on my own is beyond me. I mop up my tears with my sleeve, so grateful for this stoic delivery boy who has my solid ground in his arms.

NINE

On UPS's advice, I call the ER to alert them to our situation.

He pulls up to the entrance. We each support one of my mom's arms and lift her limp body out of the cab. She's still making noises, so I refuse to totally freak out.

A team of healthcare workers rushes over with a stretcher. Within seconds, Mom's rolling through the glowing emergency doors.

I look back at UPS with an are-you-coming look, though I'm not sure why I'd opt to involve a stranger in this problem. I'll have to dissect that one later.

"I've gotta finish my shift," he says.

That's fair. He doesn't owe us anything. The fact that he came in the first place is astonishing.

He opens the door of his truck.

I turn without a word and chase the stretcher all the way into the belly of the ER. It's crowded and noisy with machines and nurses shouting orders. Sick people are lurking everywhere.

Don't look at anything!

My eyes betray me when a hospital bed rolls past carrying a bloody man with tubes and bags coming from every part of him. My skin goes clammy. A nurse pulls a blue curtain around us, turning the spot where we stand into a little room. Everything but Mom gets blocked from view.

Five strangers poke and prod her. Someone says "airway" something, and a woman yanks my mom's head up while a guy shoves a metal hook into her mouth. My vision gets fuzzy after that. I reach for the only wall I can find.

"Mickey," a nurse says, and then arms are around my shoulders.

I'm led into a quiet, empty room by a man in green scrub pants, his long, dark-brown fingers guiding me into a chair. He tells me with kind eyes that he's a physician assistant and that my mom's in good hands. He encourages me to lie down, but no way am I playing the role of patient. I sit with my head between my knees, and Mickey leaves a cup of water on the counter nearby.

When the sick feeling mostly passes, I walk into the hall. I need a phone.

Or do I?

Should I tell Cal what's happening? He's probably over five hundred miles away by now. Also, we probably need the extra money from this job, especially after tonight's little ER trip. Worrying him won't help anyone.

But what if Mom tanks? What if they can't help her?

Tears drip onto my neck. I rub them away with my sleeve, but more come.

What if they ask me to make decisions about her care? Even after a few months of predental classes, I don't know anything about medicine. The only sick person I've ever encountered was Dad, and Mom kept me away from all the hospital stuff. This is my first time even stepping foot into one. How the heck will I know what to do?

I find a reception desk and make the call.

～

My head is tucked into my mom's hand when a lady walks into the room. She's wearing a purse and a fuzzy sweater, so she's not part of the medical staff. Must be a visitor who's got the wrong room. I don't move. She can figure out her mistake on her own. I don't have the energy to interact.

"Adia?"

Huh?

"I'm Caroline Reach, a friend of your mother's. Cal called and told me what's going on. How's she doing?"

"They say she's better now."

"And how are *you* doing?"

I breathe in a ragged breath. I'm not, like, *okay* okay, but I'm feeling better since they let me come see her. She looks much more normal.

"You look exhausted. Let me talk with the doctors and then take you home. I'll stay with your mom tonight while you get some rest. I hear you've got to get back to school in the morning."

Ugh, Avery. Did she have to remind me? I haven't done a bit of my chem studying or my linguistics essay.

But I hate the idea of leaving Mom with this stranger. I mean, maybe they're friends, but they certainly aren't blood.

"I need to be here for her."

She nods.

As the clock ticks on to midnight, I get less and less firm in my stance. It's the smells of plastic and rubbing alcohol. The constant beeping. The moaning from room 3B. And I'm just freaking cold. We're a single degree up from the morgue in here.

At twelve thirty a.m., Mickey checks in with a report. He's happy with Mom's vitals but wants to keep her resting until her surgery in the morning. She's broken her right arm.

Caroline turns to me when he leaves. "Since she'll just be sleeping it off the rest of the night, how about I give you that ride home?"

"Yeah, that's fine. Thanks."

We walk out into the parking lot in silence. In the first row of cars, UPS is perched with his legs dangled over the back of his truck. He jumps down when he spots us. "I thought you'd need a ride home at some point...."

Oh, thank god. I don't have to have an awkward ride with this random lady and her floral perfume. I turn to Caroline, whose lips and brows are pinched.

"This is Miller. He's our— He brought us to the hospital earlier. Miller, this is my mom's friend Caroline."

Caroline nods. "Nice to meet you, Miller. Thank you for helping Sam out."

He nods back.

"I'll take you up on that ride. Caroline can stay here with my mom."

Caroline's throat hums with uncertainty. But I'm nineteen. I get to make my own decision.

"I don't think we should leave Mom all alone anyway. I'd rather you stay. Please call my—uh, Mom's phone, which I'll have at the apartment, with any change. And if she wakes up, could you tell her I'm going to find a way back here in the morning, first thing?"

Caroline nods, still looking pinched, and promises she'll reach out with any news.

My guts twist as I climb into Miller's truck.

Am I actually going to leave my sick mom with a stranger?

Yes. Cal wouldn't have called her if he didn't trust her. And I really don't want to go back in there. I'll get some rest and several more layers of clothing and come right back.

"How is she?" Miller asks.

"Doctor says she had opiates and some neuroleptic something in her system but not at toxic levels…it wasn't, like, a suicide attempt, I guess. Just a bad drug interaction. She's fine now. Just super sedated, and her arm is broken. She has to have surgery tomorrow."

"Glad she's okay."

"Yeah. Thanks for your help. I figured I'd never see you again when you bailed like that."

"I didn't bail. I had to finish my job."

"I know. It's cool. How long were you waiting?"

"An hour or so."

This answer makes me feel a little warm in my cheeks. I have no idea how to respond. I'm genuinely touched but my appreciation may not come out right since I'm also humiliated about losing my cool earlier.

"So you don't know how to drive?" he asks.

I sigh. It's a problem. I get it. But driving kind of intimidates me.

"I have my license and all, but I've never had a car."

"So?"

"And my parents were really busy with their jobs. I never got much practice."

He nods his head for an annoyingly long time. "You think maybe this experience would suggest that you need to try harder to get comfortable?"

"I don't expect anything like this to happen again." For the love!

He makes a sound, but I don't engage with it. I don't need to hear a lecture right now.

He pulls into our apartment complex and cuts the engine.

"So...thanks for staying up late to give me a ride."

"It's no problem. Sunday's my day off."

"Only Sunday?"

"Mondays too, but I usually request overtime. I like to keep busy."

"There are more fun ways to keep busy, you know."

"I like the work."

Good for him, but I don't get it. A paycheck is nice, sure, but not at the expense of lounging. "Do you get paid well, at least?"

"It's a decent living, yeah."

"How much do, say, new people get paid?"

"Not sure. I think it's reasonable. Why?"

"I might need a job." And being Santa's helper seems like an ideal gig.

"I don't want to say I told you so, but this does again prove my point about knowing how to drive. You will need to get there somehow."

"Ugh. Never mind. Enjoy your day off." I grab the door handle.

"Hey." He rakes his hand through his hair. "Are you going to be okay?"

I shrug.

"You don't seem like you're used to being alone."

I drop my head against the window glass. It feels cold and uncomfortable—like my whole life.

Miller's right, I really don't want to be alone. But I've been the needy girl before. It bites.

"Did you want to come up and help me clean some vomit?" I joke.

So much for feminine charm.

To my surprise, he pulls into a parking space and gets out.

I get out too.

TEN

After shoving a pile of dirty clothes under the couch, I turn on the apartment lights.

"I found my mom passed out in her room."

I poke my head inside to see the damage. The smell triggers my gag reflex. Pressing myself against the hallway wall, I beg my mind not to go back there. We don't need two big-girl meltdowns in one evening.

"Do you have baking soda?" Miller asks, not looking phased by the unkempt state of my residence.

I search the cabinets and find him an Arm & Hammer box.

"It neutralizes the smell." He dumps it over the mess on the carpet. "Got something I can scrub with?"

We pull baskets and brooms and picture frames and tons of other junk out of the utility closet until we find the steam cleaner. Miller takes it from me and goes to work. He blocks me from helping. Horror twists my insides as I watch him go at the yellow chunks. It's like a dude watching you poop. You can't come back from that.

"I didn't really mean for you to clean that up," I say when he's done.

"I like to clean."

"So you like working and cleaning?" He is rapidly becoming the strangest guy I've ever met.

"Can I get you a hot drink?"

"A hot drink?"

He nods.

I try not to look weird, but my heavens. He wants to give me something warm and comforting. "That would be nice."

He fills a pot with some milk and situates it on the stove. I'm already enjoying the view of him standing over the cooktop when he takes off his hoodie, exposing the shapely limbs beneath. For a skinny boy, he's got some serious definition. His muscles ripple as he stirs some sugar into the liquid. His hand does things with the wooden spoon, all the squeezing and back and forth motions, that make my jaw slacken.

Maybe it's because I'm watching a male from my generation pretty much cook, or maybe it's his stoic manner, but he seems overly mature, the kind of person capable of making big decisions with confidence. "How old are you?"

"Twenty-four."

"Oh."

Twenty-four sounds so much easier than where I am.

Those muscles reach to click the burner off and retrieve a mug from the cabinet. He fills the navy ceramic just to the top. So many skills.

"How old did you think I was?"

"My age."

"Which is?"

"Nineteen."

He slides the sweet milk across the counter. "This should make you sleepy. Works for me, anyway."

I have to coach my arms into working before I can attempt a sip. This is still shocking and otherworldly. "Do you live with someone?"

His head shakes.

The milk misses my mouth and dribbles down my chin onto my shirt. Why am I so tense?

"Where are you in school?" he asks.

"Avery University. Have to go back tomorrow to wrap up the semester." I blow out the immediate stress that presses against my ribs and give up on my drink.

"Tough semester?"

"I kind of hate school."

"Why?"

"I guess I'm one of those people who *doesn't* like to work. You were probably amazing at college."

He turns back to the stove. I take the opportunity to stretch the kinks out of my arms.

"I should probably get going so you can rest."

My inside frowns.

He takes the dirty pot to the sink. Then his fingers do the unthinkable: they scrub.

I'd enjoy it more if he didn't have that very same look on his face that my mom had the last time I saw her, that distant stare. I wanted to bring her back. It's why I wanted those bottles....

"Will you help me with one more thing before you go?"

"Well." The faucet stops. "It's one a.m., so I guess all my other plans are shot."

"Perfect. We're going to need that pot."

After drying the pot, he flips the handle around his fingers and slides it onto the burner.

"Have you been practicing that move at home?"

"Only a couple times a day. I had a feeling it'd come in handy."

"What other tricks do you do?"

"Well, let's see. I'm excellent at both playing and programming video games."

"So you *are* familiar with the concept of fun."

"On occasion, I've experienced it."

I grab a hunk of fresh ginger and peel away the skin with the tip of a spoon. The air takes on the root's soapy goodness. "Good to know. More importantly, can you mince?"

"Come again?"

"Mince. That fast, choppy move that makes food into tiny little pieces."

"You want me to cut this?"

I nod.

He accepts the ginger and knife.

I add some sugar and water to our pot.

Warming milk may be about as far as Miller's culinary skills stretch. He bangs on the cutting board a few times, leaving a pile of chunks, then fumbles over the pieces, unable to reduce the size any further.

I shoo him aside. Palm over blade, I take seconds to turn his chunks into specks.

"So you're a chef," he says, picking up the stirring spoon.

"When my mom's not popping pills, she enjoys a good sesh in the kitchen. You happen to be standing beside her number one pupil. And she hates to mince, so it's my specialty."

"What have we minced all of this weird-smelling yellow stuff for?"

I scrape the bits into the simmering sugar water. "It's called ginger, and we're making it into ginger beer."

He makes a face.

"Ever tried it?"

"Not that I recall."

"It's like root beer, only not as good. But you have to have sassafras root bark to make root beer, which is tough to find. Or you can do it with root beer extract, but that's boring, so Mom and I prefer to make ginger beer."

"How does it ferment?"

"Look at you sounding all smart."

He sticks out his lip and I poke it.

Did I just do that? I'm never this comfortable around the opposite sex. I rub my thumb over the dot of wetness, wondering if it was as odd for him as it was for me.

He goes on stirring, seemingly unfazed.

After forming the syrup, we mix it with brewer's yeast, lemon juice, and filtered water.

"Now we pour the liquid into the bottles you delivered today."

"Yesterday."

"Fine. Yesterday. Then you keep it in the cabinet for a few days until bubbles form, and voilà! Homemade soda."

"So this is what you desperately needed the other day? Homemade drinks?"

"Among other things. It isn't the drinks that matter. It's the experience. My mom, as you can see, is going through some stuff. I wanted to make her smile."

He stops, and his gaze soaks through me like warm rain. It loosens me, as any good drenching will do.

"I'm sorry I was rude to you," he says, at the same time I say, "Do you want to stay?"

I'm not asking because I want to get freaky with him. I was thinking more like he sleeps on the couch so I don't feel so alone in this foreign place...and this is my first solid social interaction since I left for college. I'm not ready for it to end.

I don't think he heard me, because he offers no response. His sea-glass eyes pore over me. Blabber creeps up out of my throat to attack this awkwardness.

"It's fine. I'm sure most people you put in their place deserve a little dose of Grinch." I smirk.

"I'm not mean."

"The Grinch wasn't mean either. He just didn't like people."

Miller's whole face drops. Oops.

"Hey, I'm teasing." I step beside him, trying to catch his eyes, which refuse to come near me. "You rescued my mom. I know you're not a Grinch. Seriously."

"Christmas brings out the crazy in people."

"That's fair. It probably does. Anyway, I really appreciate you being there tonight. In fact, I owe you big time, like foot-massage big." I don't touch feet.

He grabs his keys. "I should get to bed."

I want so badly to ask him why he's putting up walls now, but I barely know him. And apparently, we aren't on the joke-around level yet, so we definitely aren't on the confide-stuff level.

He opens the front door and turns around. Propped against the frame, he lingers.

Does he want to stay?

"I could… Do you want a foot rub, really? I was sort of bluffing."

"You're a thoughtful person, aren't you?"

Oh. "I try to be."

"I get the feeling it's not something you have to try to do."

This is not normal guy behavior. He reacts to being offended by saying nice things? I don't know how to respond. I can bat a lash to compliments about my looks, but this personality compliment hits harder. My cheeks flood with heat. Everywhere does.

It's not a feeling I thought my body would permit again, and it's a sweet surprise.

He steps closer, his eyes sweeping over me in a confusing way. A tormenting way. I kinda want to be real thoughtful to his face.

"How about a rain check on that foot rub?" he says, reaching for the door handle.

"Yeah, I can do rain checks." My lashes bat in earnest. When they open up again, he's gone.

But his hoodie isn't. I might be wrapping myself up in it to sleep. I can't confirm.

It is on my body though.

ELEVEN

I dig through Mom's purse for her phone and plug it into an outlet. I'm dying to talk to my best friend. We never go this long without contact.

"What you need to do," Jemma says when I take a breath, "is get on Amazon and order another package to be delivered at precisely four p.m. today, when you need a ride back to school. It will absolutely be worth the excessive shipping fee."

Jemma doesn't yet know I'm too poor for excessive shipping fees.

I toy with the lid from one of the bottles Miller and I filled, which was a waste. Gil was nice about pushing back our trip to campus, but he didn't offer to give me a ride to the hospital. Mom's probably awake by now, thinking I'm off messing around like I don't care.

"I'm not going to summon him to my apartment like some floozy. It was just a one-night tale."

"So let me get this straight. Some reticent boy swoops in and helps save your mother's life, and you're telling me you're not hooked on him? You can't even see sad boys on TV without developing obsessive behavior patterns. At least admit that you've considered what your babies will look like, or I'll never believe another thing you say."

"Jem, I'm not going there because he's a delivery boy who lives three hours from my school. He and I would never be a thing."

"When has reality ever stopped you from pining for romance? This seems like you letting baggage hold you back."

"It isn't like that. Miller's a lot older and really mature and serious and stuff. I mean, he cleaned my mom's vomit. It was pitiful. *I'm* pitiful. He'd probably laugh at me if I tried to get with him."

"Do you want to get with him, though? Is this UPS boy, like, hot?"

The flex of his arm muscle slips into my mind. And how his lips purse adorably when he's lost in thought.

"Yes...in a brooding way. *He* isn't the point. I only told you the story so you'd know that I have interesting things going on in my life too."

"Mm-hmm. Adia, the guy went out of his way to help you—like, as in, he's a good person. I think he could be the perfect candidate for your first SGM."

"That ship has sailed. I wasted my primary steamy guy moment on the wrong guy."

"I've decided it's nullified if the guy turns out to be a closet butthole."

My stomach writhes around the memory. "Why does it matter what I do about this guy anyway? Bottom line is, I probably won't ever see him again. And I don't think he was into me anyway. I'm not really sure he's into anything. I get the feeling he's not even all that thrilled about Christmas."

"*No.* Not a Christmas-hater!" Jemma snorts. "We're only after a redo SGM here. It doesn't matter what holidays he likes as long as he has big delivery-boy muscles. Does he have—"

Someone in the background calls her name. She muffles the speaker and hollers back that she's on her way.

"Ultimate frisbee time."

"You spoiled little California girl. Just go ahead and rub it in that you're still doing outdoor activities."

"Does it help you to know that this is our only break before an afternoon of rigorous study group time?"

"It doesn't. I'm jealous of both those things." I would kill to have some friends around to make studying more tolerable.

"Gotta run. Text me when you figure out how to seduce the delivery boy."

I set the phone down and look over my schoolwork. The blank computer screen sits before me like an opponent. How can I focus when my mom's going into surgery in a couple of hours? Should I take my life into my own hands and drive her car?

My legs wobble at the mere thought. We could both end up in the operating room, and no one needs that.

Well then...if I'm not driving myself to the hospital, what am I doing?

Not pining after some boy, even if he did clean up a gross thing for me.

I fight the urge to jump onto Facebook by closing my computer. A notebook falls off my desk and onto the pile of clothes beside me. This place is chaos. It makes me want to take painkillers too. I stick my school stuff back in my book bag and grab a laundry basket.

The kitchen takes the longest. I stack and rezone until almost nothing remains on the countertops. Draping myself across the cool Formica, I enjoy the view. This place looks perfect, almost.

My final touch is the lighted Christmas balls, which I hang from an extension cord draped across the living room ceiling. *Bellissima.*

I get the toaster back out and make some breakfast.

I'm mid-munch when someone raps on the door.

UPS stands on the other side with his hands stuffed into his baggy jean pockets. Has he been shopping since the early two-thousands? His dirty Chucks don't suggest otherwise.

"Look at you knocking."

"Only when absolutely necessary. I like to avoid getting things thrown at me for waking up sleeping babies."

"Has that really happened?"

He nods. "I leave the delivery alerts up to email now."

"Makes sense. So what are you doing here?" I squirm, causing his eyes to drop. I follow them down.

Oh lord. I'm still wearing his hoodie. *And* a boob shirt, a low-cut tank I would never wear in public. The girls are basically big, pale eggs propped up in a nest.

I lay an arm over my chest like I'm in thinking pose. What is there to think about exactly? The smoothest way to explain that I'm actually Adia's evil twin who can't resist wearing abandoned boy clothes when they smell like wilderness and muscles?

His lips are parted. This is the most expressive I've seen him since we met. Maybe he *is* interested.

"You probably want this." I slip off the hoodie.

His head snaps back up, and he runs a hand through his hair.

I feign nonchalance by taking a bite of toast.

"I'm actually here to offer you a ride. You said your mom's having surgery this morning. I figured you might want to be there."

I swallow the food carefully, since my chest is spasming. He came for me? "But it's your day off."

"I usually try to save my personal business for my days off. It's good ethics."

The sarcasm barely registers. I'm *personal* business.

I snatch my book bag from the floor, using it as a ta-tas cover, though I'm not sure I need one now. Miller's eyes are glued to the floor.

"I'd really appreciate a ride. Can you come in for one sec?"

Once in the safety of my room, I yank off my top and go for my favorite shirt, a worn-out tee from my first concert, One Direction. I slip on some holey, cuffed jeans that are also the divine type of holy, because they accentuate all the right areas. Top it off with black tennis shoes, and I'm ready to present myself to my *personal* new friend.

No, wait.

I smack on a little cranberry lip gloss and some mascara. Maybe I don't look like I enjoy snacking on celery, but I've got things worth noticing.

And, to give the boy some credit, he does. There's a sensation I've gotten a few times walking through campus. The polarizing drag of eyes across skin. I've avoided that type of attention for weeks, but today I enjoy it.

I look long enough to confirm my suspicion and then play coy, sauntering over to my purse. I wrap a ginger beer in a towel and stick it inside.

"You ready?" I run my hand all the way through my thick hair. It gets caught on a tangle, but I force it through.

He clears his throat. "Yup."

His gray convertible looks like something you'd see flying on sky highways. He opens the door for me. It moves up instead of out. I sit and watch him walk to the driver's side in his understated way. And maybe it's the killer car, but I detect a little swagger. The boy's smooth and confident as he puts his machine into motion. We pull onto the road noiselessly. The car barely fits two people, so I figure that's why it's a little warm in here.

"I didn't peg you for a sports car guy."

"I love to drive."

Maybe that's why he loves working so much too.

On the highway, he punches the gas, making my stomach cartwheel. We weave around a few normal cars, and people gawk.

I can see the appeal.

When I notice the speedometer, I clutch the door handle. How can we possibly be going eighty? The engine doesn't even sound like it's on.

"What year are you in school?" Miller asks.

"Freshman."

He doesn't seem to have anything further to say.

"Did you go to high school here?" I ask.

"Yeah, Grimsley," he mumbles.

"Me too. Did you not like it?"

"High school? Does anyone?"

"I loved it."

He mm's.

"So you must have rich parents."

He stiffens. "Why?"

"Sports cars are usually expensive."

"I bought it used."

"You bought this car yourself?" This guy is in a whole different league than me. "Do you work anywhere besides UPS?"

He shakes his head.

"So UPS is your career then?"

"Does everyone have to have a career?"

"I just...you don't seem like a slacker."

"And only slackers work blue-collar jobs?" His lips pinch together.

"Stop putting words in my mouth. My stepdad's got a blue-collar job, for your information, and he's one of the people I most admire."

"So what's your problem with UPS?"

"There you go again. I never said I had a problem with it. Jeez. What's *your* problem with it?"

"I like my job."

"So you say." I cross my arms and watch the roadside.

I hear him fiddling with his phone in the cup holder and a podcast starts playing. He cuts off the speaker's impassioned sentence about how a circular economy is only possible if businesses are incentivized to invest. Whatever that means. Not exactly what I'd consider primo material for tearing up asphalt.

"What do you like to listen to?" he asks.

"Whatever's fine."

A techno beat finds its way through the speakers.

At the exit, we idle by a homeless person holding up a cardboard sign saying he lost his job recently. Maybe mom should get out here. As we pass through the intersection, I notice that the back of the sign has a picture of my roadkill TV. The rest of the box is in his cart. Guess I found a way to help the homeless after all.

All the slaughtered gifts I left on the highway appear in my head. So does my empty bank account. And my broken mom.

"UPS hires seasonal employees other than drivers, right?"

"Yes."

"Any chance you have some sway?"

"You want to work at UPS?"

"Is there something wrong with that?"

He shakes his head in his huffy sort of way.

"I don't like being treated like a child," I note.

"You aren't exactly an adult."

"Thanks, Dad. Forget I said anything."

"Do you really want a UPS job?"

"Well, I think I'd be good at it."

I can't tell if his lip chewing means he doesn't want to help me or if it means he does. I can't tell if I want him to decide or to keep chewing.

TWELVE

This time, when we get to the hospital, I follow Miller inside. He navigates us up to the surgery floor without needing any directional signs.

Caroline fills me in on everything I missed. My mom woke up for short intervals throughout the night as nurses came in to check vitals and draw blood. She didn't say much while she was awake, but she did ask about me. Caroline reassured her that I'd be by before heading to school. Thank god for Miller showing up.

"She'll be glad to see you."

"Don't feel like you need to stick around. I'll take care of her from here."

"I don't mind, sweetie. Sammy's a good friend. I'd like to wait until Linda arrives, if that's all right."

"Linda's coming too?" I give Miller desperate eyes.

"You should go in and see your mom," he says. "I'll stick around out here."

I'd like to tell him that's not necessary, but I don't want to be stuck here alone with these women. "Thanks," I mumble.

Mom's asleep in a hospital room with real walls and a door. Her thin face looks fancy but fragile, like a porcelain doll. Someone must have done her makeup for her. Was it Caroline?

"Mom," I whisper. I gently shake her shoulder.

Her eyes ease open. She reaches out to me, lifting the covers. I crawl into her left side, away from her injured arm, and close my eyes. We lie there lost in our thoughts for a long while. It's a thing we always used to do, and I relish the familiarity of it.

I break the magic first. "So that was scary."

"I know, honey. You must've been terrified."

I nod into her side. "What happened?"

She makes this noise in her throat that she always makes when she's contemplating whether or not she should tell me something. "I've been...dealing with...some emotional stuff lately. It's just something some adults go through when life gets stressful. I got put on some medication to help with it, and I was doing fine."

She wasn't. I could tell she wasn't. But I don't argue.

"Last night I was cleaning my shower, and I slipped. It hurt a lot, but I didn't realize I'd broken anything. I was trying to avoid going to the doctor. I really thought I had it under control. Figured if I could rest it a few days, I'd get better. The only real trouble was the pain. Advil wasn't cutting it. Cal had these codeine pills leftover from his back surgery. I took only two, but it turns out they can cause a bad reaction when mixed with my new medication."

"I'd say."

"I'm sorry I scared you, honey."

"I'm just glad you're okay. Minus your arm."

"At least I'm not working right now. I can lay low and be back to new in a few weeks."

"But it's your dominant side. How will you take care of yourself?"

"I'll manage. Cal will be home by the end of the week. Before then, I'll just learn a few new tricks."

Right. And I'm giving up sugar by willing it to happen. "How will you bake for the holidays?"

"I think people can survive without my cookies for one year."

"Even the mint chocolate ones?"

"Oh. No. Those are essential. Guess you'll have to make some for me."

"That reminds me, I brought you a gift." I hop out of the bed to get my purse.

"Adia, you shouldn't have gotten me anything." She covers her face with a hand that has a tube taped to it.

"Look." I present the bottle of ginger beer. "I made it last night."

She chuckles. "Thanks, sweet girl. I can't wait to try it." It's exactly the reaction I hoped she'd have.

"Should be ready in a day or two."

"Hey, how'd you get here? Did Linda bring you?"

I roll my eyes. "She's supposedly on her way, but we didn't come together. Miller gave me a ride."

"Miller?"

"You don't remember?"

She winces.

"He's...a new friend. He delivers packages to the apartments. That's how we met. He was off today, so he offered me a ride." I spare her the part about how it was actually her disaster that brought us together.

"That's awfully nice." Her brow pinches. "I'm so sorry about all of this."

"Don't worry about me, Mom. Let's focus on getting you better."

She nods, and her eyes dampen. That distant stare returns.

What are you supposed to do when your parent starts falling apart? I squeeze her hand tight until the nurses come and wheel her away.

It's late afternoon by the time the surgeon gives us news.

"She did great. We got the bone set with no issues. She'll be in a cast for a few weeks to immobilize it, and then we'll have an office visit to reevaluate. She's going to need some help doing almost everything. It usually takes people a while to adjust to only having use of one arm."

"Where is she now?" I ask.

"She's been moved to recovery. Once my team has her settled, they'll come get you. It'll be about thirty minutes. Any other questions?"

I shake my head.

Linda pipes up. "Will she go home with any medications or post-op instructions?"

"Yes ma'am. I've given her some naproxen for the pain. We agreed on a non-narcotic for now, but if she's having trouble, the number to reach me is on her discharge orders, along with some detailed do's and don'ts. Mostly she'll need to rest for a few days and then avoid using her right arm until she comes to see me. My office will call her with that appointment information. Pretty simple."

"Thank you, Doctor Crower," Linda says.

"My pleasure."

Back to our seats we go. I feel more relaxed knowing Mom's officially on the mend.

Does dental school involve hospitals? Hopefully not. I've had about all I can handle of sterile and sickly. I break out Mom's phone to finish out the last bit of waiting. I text Cal an update and reassure him that everything is under control. He best serves us by finishing his job assignment and getting paid. Next, I update my Instagram Stories with a happy message.

"Why do people feel the need to post every moment of their lives on the internet?" Miller asks.

"I don't know. It's just what people do. It's basically weird not to post stuff, so you post stuff."

His eyes narrow; he's unsatisfied with my lazy answer. I think about the hospital bed photo that I just posted of me and Mom. Why did I want to share that?

"I think people want to be noticed."

"But they're so busy posting about themselves that they miss out on the chance to be noticed by the people they are actually around."

"Are you one of those anti-technology people?"

He glowers.

I pick at the seat of my chair. "Do you think my mom's going to get along okay these next couple weeks?"

I'm talking to Miller, but Cracker Barrel Linda butts in. "I can check in on your mom as often as she needs. She can even stay at my place if necessary. I work part-time, but my husband's retired, so he can help out with anything."

Hold on a minute. No way am I abandoning my mom to go stay with some lady she's only just met and her husband, who'll remind Mom of how lonely she is. She needs *me*.

I need a minute to think.

Turning to Miller, I say, "I'm going to go check out the vending machine. Want anything?"

"No thanks."

"It's been hours since we ate."

"I'm good."

"Tell me you're not super disciplined about eating between meals?"

It's a test. A very crucial test.

"I just don't like single-use packaging waste."

Results: inconclusive.

"Over thirty percent of single-use packages end up in the ocean, which is like dumping a garbage truck worth of waste into the ocean every minute."

"Okay..."

I examine the tiny chip bag that drops out of the vending machine slot. It seems pretty harmless. And the munchies inside...so necessary. Oniony goodness fuels my contemplations.

So Mom needs extra help at home. I've got two measly weeks left of this semester. That hardly merits abandoning family in a time of need. I can't let Mrs. Perky McHelper do my dirty work. *I'm* going to be the one my mom leans on. She'll thank *me* for feeding her soup and shaving her pits and keeping her spirit alive with holiday entertainment.

It will be me who pulls her out of the darkness.

I should probably talk to Mom and Cal first....

But the mere idea of not going back to school today has erased the pit in my stomach. This feels right. This feels responsible.

I inhale the last few chip crumbs and lick the salt off of my fingers.

How can I get in touch with Gil to cancel my ride? Email seems rude, but he'll have to understand. My mom's in peril. I get out her phone and sign onto the Avery University server. With a quick note, the decision is made.

THIRTEEN

ack in the waiting room, Miller's crunching on carrots and guacamole out of a tin.

"Did you have snacks with you this whole time?"

"I didn't want to eat in front of you when you seemed so distressed. I figured the sight of food might make you feel sick."

"Well, give me some." The appetite's back, baby.

He passes a generously dipped carrot stick my way.

"Is this guac homemade? It's amazing."

He shrugs and passes me another. "I mashed up an avocado and added some seasoning. While I'm surely talented with a salt shaker, I think you're just hungry."

"Did you bring any other food?"

"Just a water bottle. Sorry."

"Then why do you have that whole book bag?"

His face reddens. It actually does. I didn't think he had enough emotion to get embarrassed, but somehow what I've just said has done it.

"What's in there?"

"I dunno. Stuff…keys. Deodorant. Games."

"Games? Let me see."

He rolls his eyes but lets me tug the book bag into my lap. The dude brought travel-sized Monopoly, Clue, Trivial Pursuit, and Yahtzee, plus a deck of cards.

"Do you play games on the road a lot?"

"I got those at the gas station today. Thought you might need a distraction."

"And you're just now telling me?"

He dips his head and gets all slouchy and quiet. There's this kind of tragic, beautiful look about him. The scraggly dark hair tucked behind his ear. The dry, chewed lips. The falling-apart jacket…

Also, I like a man who thinks of personal hygiene on the go.

I scoot down one seat and begin dealing cards. "I happen to be a whiz kid at gin rummy."

"I'll warn you, I can get pretty serious about my card play. I won't lose to a schoolgirl."

"Shut up and draw a card before I go get more plastic waste out of the vending machine."

The nurse calls me back halfway through our face-off.

"I was clearly going to win," I say, "so we can just call it now."

"I have way more points in front of me than you do."

"But I have less cards in my hand. Trust me on this: I won."

He shakes his head and takes my cards. "I guess I better get going."

"Oh?"

"My Roadster's only a two-seater, so I can't fit you and your mom. Linda will have to take you home."

I'm sure she'll love that.

"Well, thanks for bringing me and for sticking around. Normally I'd be weirded out by your thing for not having fun, but in this case, I appreciate it."

He mumbles something I don't hear because of the noisy bag he tosses over his shoulder. "See you around."

"Adia," Linda urges.

The nurse beside her smiles expectantly when I step toward the door she's holding for us. I look back at Miller sauntering away with his head bent. It feels like goodbye.

I hold up a finger to the nurse and chase him.

I can't believe I'm about to do this.

"Miller?"

He raises his shoulders and turns, hands buried.

"I've decided I'm not going back to school while my Mom's injured, so can I give you my number? You know, in case you hear anything about a job."

"Um. Okay."

"Give me your phone, I'll type it in."

"Left it in the car."

"What's your number then? I'll send you a text."

He shrugs.

"What does"—I repeat the shrug—"mean?"

He sighs. "I don't have a phone."

"Yes, you do. You just said it's in your car. Plus, I've seen it."

"That's actually an iPod."

I eye him. What kind of grown person doesn't have a cell phone these days? Well, one that didn't get confiscated by a tyrannical teacher.

"iPods are very practical for what I need. And have no monthly fee."

"So you can only be contacted by email?"

"I can get iMessages too, as long as I'm connected to Wi-Fi."

"Fine." I give him a teasing smile to ease his catlike posture. "What's your email then?"

On my way back to see Mom, I shoot him a message.

Secretly, I might be glad I need a job.

FOURTEEN

Mom ambles into the living room and winces as she sits on the couch.

"Is it time for the naproxen?" I ask.

Linda hands me the discharge papers. "Check the sheet. I'll be right back." She wanders into the hall.

"Can I get you anything, Mom?"

"Water," she says in a scratchy voice.

"Do you want a cough drop for your throat?"

She nods and starts to lie down. Linda catches her head and sets a fluffy bed pillow beneath.

Someone knocks on the door. I beat Mrs. Perky to it and find a light-brown skinned lady with a casual smile on the doorstep. She's holding food containers.

"I'm Betsy, a friend of—"

"My mom's. Come on in." I walk back inside.

Linda has tucked Mom in with blankets and gotten her water. Does she have telekinetic powers? How is she doing all this so fast?

Betsy places the casserole dish in the fridge. "This is baked spaghetti, and I taped heating instructions to the lid. I also brought ginger ale, fruit salad, and a baguette."

"Thanks. This is very nice of you guys"—I take the discharge sheets out of Linda's hand—"but I can take it from here."

Linda smiles. "You sure, darling? We don't mind staying for a little while."

"I've got it."

"Such a wonderful daughter. I hope I get daughters-in-law just like you." Linda comes at me with one of her hugs.

I give her a quick squeeze and mimic her hum.

Betsy says, "I've started a sign-up for meals. I'll include you on the link so you know what's coming. What's your email?"

After I give Betsy my email, Linda gives me her number in case I "need anything." I won't. I lock the door.

Mom's sleeping by the time I successfully shoo them away.

I sit on the recliner and open up my computer. Time to settle up with my teachers and rescue my phone. After emailing all my professors, I look up the phone number for the admin office.

"Yes, hi. This is Adia Bell. My phone was left in your office last week. I was going to pick it up today, but it turns out I'm not able to return to school due to a family emergency."

A gentle male voice responds, "Oh, I'm sorry to hear that. Hope everything's okay."

"I think it will be. But having my phone would help. Is there a way I could get it mailed?"

"Oh. Sure…how quickly do you need it?"

"The sooner the better." Especially if I'm applying for jobs.

"I can overnight it if you're comfortable with the shipping fee. We can tack it on to your student account. What's your student ID?"

"Sounds good." Except for the whole I'm-broke thing. He types as I drag my student number out of the back of my brain.

"Hmm. I'm looking at your account now, and it looks like you're overdue for a tuition payment."

"Oh, okay." I try to hold my voice steady. "Can you go ahead and mail the phone and add the cost to my statement? I'll make a deposit right away…as soon as I can."

"Sure thing. Good luck with your family situation, Miss Bell."

More like, good luck with the mild heart attack I'm having.

I need that job pronto.

~

By the next morning, Mom has livened up enough to be angry with me.

I bring her an iPad.

She pushes it away and says, "I can get these things myself. You should be at school."

I ignore her. She's helpless. It's ridiculous to think I'd leave her like this. "I'm going out to find a job."

"I never meant you needed to start working right away, Adia. School comes first."

"I know that. I'm just...taking advantage of the seasonal job postings. I'll be out for a couple of hours. Text me from the iPad if you need anything. I'll have your phone with me."

"I want my phone."

"I left mine at school. They are mailing it to me today or tomorrow, but if you want to be able to get in touch with me this morning, I need to borrow yours."

She drops her head into her hand.

"I need these too." I grab her keys.

I can do this.

In the parking lot, I stare down the big white heap of metal. Where do I need to go that makes this machinery necessary? Michaels probably isn't nearly as fun if you're working there. And if I worked for Ms. Pearl's bakery, I'd have to wake up at like three in the morning. Plus, I wouldn't be able to resist the Danishes, so I'd probably gain more pounds than cash.

Those gigs aren't worth the risk. There are plenty of options right across the street.

In the daytime, the journey across the highway is scarier. I wait and wait for the traffic to break, and finally, when I can only see one vehicle coming from a long way off, I sprint. If I'm to do this every day, I may need to enlist the services of a crossing guard.

At least the daylight hike through the bushes is easier.

Instead of speaking to a manager at The Home Depot, I purchase a wreath. I doubt I'm qualified for a hardware store job. I craft. I don't do home maintenance.

The hiring manager for Kohl's is out for the morning, but the service desk lady says I can submit an online application. She owes me, since it's basically her fault I'm in this whole mess.

"Do you know how much the starting pay is?"

"A dollar above minimum wage, I think."

"Which is…"

"Like nine dollars or something. You can make more if you work overnights, or if you have specialized experience. Do you have a fashion background, by any chance?"

"I knit."

Her face sours.

I'm not working overnight. Sleep is too important to me. How many daytime work hours will it take me to make up the fifteen hundred dollars I've spent? At nine dollars an hour, I'd have to work, like…thirty hours a week for the next six weeks—my whole winter break.

How much do they take out for taxes? Do students have to pay those? And do I need to pay my whole school fee all at once?

Probably yes, which means I'm going to need to either make more money per hour or give up any hope of having an actual Christmas. If I work for minimum wage, I won't be able to take care of Mom, or help with the Twinkle Dash, or binge watch Christmas movies, or bake for everyone…or sleep at all glorious hours of the day.

How much do grocery stores pay?

I walk into Food Lion with some hope and walk out with a bag of donuts. I'm screwed.

My mom's phone buzzes.

[Maybe: Samantha Bell]: I'm stuck in a nightgown. Heeelp
Samantha Bell: Be there in five!

I secure the wreath and donuts, one under each arm, and bound across the highway, reaching the apartment with a small rash, two side stitches, and a bag of armpit-shaped cake. But my life is intact and it only took me four minutes, so I'm amazing. Could highway sprinting translate into money somehow? Is there a YouTube audience for that?

Miller's truck is on the apartment curb, his little LEGO man dangling from the rearview mirror. I don't see him anywhere, and I don't have time to search.

Mom is curled into a sullen heap on her bed, halfway in and halfway out of her nightgown. The thing is tangled so badly I consider cutting it open.

"What exactly happened here?"

"I think I went the wrong way through the hole a few times after I got frustrated. I'm so darn helpless I can't stand it. I need to do something."

"Uh, could you wait until I've unknotted your upper half?" I hold her still.

"Sorry. I just really need to get out of this house."

It's not a house. It's barely more than a closet, which is definitely the problem. I've seen cabin fever before. Drew gets it every time we go on a road trip.

I weave Mom's arm through the hole of her shirt several times and unwind the fabric until finally it's back to normal and slips over her head.

Sitting behind her and navigating her legs into spandex yoga pants isn't pretty, but we manage. She looks like a stick in them, so I make a note to add extra cream in her coffee.

The baggy winter coat easily fits around her cast. Once geared up, we go outside for a stroll.

Miller's truck is gone. Guess he didn't come to offer me any jobs.

Mom doesn't say much and neither do I. Maybe we're both afraid to voice our thoughts because if we combine our worries it will be too much to carry.

This is a far cry from the last time we walked. Back then, it was a clear summer day. Mom was busy at work. I was almost fully prepped to leave for school. The future was a stream of light. I had no idea that everything I liked about my life was about to be stripped away. Can we rewind three months and stay there?

I close my eyes and try to go back. When I take a deep breath, my nostrils fill with the scent of urine, probably from the dirty bridge we now live beside.

FIFTEEN

The next afternoon, I bring an extra creamy coffee to Mom's bedroom. She passes me her empty plate of lunch. I clean up the kitchen and sit at the island. What now?

Job hunt or schoolwork? How do I choose between such fantastic options?

I start an online application for Michaels and quickly lose interest. Why do they need to know about job and education experience for a prospective cashier? I have no experience or degrees. Still want to hire me?

Ugh.

I get out my computer and pull up the chemistry study guide. Who knows when I'll sit for the exam now, but I suppose I can knock out studying while I wait to hear back from professors about my absence.

That reminds me. I still need to email Professor Frume a doctor's note from Mom's hospitalization. Who seriously asks for that? And how do I get a doctor's note after the fact? Should I go into the ER with a piece of loose leaf?

Anyway, reduction-oxidation. *A strong acid is one that entirely dissociates into protons in a solution. So HCl becomes hydrogen and...* I wonder if mom would be up for driving me to the Twinkle Dash meeting tonight. I can't believe I'll get to help plan it this year. Yay!

An email alert pops up on my computer screen. My iPhone has been delivered!

Is Miller here?

I dash out the front door. A small box lies abandoned on the ground. The back of Miller's truck disappears down the road.

He couldn't even take a hot second to say hi?

～

Mom refuses to take me to my Twinkle Dash meeting. She wants me to do schoolwork instead and basically be miserable even though I've bent over backward to help her. I have no one else to ask, because all my friends are at college. Boo.

Maybe Miller would give me a ride. I sneak his number off of Mom's phone and add it to my contacts.

555-6710: Hey stranger… This is that cool chick from the apartments

He doesn't respond. Maybe he's confused.

555-6710: It's Adia. Use this number for me from now on

Still nothing.

I call Mrs. Karen to say I can't make it to the meeting. She promises to pose my suggestion of a cookie booth and to send me any relevant meeting notes.

If I can't go out and have fun, I'm going to stay here and show Mom exactly how much she needs me. I heat up the donated meal du jour, a chicken and rice casserole, and throw together a side salad from what we have in the fridge. While she's eating, I wash her sheets.

I get a plastic bag and tape it around her cast to prepare her for a bath. She sits with her eyes closed while I pour water over her back and lather her hair. My endless knowledge of the latest Hollywood news entertains her. She attempts to dry off by herself. After she drops the towel three times while trying to wrap her hair, I intervene. I brush and braid it for bed. She claims her arm doesn't hurt, but she winces as I pull on her nightgown. I check her discharge instructions and get her two more naproxen.

"Do you want to watch *About a Boy* with me before you go to bed?" I ask.

"I can barely keep my eyes open. Maybe tomorrow."

She's still looking too thin. I make her some of Miller's sugar milk and tuck her into bed.

She licks the froth from her upper lip. "This is nice. Thank you."

Miller for the win.

I wait for her to finish the drink, turn out the light, and carry my exhausted self to my own bed. I skip my bedtime routine. It's a lot of work caring for another human being. Plus job hunting. And making my brain bigger.

And Cal won't be here to help for three more days.

I need to rest up.

I check my texts one last time for a response from Miller, since he's definitely off of work by now. Nothing. I don't get it. I thought we were friends. Or approaching friendship, at least. And these days, I'm not that picky.

SIXTEEN

On Saturday night, three of Mom's church friends show up with snacks and park themselves on our couch. Everyone has a better social life than me. The room gets real crowded, real quick. I relegate myself to the bedroom designated for me—and any and all guests. My boredom goes from bad to worse.

I look Miller up even though I'm done with him. This is purely a fact-finding mission. Is he always closed off, or is it just with me?

Without his last name, I'm unable to find him on any of the socials. Even the online version of him keeps me at a distance.

All my high school friends and college acquaintances seem to be in the thick of exams or holiday travel planning like normal nineteen-year-olds. I'm so lame. Or Facebook is. I close out the site.

The ceiling isn't any help. Time to consult Dr. Google, my favorite psychiatrist.

What to do when you're bored out of your skull.

All kinds of lists appear on my screen. I pick one at random called "15 Ways to Bust Boredom."

1. Paint cool patterns on your nails.

Nah.

2. Write poetry.

Blah.

3. Set some personal goals.

Or I could bang my head against this wall.

4. Learn how to take better pictures with your iPhone.

Hmm.

That's a skill I've wanted to improve for a while. The video begins....

Thirty minutes later, I'm putting my new knowledge into practice when a link to the UPS employment page pops up in my texts.

Miller: Got you a job. Fill out this application. You start Monday. Greensboro West store

He does know how to text!

I don't type that, because I haven't yet decided if Miller possesses a sense of humor.

Adia: Oh my gosh. Thank you!
Miller: NP
Adia: Also, can I get a ride?
Miller: ...

For the love.

Adia: j/k

I consider asking him if he plans to have any fun on his day off tomorrow, but I think better of it. I don't want to look like I care.

He doesn't text me anything else. He most likely doesn't care.

I turn back to my new hobby and spend the next twenty-four hours obsessing over it. Who has time for boys when they're discovering their new passion in life?

~

To be safe, I wear khakis and closed-toed shoes to meet my boss Monday morning. I show up at seven a.m. to a dark store. When I knock, no one answers. Mom is, fortunately, still waiting on the curb.

"It's locked. What should I do?"

"Let's wait a minute and see if anyone comes."

Fifteen minutes later, a Latina woman with short choppy hair and marked creases around her eyes rushes past my mom's car with a handful of bags. I make Mom swear she'll call if she needs anything, and then jump out of the car to introduce myself.

"I'm Adia, the new employee."

"Oh, yes. Sorry I'm late. It's been crazy at home. My daughter Camila's in a play, which I'm trying to help run, and we're short here at the store. I'm Rosa, by the way. How are you?"

"I'm great. Thank you for giving me this opportunity."

"Thank *you*. You're doing me the favor."

"Can I hold something?" I ask while she struggles with the lock.

"Thanks!" Her lunch box and coat land in my arms. She pushes the door open and scurries around clicking on lights. The shop smells like fresh cardboard. After turning on the register, she summons me to follow her to the back.

"Sit, sit. Have you eaten? I have fruit and muffins. I always bring extras to share."

"Um..." I didn't have an appetite when I left the apartment this morning, but now that I've met my very nonintimidating boss, I'm much more open to food. How many muffins is it cool to claim?

"Take as many as you want, please," she says, like she's a mind reader. She pops the lids and sweet blueberry wafts into the air. "Now, we need to get you settled. All you need to know before we start is to be friendly and be careful. We don't want any injuries. Some of these packages, even the small ones, can be quite heavy. The rest I will teach you as we go along. Sound okay?"

I nod and do my best to politely nibble the one muffin I've grabbed.

Our first customers come through the door right at eight when the store opens. I watch Rosa key in the transactions, print labels, and process packages. By noon, I'm confident enough to try it on my own so she can take care of other tasks around the store.

I only have to ask one question during the lunch rush.

"I'm glad you're here, Adia. You're a fast learner."

"I like it. I feel like a little Christmas elf."

"It's nice to be doing something positive, for sure. I'd hate working somewhere depressing, like a debt collection agency. It can get pretty busy here this time of year, though, and then people get cranky. That gets old."

"Maybe we could decorate a little. Keep people in a cheerful mood."

Rosa stops stocking a shelf and wrinkles her brow. "Oh, my gosh. I hadn't realized I forgot to do that. There's a box of stuff in the storage closet. Let me grab it, and you can go crazy."

The string lights and garland I drape along the counter definitely liven up the place. I skip the broken Santa, planning to craft a wooden reindeer statue sometime this weekend as a replacement. My mom taught me how to make them from leftover Christmas tree branches. They're cheap and adorable.

While I'm tying jingle bells to the garland, a guy, whose teal shirt bears the UPS logo, stops beside me. Do we all get teal shirts? That'd look way better on me than brown.

The guy is Korean, at least partially. He's a little taller than Miller, with a giant smile that conceals his eyes. Earrings sparkle in both his earlobes. I recognize him right away. My friend Jessica dated him in high school, which made her the coolest girl in our freshman class.

"I've been thinking we needed some holiday spirit around here. Kudos, Jingle Bell." He gives the bell ornament I've just hung up a jiggle.

I stand back to admire my hard work. It does look lovely. "Thanks."

"I'm Harry. You must be Jane's replacement."

I stick out my hand to return the shake. "I'm Adia. We went to school together. I was a few years younger."

"You sure? I think I'd remember a face like yours."

I laugh off his comment. Back then, I had a hardy case of cystic acne and avoided most of the popular kids in the hallways. Accutane didn't enter my life until senior year.

He says, "Let's get the Christmas soundtrack going while we're sprucing things up."

Yes. Harry knows what's up. He disappears, and a few minutes later Michael Bublé croons a Christmas carol over the sound system.

Jemma has got to hear about this. Is cell phone use acceptable here?

I decide to wait until I'm off the clock.

I'm situating the nativity set when Rosa comes out of the back with a load of papers. I offer my assistance, and she beams at me with her warm brown eyes.

"So what's up with you and Miller?"

"Miller?"

"You know, the guy who usually avoids conversation but risked it to ask me to give you a job."

So he's a loner at work too.

"We're friends, sort of." More like I'm some girl he took pity on for a minute.

"Miller doesn't have friends. I've known him six years and never seen him talk to anyone if it wasn't absolutely necessary. I think that's why he avoids me so hard—because I force him to interact. Have you known him awhile?"

So it's *not* just me. It's not me at all. It's him.

"I met him a week ago, actually."

"Oh." She studies me for a moment, then smirks.

"What?"

"Oh, nothing. Nothing at all."

I turn back to my organizing. Does Miller really not have any friends?

That's tragic.

If college has taught me anything, it's that not having friends blows. You end up eating lunch alone and bumming awkward rides and getting caught up with the wrong type of guy.

But Miller has something here that I don't have at Avery, an ally.

I'm going to jingle bell rock this boy's world.

I'm going to find Miller a friend.

SEVENTEEN

I've had a few too many cups of caramel coffee from the break room by the time Miller pulls into the store's back lot to park his truck for the night. He's setting something inside when I accost him.

At a full-speed run, I swoop him into a hug. "I love my new—"

An elbow to the stomach knocks the breath out of me. I fall on my rear and look up at Miller, who's in full-on bear stance. "Shit, Adia. You can't sneak up on someone like that."

"I was hugging you! Do most perpetrators start their acts of violence with affection?!"

He sticks out a hand and tugs me to my feet. "I'm sorry."

I brush off my butt. "I'll forgive it, but only because I love the new job you got me."

He raises an eyebrow.

"What?"

"Is there anything you don't get excited about?"

"Whatever. Today was fun. And Rosa's really nice."

He shuts the doors of his truck and walks toward the building. I scoop his arm into mine, ready to deliver the first element of my Christmas surprise. He stiffens.

I drop his arm. Maybe I'm being too much? Or do I smell? I think I put on deodorant this morning. Clamping down on my underarms just in case, I follow him toward the building.

He drops his keys into a mail slot.

"Did you know that every Wednesday they do this trivia night at The Drowsy Poet? I used to go all the time. They have the best coffee in town and a lot of people come to the game nights. I thought that since—"

"I actually need to get home. You have fun."

"Oh."

He practically runs away from me. No goodbye. No "glad you had a good day." Nothing.

It's okay. He doesn't know any better.

But helping Miller is going to be much harder than I'd hoped. I really thought trivia might be his thing, since he likes to state facts. And it was Christmas music trivia night too. Oh, the delight!

Miller avoids me the rest of the week. Does he know I'm up to something?

It's kind of entertaining watching him dodge interaction. It's like looking in a magic mirror of my own recent past. Only, I had a good reason to hide. What's he so afraid of? That I'll overwhelm him with my thoughtfulness? That I might have other family members, thereby increasing the potential for health emergencies?

If I'm going to make any progress with this boy, I'll have to bide my time. Something will come along. It's the holiday season, after all.

EIGHTEEN

The first weekend of December hits me with the same feeling it does every year: total elation. I give my dear mom until about ten a.m. Saturday morning before I bombard her room about going to Mistletoe Meadows.

"Please come. It's the Christmas Tree Festival. I'll die if I miss it!"

"Adia, I have a broken arm. I'm not up for walking around a mountain."

"You need to get out."

"Then we can go for coffee sometime. I don't have the stamina for a late night or a crowd. Plus, Cal's getting home tonight. I'm sorry."

Ugh. I slam my bedroom door. I have been at her beck and call for a week, and she can't do this one thing for me? I throw a pillow against the door. I need a pick-me-up before I explode.

But retail therapy is out. I guess there's always crafting....

The cookie booth! Mrs. Karen said my refreshment idea was a huge hit at the Twinkle Dash meeting, and the race director assigned me to organize the booth. Naturally, we need themed goody bags. Computer paper won't do much for presentation, but I can use it to make a prototype. I grab some out of my desk.

My reindeer box takes me over an hour to construct, but it comes out adorable. With some glitter antler handles and fun paper, it's going to pop. I can't wait to show it off at Monday night's meeting. Jemma can take me since she'll be back in town. Yipee!

I burn daylight searching Pinterest for other decoration ideas for the booth. If you can't waste time planning over-the-top events for the holidays, when can you? Eventually I get tired and stretch out on my bed to watch *White Christmas*. Even though it's one of her favorites, I'm definitely not inviting Mrs. Life-ruiner to join.

We could be at the festival right now. I squeeze my pillow.

"Honey." My mom shakes me awake.

I'm doing that wide-eyed stare that happens when your brain's conscious and unconscious parts are trying to switch places.

"That Miller boy is at the front door."

Seriously? I pop up. "What time is it?"

"A little after four."

A two-hour nap! Not exactly a good use of my diminished free time, but whatever. I need to focus on the real issue: my bedhead.

I feel out the problem. It's sizable, sticking off the back of my skull in frizzy tangles.

"Tell him I'll be there in a minute."

I manage to play it cool until I'm alone. Behind a closed door, I tear through my bag, looking for a clean tee. I need to spend a little more time on chores for the next few days.

I resort to a chunky sweater and my favorite jeans. Then I brush like a madwoman. It usually takes a lot of time to get all the tangles out, but I can hear the awkwardness of the silence on the other side of this door...even I'm uncomfortable. I give up and sequester the knot of hair with a scrunchie plus two chopstick pins that I find at the bottom of my purse. The updo actually turns out looking kind of cool in a free-spirit sort of way. I quit while I'm ahead. Time to seize the moment.

I strut into the living room. "Hey." My hand reaches for the couch but misses, and I nearly tumble into Miller's lap.

"Hey," he echoes, eying my recovery.

"What's up?" My second attempt at a casual lean is successful.

He rakes his long fingers through his hair, and I get this feeling like he's about to bail. "Will you do me a favor?" he says.

"I don't think so. You don't seem like the type who deserves it."

"That's fair. I'm probably not." His eyes hit the floor. I take the opportunity to study his face. He's got this slight gap between his teeth that you can only really see if you're up close. Embedded between his eyebrows is a permanent burrow, probably from too many brooding thoughts. He's definitely thinking one right now.

"I'm teasing, dude. Lighten up. Tell you what: I'll do you a favor if you do me one."

His eyes narrow.

I smile.

"Fine," he says.

"Do you want to know what my favor is first?"

"No. Do you?"

"Does it involve illegal activity or cats?"

"Nope. Don't think so."

"Then I'm in. My mom has no desire to be involved in my life this evening, so I would prefer to be elsewhere."

"How is she?" he asks quietly. He glances behind me at Mom, who is fiddling around in the kitchen. I don't care if she heard me.

"Better. Well taken care of."

"Seems like it." He nods toward the kitchen.

Wait, what?

A boastful platter of chocolate chip cookies—which I'd love to taste if I wasn't busy conceiving an anger baby—sits atop the counter. Mom made dessert? Without me?

What the devil?

Music curls through my awareness, as does the crackle of a candle. The living room has even been picked up. Guess my stepdad's return is important enough to merit some enthusiasm.

"Let's get out of here."

Miller pulls his car into a neighborhood. The Christmas decorations have really come out since last weekend, and I am all for it. The bigger, the better. I'm talking property line to property line illumination. On this street, a massive snow globe takes the cake. I let go of everything that's bothering me and give in to my childish wonder. It's like reconnecting with an old friend.

"Look at that puppy!" I point.

"All those lights adversely affect the brain's melatonin production. Excessive nighttime outdoor displays can lead to increases in human anxiety and headaches, and they disrupt the ecosystems of nocturnal wildlife."

"You're being extreme."

"It's science."

"The holidays also make people's spirits bright. I'm sure that's scientific too."

We stop at the house next to the snow globe.

It has two tasteful (ahem, boring) lighted topiaries in pots on the porch, and that's it. The subdued display would probably appease Miller, but his eyes are glued to the road.

"Set the package on the porch. Scan the bar code with this." He hands me a big black clicker thing. "Type in the date and time, press confirm, and your favor will be complete."

I narrow my eyes at him. "This is all you need me to do? Set a package on a porch?" He is *so* in for a rude awakening when we do my thing. "You sure you weren't just missing my excellent company?"

"You got me. Now don't drop the package. My satisfaction score is irreproachable."

I probably shouldn't mention the tractor-trailer vs. shopping cart incident right now. "You use really big words for a delivery boy."

"I listen to a lot of podcasts. Now go. You're slowing us down."

I wink at him from the porch as I execute my mission to perfection. I'm not sure what is so special about "Maureen Johnson" that Miller needed me to deliver her package, but I don't feel like questioning it. I'm going to the tree farm, baby!

NINETEEN

Despite the chill in the air, a window roll-down is essential. I reach across Miller to get his open too. He shies away from my touch.

Jeez, it's not like I was trying to cop a feel.

"You do know we're not in the city of Greensboro any longer, right?" he says.

"We're almost there. Just stay straight."

Twenty minutes later, I see it. "Turn here!"

He slams on his brakes to make the left. We idle on the dirt path behind a long line of cars. There are hillsides of dark green treetops for miles. Along the road, ribbons and white lights festoon the feathery pines. I stick most of my torso out the window and snap away on my iPhone, practicing my focal points and balancing the weights of objects in the photos. I juxtapose pieces of things. Our gunmetal gray hood engulfed by ancient trees. The blurred energy of happy people in the distance. No angle quite captures the mystical haze haloing the tips of the highest firs.

I snap a pic of Miller's narrowed brow before he covers my camera with his palm. "What is this?" he asks.

"A Christmas tree farm."

"I can see that. I meant the crowd."

"Today's the Mistletoe Meadows Tree Lighting Festival. They always do it the first weekend in December to kick off the season. Once it's really dark, some lucky kid gets to climb a ladder to place a star on top of this enormous tree that has, like, thousands of lights on it. Then they turn on the power and the whole sky lights up."

The leather beneath him creaks.

"You'll love it. It's a whole thing."

"There's nothing I can do about it now."

First things first: refreshments. After we park and pay our entry fee, I lead Miller to the picnic area. A crew of people is hard at work prepping a stage near the tables. I figure out from someone nearby that a live band comes on at dusk. Miller's side-eye at my squeal gets a pass, but he better shape up. He *will* be my dancing partner. It's half the reason I brought him out here.

We finally get to the front of the concession line, and I order cinnamon donut holes, hot chocolate, and a big ole popcorn. Miller declines any food but slips his debit card through the window. I snatch it and stick it in my bra. He already won this fight at the welcome counter. It's my turn now.

We take my food and head to the hayride. Miller somehow resists the urge to sample a single kernel out of the popcorn bucket he carries for me.

"You sure you don't want some? I wanted to taste everything, not eat it entirely by myself."

"I'm good."

"It's going to be a long night if you resist nourishment. Tree hunting takes some stamina. We are on a mountain, you know."

"If I'd known the plan, I would have packed something."

"Is this a single-use packaging issue again?"

He gives me the shrug. *Gah!*

"If I promise to not eat packaged goods the rest of the week, will you try one donut hole?"

He shakes his head. It's not a no; it's a weakening resolve.

"Please, Mr.— Hey, what's your last name?"

"Do you want my name or my compliance? You can only get one."

"I definitely choose the donut. Look how sad he is. He needs the big, stubborn man to give him a chance. Let him live his little donut destiny."

Miller holds out his hand. I stick the three remaining balls into it.

"You're pushy," he says around a mouthful of dough.

"Only when it comes to Christmas activities. You needed to experience the full effect of the tree farm. Now help me finish the popcorn."

"No convenience eating for a month."

"A whole month! You better be planning to cook for me."

A handful goes into his mouth in one big bite as we approach our stop. He smiles with chubby cheeks. I throw a kernel at his forehead.

Miller gets off the tractor first, then reaches out his hand to help me down. How chivalrous. My heart pitter-patters as I reach down to my gentlemen caller. But he ruins the moment by flinching when I touch him.

I huff and march toward the worker giving out hacksaws.

If you don't want to touch someone, don't offer to touch them. Just like if you don't want to look at someone, walk away as quickly as you can without checking behind you. It isn't rocket science.

"Adia, wait."

I duck between the fingerlike branches of two Fraser firs and angry hunt. *Why would anyone even take me near a tree this massive? Do I look like I'm made of money? That one's so perky it should be punched...fatty...and you're super sucky for no specific reason. Ugh.*

Miller halts my rampage. "Hey."

I turn the other direction. He comes around to block me again, careful to avoid the wild saw blade.

"Come on, Adia. Stop for a second, okay?"

"Make me. Oh, wait, you're too grossed out to touch me."

"It's not like that."

"I didn't ask you to touch me or anything. I didn't even want you to. But you don't have to act like it's so awful."

"I don't think it's awful! Listen, can you stop walking, please?" He brushes my back with his fingers.

My heart skitters at the sensation.

I turn around and throw my hand on my hip. "What?"

"Can we talk somewhere more private?"

My cheeks redden, and then I get embarrassed that they are reddening, and that makes it even worse. This whole situation has me on tilt. Why do I care so much that a stupid boy thinks I'm gross?

I breathe out a cloud of hot breath and walk with him farther into the trees until we get out of everyone else's earshot.

Everything on him gets droopy, like a parched plant. My pity climbs into the driver's seat.

"Whatever it is," I say, "just lay it on me. All of my friends have lots of issues."

He looks me over for a minute, mostly right into my eyes. Now I'm the one who wants to flinch.

"When I was younger, I got beat up, okay? A big group of guys got pissed off at me and put me in the hospital. Ever since, I'm skittish if people touch me when I'm not expecting it."

I nod, wanting to feel sad for him but unable to let go of the fact that it doesn't explain why he flinched just now, since he initiated the touch. "Did they get in trouble?"

"I never told anyone."

"You mean you let them get away with hospitalizing you and traumatizing you for life?"

He bites his lip. "Let's go pick a tree."

"Wait. I want to know why you never said anything."

"Haven't you ever just wanted to move past something?"

Douche Face pops into my mind.

I let it drop and follow Miller back toward the other people. This discussion isn't over, though. Miller hasn't moved past anything. He's drowning in it. The signs of distress are all over him, like how he's clawing at his neck skin right now.

But I want this to be a fun memory.

"Person to find the ugliest tree doesn't have to cut it," I say.

"You want the ugliest tree?"

"Yeah, it's the Charlie Brown factor. You find the one that looks the worst, because it feels the best to dress it up. Plus, they might cut me a deal on the price."

He finds one with a gnarly hole. I find one that's half brown. But when we simultaneously spot one that's hunched like it's having a full-on pity party for itself, we know it's the winner.

We saw together while I sing songs with the word "cut" in the chorus. Thank you, *Footloose* and Carly Rae Jepsen.

"Can you stop making me feel worse about this than I already do?" he whines.

"You feel bad about this?"

"We are deliberately killing a vital part of our ecosystem. I'm in physical pain."

Aw. I resist the urge to pinch his cheek, since touching is evidently a no go. "But Hunchy's fulfilling his destiny. Just like the little donut hole."

"You cannot call a tree an insulting name while it's down."

"Fine. What would you name him?"

He shakes his head. "Since we're at its funeral, we should call it by its formal name, *Abies fraseri*."

"Be honest. Did you start this entire argument so that you could show off that you knew that?"

"I'm not that cool. I heard it on a podcast yesterday."

"I see. Let's take Abies to the tractor then."

Miller heaves that bad boy onto his shoulder in one motion. Hello, mountain man.

My phone can't help but capture that visual.

We set Abies on the trunk of Miller's convertible and strap her in. It's a tenuous setup, but Miller seems confident the tree will make it home.

"This car is crazy," I say, pinching off a sneeze.

"It gets me around." Miller opens the driver's side door and starts to get in.

"Hey. What are you doing?"

"Getting in the car."

"But we're not done."

He looks back at the mass of bodies swarming around the farm. "We've done what we came here to do."

"Not at all. There's lots more, and we've got to be here for the tree lighting part. Please." I do my best pout.

Concern veins his forehead.

"Look. It's just you and me, okay? All those people...they're just decoration. We can pretend like they aren't even there."

"I don't care about the people. It just seems stupid." He sits down.

I duck down into my side of the car but don't shut the door for fear he might drive off. Time to get real. "The first time I came here, I broke my toe. I was five, and it was just me and my mom. We managed to cut down a tree all by ourselves, but I couldn't carry it very well. Dropped that sucker right on my big toe. I didn't tell Mom how much it hurt, just kept going. My foot was black and blue for weeks."

Miller pokes out his lip.

"But I was proud of that toe. My dad had just died and that toe was proof that me and my mom could get along okay on our own, that I was tough enough... Mom and I come here every year. This place reminds me of a layer of myself that I forget about most of the time. This gutsy layer." I lean my head on the door frame. Abies's needles brushes across the side of my face. "I sound crazy."

"I don't think I've ever thought about any place with so much feeling."

"Well, I love this place. I love that I can count on it. Unlike everything else in my life. I mean, I didn't even know my mom and stepdad had moved into an apartment while I was away at school. They got rid of our house and my dog without telling me. It's like I traded everything I knew for the chance to get a degree. But if someone had told me that was the price, I wouldn't have paid it. I loved my life before."

He stares at me, expressionless. His silence stings. He probably thinks I'm obnoxious and whiney, and he's deciding how to bail. My arms prickle.

"They gave away your dog?"

"Yeah." I blink away a tear.

"Unconscionable."

"Un-what?"

"Unconscionable. It means that's not right."

I chuckle. "Yes. Totally unconscionable."

"You really get into all this cheesy holiday stuff, don't you?"

"Every bit. I want all the bells and all the whistles. Every year. Forever. Holidays are the one thing I can count on not to end."

"Man." His face crinkles as he shakes his head at me. "Okay."

"Okay, we can stay?"

"Because you lost your dog, I'll subject myself to this madness."

Thanks, Wizard, for the parting gift.

TWENTY

I can't stop myself from bouncing around Santa's workshop and cooing as we tour the Christmas displays. It could be the influence of the second hot chocolate, which I picked up on the way inside.

Mistletoe Meadows does a fundraiser every year to raise money for cerebral palsy since one of the owner's kids has it. All their sponsors get to decorate a tree in the barn. The trees are so clever! I pull my phone out for a shot of the lawn and garden store's tree made entirely of outdoor supplies, mostly pots and metal chairs spray-painted green. Lee's Tire Shop made a tire tree with air fresheners as ornaments. Even Miller laughs at that. The sound is inspirational, a chesty bellow that makes me want to tickle more out of him.

But tickling is probably off-limits. What are his boundaries? High fives? I wonder if he's ever kissed a girl. I wonder if he's ever even hugged one.

He's probably not a hugger.

I sneak behind my phone camera when he catches me watching him.

The next tree has dainty little candy boxes dangling from its branches. I sniff one. "This one's got chocolate on it! Real chocolate. It's officially my favorite."

"I like that one." Miller points to a tree in the corner with nothing but a lumpy burlap bow at the top.

"It looks like some dude showed up without any decorations and made do with a bag he found in the trash."

"Yeah." A chuckle escapes him. It's like watching Christmas joy slip into someone's soul.

We get to the stairs, and I swing around the banister. "Time to visit the big man."

"Come again?"

"Santa. Let's go see him."

"You know that at your age he could get arrested for that."

"I'm nineteen."

"Yeah. Public indecency."

"Whatever. Just humor me. I want one good pic and then we can go."

I pass him the phone and skip up the stairs to get in line.

It's excruciatingly long. How did I ever last as a kid? Probably my mom's bag of tricks. She had everything in there. Playdough. Coloring books. Suckers... I really wish she was here.

But she's not up for mom stuff lately.

"What do you want for Christmas?" I ask Miller.

"I stopped wanting things years ago."

"So what do your parents give you then? Boring money?"

"They don't give me anything. I don't want anything from them."

I flinch at his change in tone. I've hit a chord.

"My dad stopped talking to all of us a long time ago, when he succumbed to his vices. I stopped talking to my mom when I was seventeen."

"But you were a minor."

"I got emancipated and moved out."

"Why?"

"She isn't awesome."

I need to sit down to take this in properly, but we're almost to the front of the line. "Was she upset that you left?"

"I don't know."

"So you haven't seen her in the last, what is it, seven years?"

"Haven't heard from her since the day I walked out. She doesn't know where I am."

What is the world without parents? I reach for Miller but catch myself before he notices. "That must be rough." I try to comfort him with my eyes.

"I'm better off. I can take care of myself just fine."

The boy has maturity on lockdown.

"Do you miss them?"

"I don't miss feeling like an afterthought, no."

"But—"

"Your turn, sweetheart," interrupts Santa's helper.

"Hi, Santa!" I say cheerfully to cover up the awkwardness I'm feeling. I'm taking a classic Christmas photo, because it's funny, and that's what you do to make memories, dang it!

But I don't sit on his lap—that would be way weird. Instead, I lean beside him and smile. Miller fiddles with my iPhone, unsure what to do.

"Swipe left over the screen to open the camera. Then hold it steady and press the white circle at the bottom."

Santa's helper is fiddling with his own contraption. He's got it angled in an awkward—suspicious—way. I become very aware of my cleavage. This sweater is baggy, and with how I'm leaning... One glance confirms that my girls are out there for him to see. I shift back, but I'm pretty sure the creep got a few shots first.

"Okay then." I step away from Santa, feeling my cheeks turn the color of his coat.

"The picture's blurry," Miller says.

"It's fine. Let's just go."

"Hold on. We just waited like forty minutes. We at least need a decent picture."

"I'm good." I pull him away.

"Well, now we've wasted all that time."

I lean in so only Miller can hear. "Look, if you want a clear pic just ask the elf dude. But be prepared for mostly chest. Let's just go."

"What?"

"He was doing that thing people do with cell phones when they're trying to take pictures of someone without them knowing."

"Hell no."

Miller pushes past a dad trying to snap a photo of his toddler squirming out of Santa's hold.

"Where's your phone?" he demands in a tone that gets the elf guy to cough it up without argument.

"Put in your code," he says.

Once the guy has done so, Miller pushes it toward me.

"Find the photos."

Sure enough, there I am. He was nice enough to capture my confused face in the stolen image. I delete it and three others he took before I noticed.

"You probably shouldn't hire perverts to work with children," Miller tells Santa and throws the phone at Douche Face Number Two, who goes ghost white.

I flee the scene. Miller follows me to the back of the building, where I choose to stop since I'm dizzy from all the blood pooling inside my inflated heart. My honor has been defended.

"Thanks for that."

"That guy was a chump."

I giggle.

"It's not a laughing matter, Adia. Who knows what he could have done with those photos. What if he'd posted them online? Once that kind of thing's out there..."

So serious. I wish I could tackle him...or at least move the straggling hair away from his left eye.

Instead, I say, "I don't need a picture with Santa when you've just become my Christmas hero."

I make a stunned face and hold out the phone for a selfie of us.

He snatches it away before I can.

"I don't like having my picture taken."

"This hardly counts."

"Just please don't take my picture."

"Okay."

We are from different planets. I wish I could have filmed every second of us on this mountain. I love some moments so much, I never want to move on from them.

Up above, a sparkly purple curtain draws down upon the orange and yellow remnants of daytime. String lights don't compare to that twinkle.

"Look," I breathe.

We gaze in awe.

The thump of a bass begins.

I rub my increasingly itchy eyes and stand. I keep rubbing until I'm crying. Perfect.

Miller peels his gaze away from the morphing sky. "Are you okay?"

I sneeze. "My eyes hurt."

"I think the trees are turning on you."

"They would never do that."

"Well, you're reacting to something out here."

"What, like allergies? I don't have allergies."

"Let's take stock. Watery, itchy eyes. Sneezing. Does your throat hurt?"

I frown. How the heck did I catch allergies?

I consult Google. Miller's right. I've got all the symptoms, and apparently it can begin at any age.

"This is so tragic," I whine, rubbing my eyes again.

"Let's get out of here."

"But I wanted to dance."

"You're maddening, woman. Come on."

He leads me to his car. My lip juts out to its full potential. With that and the allergy tears, I'm really selling this pout. He rolls his eyes and ducks into his car. After some shuffling, he comes back with something in his hand.

"Here."

It's a container of Benadryl.

"You really come prepared."

"Everyone should keep a well-stocked first-aid kit. You never know when you're going to run into trouble. Here's some water, if you're not a germaphobe."

I'm not, but somehow putting my mouth where his mouth has

been feels too intimate. I don't want him to think I'm enjoying it or some weirdness. But if I open the steel lid and drink from the rim, he'll probably think I think he's gross, which I know from recent experience feels crappy. I debate for so long, he pulls the bottle back.

I hold firm. "I'll take it. Thanks."

By the time we get back to the gathering, my eyes have stopped watering.

"You patched me up. Again." The mom. The puke. The job. The sleazeball. The allergies. I'm beginning to think Miller might be the cure for everything.

TWENTY-ONE

Miller plants his butt on a picnic table near the band—which is currently rocking out with an electric fiddle—and refuses to budge.

"We don't have to touch."

He blows out a breath. "That's not the issue."

"Then what is?"

"I don't want to do it."

I scowl. "But dancing feels *so good*. Don't you want to feel good?"

"I feel good sitting right here." He crosses his arms and leans back.

"You don't get it. There's, like, normal good, and then there's the dancing high. It isn't something you can understand until you give yourself to it. Come on."

"Adia, I'm not dancing in front of all these people, okay?"

"Fine." If he's going to cement himself to his fears, I need to get drastic. "I'm going to show you what you're missing. You better keep your eyes on me."

He obeys, dragging his gaze from the ground all the way up my body. It's like a matchstick stroke. The smolder mingles with the party energy leaving me effervescent already.

If there's any kind of Christmas music I can get down to, it's countrified Christmas music, so I've lucked out. I loosen things up with a few tame shoulder pumps on my way to the dance floor.

The band is fantastic. They have two guitar-playing singers, a guy and a girl, which makes for some stellar duets. Accompanying the vocalists are a fiddler, a drummer, and a keyboard guy, who throws in all kinds of techno sounds like bells and chimes. The music crawls through me.

I turn my moves toward Miller, and we lock eyes. He shifts under my gaze, like even eye touches are too intrusive.

Alongside a fast-thumping beat, the singers croon about getting jolly, so I do. Every fiber of me shifts into motion.

In high school, this one rich kid had hippie parents. They let him have dance parties every weekend in his basement. It was an excellent education. It's where I learned this body roll I'm doing.

Miller's brows rise. I use more rolls to lure him out of his repression.

His dark head starts to bob, and I mirror him. His feet strike the grass, embracing the music. I press on. His waist seems to be subtly following my movement. When I twist my hips in a slow, popping swirl, his hand goes to his lips, dragging the bottom one down to expose clenched teeth. Though I'm alone, I can feel Miller's attention on me like the glint of clashing body parts. What is this exchange?

Maybe this isn't dancing, but it's something. *It's something good.* It deserves a name.

Eyefrisking: Locking eyes with another person and accosting their visual senses with your nefarious moves.

I eyefrisk until my legs are too weak to function.

"How's the dancing going?" Miller asks when I sit down.

"Good." My voice is breathy and unstable. How can he sound so calm after all that? "How's the not-dancing?"

"Just fine." His voice cracks. *Ha.* I knew I was getting to him.

"You want to get out of here?" I ask. I think I've done about all the merrymaking this body can handle for one evening.

"We can stay."

"Nah, it's fine. Let's go. I don't really need to see a big tree light up all that bad." I walk toward the parking lot to keep from fixating on his damp lips.

"You're a good dancer," he says, catching up to me.

"Thanks." My body resumes the flush it had on the dance floor.

Where do we go from here? I know we didn't kiss or any of that couple stuff, but we definitely got *personal* back there. I feel like we're on a different level now. The air between us is harder to breathe.

We wiggle into the tight seats of his car. Our arms brush for a brief second, and I know I don't feel the same about Miller anymore. I care about him. I care what he's doing tomorrow and what he thinks about my dancing and whether or not he's going to go back to pretending I don't exist after tonight.

I don't want to go back to lonely.

Miller slowly weaves us out of the parking area and away from the farm while I monitor Abies. We hear the collective cry of hundreds of voices counting down from ten behind us. I peek back. Miller pulls to the edge of the dirt road and puts the car in park.

"Come on."

He crawls out of his window. I follow him to the trunk, where we recline against the windshield with our legs propped up on Abies. The wind howls through my brain. To block out the chill, I scoot as close to Miller as I can without touching.

From our private spot fifty yards away, we watch a shining star finish its ascent to the top of a grand spruce. The countdown nears zero. The star perches. Then, *bam!* The whole area goes bright. And not just the tree. Soft-white, glowing bulbs rim the whole barn like icing on a gingerbread house, and illuminated garland connects the trees along the gravel road. The effect is way better from afar. My breath hitches.

But it isn't because of the visual delight. Miller's hand is sneaking into mine.

His palm is rough, the little knobs of callus scratching across my skin where we join. Our fingers knit together. This is what I needed tonight. Not the lights or the warm cocoa or the music or any of that. Just a closed-off boy reaching out for me. It's pure magic.

I'm too afraid to look at his face for fear I'll scare him off. I lean against his shoulder. "Tell me something about you," I say. "Something you like to remember."

With how loud the wind is, he has to tell me the story like it's a secret. His warm breath coats my earlobe. "I helped start a tech company called Innovise when I was fifteen. It got fairly big."

I've heard that name. "Is that the huge building near the interstate?"

He nods.

"You helped start it?"

As he talks, his lips graze my skin. My hormones start playing Would You Rather? with my brain. I learn as much about Miller's first job as gets past my poor concentration. He had been doing programming work for his high school...would I rather him run his tongue across my ear or my neck...a teacher put in a good word with a friend...would I rather his hand stay in mine or travel somewhere lower...he got hired at fifteen to work on the software program for a start-up market research firm...would I rather straddle him or ask the question that has just come into my head...

My lungs gulp air.

He stops talking and moves a few inches away. *Come back.* I lean toward him. "Did you feel like a fish out of water around all those adults?"

"Not really. I liked working better than being at school. Mostly because the people were cool...most of them. They didn't judge a person by looks or social status. I didn't have to be this certain way for them to accept me. I could just be good at my work and that was enough."

I picture fifteen-year-old Miller as a glum misfit. Would I have misjudged him? Would I have even noticed him at all? He was probably out-of-fashion and awkward. I picture James Leon, who I asked to be un-partnered with in history class because he wore wrist spikes and I didn't "feel safe" studying with him outside of school. Shame sets up next to the desire in my chest. At an age when I was wasting my time on socializing, Miller was working a legit corporate job. He must have been a stud programmer.

"So you get along better with old people?"

The wind whips my hair across both our faces. Miller catches some and tucks it behind my ear. It doesn't stay, but the memory of his touch does—a small trail of warmth in the frost. I clench my jaw as the cold intensifies.

"I do tend to prefer people over thirty, when all the stupidity and self-centeredness has worn off a little."

"Hey. Not even twenty here."

"You're different."

"How so?" I feel like I might be exactly what he just described. The wind roars, and my shiver reflex gets the better of me.

"Are you cold?"

"Mm mm. Nope."

"You're shivering."

"I'm fine."

He lets go of my hand and gets to his feet instead of answering my question. *Darn you, survival reflexes.*

"We don't have to go, really. I can handle a little cold."

"I'm only getting a jacket."

Of course he has an extra jacket.

I tuck my arms into the sleeves. The extra layer is a sweet relief, although Miller taking my hand again would be even better. I hear good things about body heat.

"Why don't you still work at the software company?"

"Long story."

"I've got time." I lean my head back. The stars twinkle brilliantly above me.

Miller goes mute.

"What?" I sit up to face him.

He shakes his head. "Let's just talk about something else."

"Like why you don't talk to your parents anymore?" I let his jaw clench several times before I change directions. "Have you ever been in love?"

He gives the most unconvincing no I've ever heard.

"Who was she?"

"I've never been in love."

"You've been in something. Tell me."

He shakes his head.

"Is it that girl who lives in my apartment building?"

"Who?"

"The redheaded bombshell with the tats...the one with the white convertible."

He wrinkles his brow and, after a second, raises it. "No. Definitely not her."

"Then who? Tell me," I beg.

"Adia, you might be the first girl I've ever had a real conversation with since I even had those kinds of feelings for girls." He smooths out his jeans. "What about you? Have you ever had a boyfriend?"

That terrible night busts into my consciousness. My lip starts to tremble.

"Adia?"

What the heck? Why am I getting upset? Why do I have to be so emotional at the worst times?

"Did something happen to you?"

The tears break free, spilling down my cheeks. I wipe them away.

"Dammit." He turns his body toward me, moving his face into my view until I look at him. I get his hand back. "Tell me what happened."

"That's real fair," I mumble.

"Just do it." His jaw is clenched.

I don't like angry Miller, so I give up on my case. "I met this guy named Charlie in one of my classes this semester. He seemed cool."

Tears pour. I'm not going to be able to say all this crap out loud. I look away. A cloth tissue appears in my face.

Sloppy, snuffly chuckles escape from me. Who on earth is this guy? I snatch the handkerchief and blow out a wad of snot. It's getting real up in here.

After my nasal passages are cleared and my tears have slowed, I start again.

"He was the first big-deal guy who ever paid attention to me. It's the typical story. I wasn't exactly popular in high school. Other than one summer camp fling, no boys looked my way. So when Charlie did, I got caught up in it. I thought that college had, like, adjusted my lighting, I guess. I really believed we had an actual connection. And he was everything I thought I wanted. College athlete. Perfect face. Buff. Rich parents...charm for days. The works. I started crushing hard. I held Charlie up so high, I couldn't even see him. I never stopped to think about how little of him I actually knew. I just lapped up any attention he gave me, all the subtle touches in class, the flirty innuendos. He was priming me all along." My stomach twists. "When he invited me to a frat party, I thought, *This is my night.*" Miller's hand squeezes tighter. "I figured it'd be the night we went from flirting to confessing our feelings for each other. I'd been missing my high school friends, and this was the first time I didn't feel so alone."

Now that I'm free-flowing, Miller drops his gaze, looking out at the trees.

"I'd made this—ugh—dumb promise bracelet for him. I don't know what I was thinking. When I told him about it that night, he laughed. I felt like such a dork, but then he put his arm around my waist and showed me off to his friends and all was forgotten. I wanted the night we started dating to be dreamy and perfect. I schmoozed his friends. Tried the drinks. At some point, he asked me if I wanted to check out his room, and..."

Hot tears cover my face again. I hold my breath trying to keep them in, because with them comes a searing pain ready to drown me.

Miller squirms.

"What did he do?"

"I mean, nothing...and everything."

He pulls my hand into his chest and waits.

I look out at the stars and take a deep breath.

"I know this sounds dumb, but one minute we were kissing and the next I was beneath him. I didn't stop even though I wanted to. He seemed so into it, and, you know, picture-perfect night."

I scoff at myself. Miller is looking away, but when I try to pull out of his grasp, he holds firm.

"Afterwards, there was this feeling of confusion. Probably because this change came over him when we were done. He had this look of... of..." Charlie's lips curl upward in my mind, exposing his big teeth. "Victory. I'm reminded of it sometimes when I look at myself in the mirror before a shower, and it makes me nauseous. Then I can't look at myself. It's weird. I mean, it's my own choice I'm disgusted with, but he's all over me sometimes, like this coat of slime I can't wash off."

"He's an asshole."

"I know. I figured it out quick when I told him I didn't want to go back down to the party and he ditched me for his boys. I had to walk back across campus alone in the dark. And to complete the nightmare, when I got home, I opened Snapchat...."

"No," Miller whispers.

I take a few moments to catch my breath. This part of the story has dug into me so deep, I'm almost numb to it. "I don't know if it was worse to be scarred by the external visual of that moment or to know that someone else was there spectating it."

"Hell no. He did that online?"

"No. It was his friend who posted it. For all of his thousands of followers to see. And even though my face wasn't showing, everyone knew I was with Charlie at that party. Since then, I've felt so exposed on campus. My biggest humiliation got shared with the world." I scoot away, needing to hug myself. It's the same thing I do back at school when people stare too long or whisper when I pass. Maybe they aren't even talking about me, but it feels like they are.

What does Miller think of me now?

It must not be good, because he shoves the car as he leaps off of it. He pulls at his hair and paces. His knuckles collide with a tree trunk.

Somehow his fit of rage stops my tears, like some of the burden of what happened has been yanked away.

Every part of me, especially my eyes, feels raw. I nestle myself into Abies's side, focusing on the piney scent and the cool air and nothing else.

"I hate being a person," Miller hisses, rattling the car again as he pushes against it. "People are so damn destructive." He stops moving and gazes up at me. He looks...devastated. "Did you report the attack?"

"He didn't attack me."

"His friend sure as hell did. You should have reported that post to the school. It's harassment."

"And further increase people's scorn? Charlie's a campus icon. I'd become worse than a slut. I'd be a pariah."

Miller squeezes his fists against the hood so hard I prepare for a crack. Caught in the funnel of his anger, there isn't room for self-pity. I sit up.

"Don't ever call yourself a slut," he says between his teeth.

"I know. But if I hadn't—"

"No ifs. That guy's a bastard."

"So you don't see me differently now that you know all of this?"

"The only thing I see is a crime. You're..." He blows out a breath.

His eyes cover me with sadness. He crawls back up onto the car and lies beside me, looking up at the enormous black sky.

"I'm what, Miller?"

"I would never do something like that asshole did to you. If I kissed you, it'd be because I had no choice but to kiss you... Because if I do have a choice, I won't risk it."

He just uttered the k-word. Twice. Something about that word coming from his lips feels much more intense than anytime a boy has ever actually planted one on me. But he basically said he's actively trying *not* to kiss me. This leaves me unsure of where to put all my feelings.

When he reaches out his arm, I put them all there—right in the warm pocket of his side.

"Tell me about college. Where do you live? What are your classes like?"

I tell him about how I find most of my classes either mind-boggling or incredibly draining. I tell him about my eccentric room-mate. He laughs as I describe the cafeteria funk and how I have to plan my showers around my meals. It's nice to talk about it with someone who isn't in college and adjusting way better to the independence.

It's nice to talk to a guy like he's a friend, to not have to sugarcoat myself. Miller seems like he can handle the full extent of me.

He doesn't shy away from it, anyway. He asks so many questions that I end up talking until my mouth forgets to move and all the thoughts float like little butterflies into the atmosphere, transformed and free.

TWENTY-TWO

When a whole-body shiver runs through me, my mind snaps back to consciousness. Daylight fingers its way through dense tree branches. The evidence trickles in. Convertible. Mountains. Miller.

We fell asleep together.

I let the full weight of his body pressed next to mine, the tingly lightness, consciously register up through my nerves.

I like him. Inexplicably, I *really* like him. I never could have imagined I'd be into a loner delivery boy. But now I see my error. He's more than his surface.

Miller treats me like I'm meaningful. He talks to the depth and potential of me. Where he's been digging feels loosened and refreshed. He has a way of expanding me. He's...sustenance.

His beanie has fallen off and his dark hair is scattered every which way. Between his pale pink lips, the slightest cloud of breath forms with each exhale. They're a pretty shape, his lips, sloped toward two sharp peaks at the top. The edge of a cliff.

Using my free hand, I feel around in my pocket until I manage to snag my iPhone and situate it in my palm. I want something to dwell on later. Miller doesn't ever need to know.

I angle the lens where I think it will capture his face the best. The camera clicks away.

His chest rises and falls in peaceful serenity for a few minutes, and eventually I nudge him awake. "Hey, Miller. It's morning. I need to get home and check on my mom."

"Shoot." He flies upright. "Is she going to hate me?"

"Knowing my mom, there's a good chance she fell asleep early and hasn't noticed I'm gone."

My phone rings.

"Well, she might have just figured it out."

I hop off of the car.

"Hey, Mom."

"Oh, thank god. I thought something terrible happened. Where are you?"

"I'm at Mistletoe Meadows still. Accidentally fell asleep on Miller's car while stargazing."

Miller eyes me. I brush him off.

"Are you being careful?" she asks.

"Yes. Of course."

"Okay. Well, next time text and let me know so I don't panic when I notice you missing."

"Sorry, Mom. This really wasn't planned."

"Mmm. Okay. Tell Miller to behave himself."

No thank you. This girl would prefer a little misbehaving from the boy with the pretty lips.

"When are you headed back?"

"Soon."

"Sounds good. Cal's cooking pork and beans for lunch."

"Okay, cool." It's not my favorite, but I'll pretend I love it like always. It's an old family recipe that brings him pride.

We hang up.

"We're good," I announce. "I need heat."

Miller starts the engine, and I lean near the vent, awaiting the hot air.

"Your mom's pretty laid back."

"She's pretty absentminded, so I get away with stuff by default."

It's really more than that. My mom hasn't questioned my decisions for a while now. Somewhere along the way, she shifted from giving me opinions to letting me form my own. She says I can handle myself. She has more confidence in me than I deserve.

The reins are too loose, I'd say.

Miller starts a song on his car Bluetooth that I recognize from last night.

"I looked it up while you were dancing. The original artist is Imogen Heap."

It makes me feel special that he downloaded a song I danced to, even though it probably has nothing to do with me. It's more likely that it's just an uncommonly sullen holiday song.

I lean against the window and watch the passing marvel that is the great outdoors. All the evergreens stand out in their tufted glory. The ground is a naked, vulnerable brown, every trial exposed for the world to notice. It crawls and turns, like it's chasing after us to stay and keep noticing.

We pass a rusty warehouse surrounded by a giant empty parking lot, a sad place with little shrubs growing up between the cracked slabs of asphalt. Miller pulls off the road.

"What are you doing?"

"Letting you drive."

My insides clench. I can't try to drive in front of Miller! My heart starts racing. "I'd prefer not to."

"Which is why we're going to practice."

"No thanks."

"Yes."

"I'm not doing it, Miller."

"But you are, though. Look around. There are no other drivers for miles, and my car runs as smooth as they come. You'll be fine."

How much does this *smooth* car cost? I flash him a face that's halfway between a plea and desperation.

"There's nothing to lose."

Except for my dignity...and our lives...and a bumper or two.

"You can't go through life having to rely on people to get you places."

"I'm not planning to go my whole life mooching rides, just until I get a car and it actually matters."

"The incident with your mom would suggest it may be useful to learn *before* you get a car."

He gets out of the driver's seat, motions me over, and waits.

Baby steps. I slide over the joystick and set my hands on the wheel. The panic flares. I shake my head. "You draw the line at dancing. I draw it at driving."

"Okay."

Thank god. I've won an argument with him.

He leans back into the car and reaches for something. I focus on his woodsy smell and not the fact that his everything is near my everything.

A song starts on his stereo, a guitar solo morphing quickly into a breathy ballad.

He hops back onto the asphalt and holds out his hand.

"What are you doing?" I know what he's doing. I'm just stalling while I recuperate from the full-body flush.

"May I have this dance?"

Well, I'm not going to say no, even if it does put me in a crisis situation immediately afterward. I take hold of him. One hand guides me up out of the seat. The other wraps around my waist.

We sway. The wind tries to deter us, slipping its icy fingers in and around our bodies, but I keep a firm grip on Miller's neck. His hands travel along my back. I wish I could feel more than a hint of it, but I'm wearing one too many layers.

On a particularly long, airy note, Miller leans me back, suspending me upside down in the breeze. My clothes ride up so that I can feel his heart picking up speed against my stomach. When he scoops me back up, I'm dizzy. Where did he learn that little trick?

My fingers catch the soft hair at the nape of his neck, and I scoot closer to block the wind. His chest expands. He drops his forehead onto mine, giving the ground a hard stare.

We hold each other like this for the rest of the song. He's close enough that I can hear every breath. They aren't at all steady.

Neither are mine.

The singer is talking about unrequited love. A one-night stand. He's singing my soul's pain. Deep in the dark of my chest, I ache, but Miller's fingers uproot the rot. He's much different than Douche Face. Douche Face never asked about my opinions or feelings. He didn't want to know my history. He definitely never tried to teach me anything.

I lean a little closer to this boy I really like.

He stops moving. His perfect pink mouth breathes against mine. So close.

My heart somersaults.

His hands disappear, and then so does his whole being. He grabs his head and walks away toward nothing.

I fall against the car, head back, eyes closed. Even though we didn't kiss, it feels like we did. My whole body buzzes, including my lips. I lift my fingers and run them across the tingling.

What am I doing here? I go back to college in six weeks. This isn't the time to fall for a guy.

I guess I'm glad he didn't kiss me.

A desperate "hey" catches in my ear. My eyes flutter open at the exact moment Miller scoops me up into his arms and presses me against his car. He lays his lips achingly slow against my shoulder. His body surrenders around me.

My eyes shut again.

Miller isn't suggestive or aggressive with his embrace. He doesn't take anything. Only gives. His lips hold firm to my inner shoulder as a part of him transfers.

I try to do something more than be kissed, but I can't. I'm too stunned. I will my legs not to buckle so that I can savor being wrapped wall-to-wall in the desperate arms of this boy I really like.

The intensity of it all, him, becomes too much to sustain. I whimper. He releases his hold on me. Sweeps his hand through his hair. Steps away. This is good, since I could really use a minute. I've never been this hot in winter.

TWENTY-THREE

I don't go a mile over thirty-five the whole way home, but Miller is patient. He predicts when I'm going to have trouble and gives me plenty of warning and direction.

My heartbeat settles about halfway through. I begin to trust myself. I don't even tense when I have to change lanes to make the final turn.

We pull into the apartment complex, and I breathe a sigh of relief. I didn't kill the car. I slam on the brakes when I pass my favorite person's red Audi in the parking lot.

"Jemma's back!" I pop open the door.

"Jemma?"

"Yes! She's my best friend, and she's home for break."

"Well, park the car before you go see her."

"Oh, sorry." I find a space with open spots around it, but it turns out I don't need the room. I stay perfectly within my lines.

Miller tugs his beanie down over his head and comes around the vehicle looking at his feet. His hands are in his pockets, of course.

I play with the edge of the door. "Thanks for doing that with me. It definitely lifted my spirits."

We stare at each other with that awkward question. How do we act now that it's unclear what we are to each other?

He turns away first and scans the parking lot. Then he pulls Abies off the car. "I'll bring this up for you."

I follow him up the steps, admiring the way he easily handles the six-foot heavyweight.

He sets it next to my door. "Got it from here?" He chews his lip.

I nod.

"Well, have fun then. See you at work."

"Yeah."

I watch him hurry down the stairway.

That was a completely unsatisfying goodbye. But what did I expect? Leaps of joy? Showers of kisses? That's not his style.

Jemma catches me in a hug at the door. "Did I just hear a man on your doorstep?"

"It was the UPS guy." My lips curl into a grin.

"You little slut. You've been keeping juicy secrets from me."

"I haven't. I didn't have anything to tell until last night." A smirk spreads across my face as the full impact of what has transpired hits me. "He does have nice delivery boy muscles, though."

"You've seen him naked!"

"No," I say lowering my voice. "But they were wrapped around me a couple times."

"That's it. You're making me coffee and spilling everything."

"I'll take one too, and let's make ginger snaps," my mom calls, that lovely tinge of joy that I've been missing present in her voice.

Okay, holiday. I see you.

Finally.

I don't see Miller's work truck the next morning when I pull up to UPS. He must have decided to work his day off. I let myself in with the key Rosa gave me and get to work turning computers on and checking inventory.

Harry shows up around eight-thirty, which I think is technically late, but Rosa isn't here to notice.

"Hey, Jingle Bell," he says.

"Hey, Harry. How was your weekend?"

"Cool, cool. I got up with some people." He sits beside me and pulls out his phone.

I keep up with the task list Rosa left for me. Harry doesn't seem to have one.

"You going to this?" he asks, showing me the e-vite to the holiday party at headquarters.

"First I've heard about it, but I could get behind a good office social."

"It's usually pretty epic. I'll send you the link. What's your number?"

I get his forward and then another later in the morning from Rosa. The party is Eighties themed! Miller and I can get all tacky and have a hilarious memory. Sigh. I wonder if he'll dance with me. I'm definitely willing to try eyefrisking again if necessary.

Something hits the back of my head. I turn to see a tiny paper ball on the floor. Harry giggles from the kitchen, a straw hanging out of his mouth.

"You need to find something useful to do," I say. "You've got way too much time on your hands."

I'm filling out a package log when another paper ball plonks into my hair and sticks.

"Give me that." I try to snatch the straw, but Harry dodges. He makes me chase him all the way around the break room table. I've got his arm twisted behind his back and we're both laughing when the entry bell chimes.

Miller walks inside. He sees Harry follow me out of the kitchen all playful and laughing.

"Miller Blaze." Harry emphasizes the last letter.

Miller lifts his brows and then stands at the counter like he's waiting for service.

"I thought you were working your day off," I say, scrambling to get the paper out of my hair frizz.

"I am. I stopped in because I wanted to give you this." He hands me a metal travel mug decorated with tiny Christmas trees. "I wanted you to have a reusable mug to enjoy all of your holiday beverages in.

You can take this to any coffee shop. The good ones will even give you a discount for using it."

Holy sweet little cow. I stand there admiring my new favorite possession. It's heavy. "Is something in it?"

"It's a latte from The Drowsy Poet since you said you like their coffee."

I could kiss him. But maybe not on the mouth, since it'd probably freak him out. And he's all the way across the counter. And we have an audience. And it would be weird anyway to just plant one on him at this point in our relationship. Is it a relationship?

He did get me an adorable coffee cup.

I don't know what to say, so I sip. Caramel and vanilla heaven oozes into my sinuses. I hum.

"Hey…" He glances over to Harry, who is lingering beside the register, and then back to me. "I was wondering if you wanted to come over and hang out tonight."

"Tonight? I can't. I have a meeting, and then plans with Jemma."

"Okay." He does the hands-in-pocket thing.

"How about tomorrow night? I'm free then."

"Yeah." He nods. "Tomorrow's good."

He turns around and walks out without another word.

Harry comes over and leans on the counter right next to me. "Are you and he a thing?"

"I don't know. Sort of. It's new."

He stands there nodding for a minute. I'm annoyed with how surprised he looks. Is it the fact that I got any guy's attention or is it the specific guy?

Actually, what do I care? I'm hanging out with Miller again. Because he asked me to. He purposely engaged. This is huge.

I'm such a good elf.

"I'm bored," Harry says. "Let's play a game."

We spend the rest of the afternoon trying to land paper balls on various things around the shop…and helping customers when necessary.

TWENTY-FOUR

Jemma meets me at the store so she can get a look at adult Harry with her own eyes.

Once we're in her car, she says, "He's not as hot as he used to be, right? Like bloated around the face or something."

"Do you think he ever even was hot? Maybe it was just upper-classman allure."

"No. He was hot. A delicious Korean model that could handle a lacrosse stick like a cheetah."

"He was good at lacrosse, wasn't he? I'll have to ask him what happened with that. I don't think he gives a doink about working at UPS, but he keeps it interesting." I tell her about our game of spitball.

"He sounds like he's into you."

"Why?"

"Guys are only playful with girls they like." She has very little first-hand experience in the world of guys. Even less than me. I eye her. "What? I've been reading a lot of *Psychology Today* articles. They're addictive."

She flicks on her blinker and squeezes between two cars in the neighboring lane. I marvel at how easily she performs the tasks of operating a vehicle. It's like she doesn't even think about it. I can't wait until I'm that comfortable.

"I cannot believe you go off to college and somehow become a guy magnet. What is this world we're existing in now?"

"There are just a lot of hornballs out there. I'm sure you have creepers waiting to pounce on you too."

"Miller doesn't sound like a creeper."

"Maybe not. But he also has no friends, so I can't be sure."

"He doesn't have a single friend?"

"I know, right? Everyone should have friends."

"Oh, boy. You have that tone like you're going to meddle."

"Who, me?"

"Yes, you. The same person who paid her cousin to ask me out to prom."

I shrug. "Just because Terry compared you to a meatball doesn't mean it was a bad setup. He meant well."

"Though I doubt you'll listen, I'd like to say I think it's a bad idea. You can't force things that are out of your control. You only make situations messier when you try."

"Actually, some of my interventions have been very positive. Look at Hailey. I got her into swimming, and she could have gotten a scholarship for it if she'd wanted."

"Adia, trust me. Leave the boy be. No guy likes it when a girl tries to fix him."

"There you go acting like an expert on the male gender again."

"I am a very smart person."

"Book-wise."

She pops me in the shoulder, and we laugh. We get spotted by Mrs. Karen and Mr. Bob as soon as we enter the meeting, and Jemma runs over for hugs.

"...now Adia and I are both honorary members of the neighborhood," she's saying when I reach them. We take our seats as Jen, the race director, begins speaking.

I think about Miller and this whole friend business. Is Jemma right? Will I make things worse trying to help? What if I don't try? He's clearly detrimentally closed off from the world. He doesn't even have a cell phone. What kind of way is that to live?

He imparted his driving skills to me. My skill happens to be helping, and by golly, I want to use it to benefit that boy.

Who's taking me on a date.

Is hanging out at his house considered a date?

I'm going to treat it as such until proven otherwise, fancy britches and all. A girl can't wear granny panties and expect to exude confidence. It will be—and stay—my little secret.

"...the Murrays, at the end of the street where the finish line will be, have kindly agreed to spruce up the event by offering their yard for a musical light show. They are going to provide the materials if we can get someone to make the display operational. Does anyone know anything about programming?"

My mind goes straight (back) to Miller. I throw up my hand. "I have a friend."

"A shoulder-kissing friend," Jemma whispers.

"He's a programming expert. I can ask him about doing it."

"Great. Bring him on board."

This will be awesome for Miller. And it gives me an excuse to spend more time with him.

Director Jen makes a note on her legal pad. "How are plans for the cookie station coming?"

"Super. I sent out a Google spreadsheet and several people have signed up already."

"Do we have a plan for volunteers at your station?"

"Me and Jemma can handle it. Right, Jemma?"

My best friend gives me a look of apprehension.

"It's covered," I tell Jen, giving Jemma a pressured glare.

Everyone gets excited to hear that the head of the regional food bank is coming to our little fundraiser and FOX 8 News plans to feature it. For the TV spot, they want us to do a formal presentation of the money we've raised. My hand shoots up again when they ask for a volunteer to print out a giant check.

"I work at a copy store, so I can take care of that."

"Aren't you the little overachiever," Jemma chides as we walk out.

"I can't help it. Do you think it was too much?"

"You know I'm teasing. I love what a helpful person you are."

"I don't know about all that, but I'm glad you're here so you have to look me in the face when you pick on me." She pinches my cheeks together when I stick my tongue at her. I scare her away with a slobbery lick. Skipping across the sidewalk, I say, "What are we doing tonight?"

"Must you even ask? You know I pulled out all those Richard Simmons DVDs we bought at that yard sale over the summer."

"You didn't."

"I did. They *will* get used, and I *will* get my money's worth. You owe me a session."

"I will aerobics these glutes all up in your face, if you watch a Christmas movie with me after."

She hooks an arm around my neck. "Glute me up."

We hop into her car for a perfect night of dorkiness, like old times.

Mrs. Sanyal hugs me for what feels like an hour. I soak in every second.

"You've been away too long," she scolds, setting down a pot of tea. "You know you can come here even while Jemma's gone."

"How have you been, Adia?" asks Jemma's *didima*, who always visits from Bengal during the winter. She beckons us to join her at the table.

"Pretty good. I got a job a couple weeks ago."

"Oh?"

"Basically, I'm an elf. I help get presents to the right people."

Didima chuckles, her eyes disappearing inside the creases around them.

Mrs. Sanyal sets a delicate mug etched with a jewel-toned geometric design in front of me. It manages to rival the green and red combo I'm so fond of right now. "Don't work too hard. School comes first."

School... I still need to sort that out. My linguistics professor is being difficult. At our last correspondence a week ago, Professor

Frume seemed very displeased at my failure to turn in my paper thus far. Something about wanting to turn in grades before going out of town. But with work and taking care of Mom, I just can't wrap my head around it. He's going to have to understand.

After filling our bellies with tea and samosa, I'm not sure how this workout is going to go. We walk down to the basement to stretch. My stomach gurgles.

"Want to skip the exercise and go straight for a movie?"

Jemma seems less affected by the refreshments. "I guess," she says, pulling up out of a side bend.

"Can we do *The Holiday*, pleeease?"

"We can watch your sappy movie first, but then we're doing our aerobics. I need to beef up my hiking form."

"You don't hike."

"I'm going to soon. Across Europe."

"What? When?"

"I'm studying abroad next semester."

I throw myself across her lap. "You're planning to get even farther away from me. Why? Tell me why!" I'm pretending to be overly dramatic so that I don't actually get emotional. I can't stand the idea of Jemma being so far. Will she even be able to talk to me on the phone every day?

"My friend Kelsey found out about this amazing program in London for prelaw students. We get to intern at a humanitarian office of our choice, which would be huge for me. I'll get hands-on experience that will help me figure out what kind of law I want to practice. Plus, I'll be in London with access to all kinds of travel opportunities."

Smiling is painful. "How long do I have you?"

She winces. "Two weeks. I leave a few days before Christmas. I wanted to see what the holiday was like there. Plus, a bunch of the study abroad students are planning to get there early, so it will be a great way to bond before we start the program. It's supposed to be pretty intense and all."

My heart cannot take this. My best friend is going with her new best friends on some amazing international experience that she'll probably never want to come back from, and I'll lose her forever. I've got two measly weeks before a hole is ripped through the middle of me and I have nothing left to show for the life I've known for the past nineteen years.

I curl up into a ball and start the movie, but I'm not even sure I can enjoy Kate Winslet in this mood.

TWENTY-FIVE

W hen I walk through the apartment door with my head hung, Mom throws out her good arm, summoning me.

"Honey, what's wrong? Did you and Jemma have a fight?"

"She's leaving me."

"Oh?" She moves some bills off the couch so we can sit together.

"She's studying abroad in London this semester, and she won't be back until next fall."

"I'm so sorry. I know it's been hard being apart from her." Mom tucks my hair behind my ear and cups my cheek.

I love having this version of her around, the one who asks about me and folds laundry and makes food other than cereal. Between her revitalization and Cal having the week off, I may have time to do some schoolwork when I'm not at the store.

"Where's Cal?"

"At a hockey game with some friends."

I get up and go into the kitchen, hoping there will be something left of the savory smell that welcomed me home. My mom quietly observes my nervous rummaging.

"I know this college transition has been hard for you, but you'll adjust." She comes over and pulls out a container from the fridge. "All it takes is a few new friends. I've met some great ladies that have made being an empty nester bearable. They're so supportive. This is Mary's potato soup."

The church ladies. I roll my eyes, which my mom can't see. I'm no longer in the mood for something savory. Too bad I've had no time to bake.

"They've all been through the same thing, so they really get me. It's nice to be around people who understand."

"I don't think anyone at Avery understands me."

"Adia, you're one of the most social people I know. I bet there are students all around who would love to be friends with you. You just have to go find them. College is a big place."

"Tell me about it." I push away the bowl of soup my mom sets in front of me and slump over on the island.

"Your brother comes home tomorrow. How about we all go out for pizza?"

"I can't tomorrow," I mumble into the counter.

"Wednesday then?"

"Fine." I still sound mopey, but the idea of going out as a family does have appeal. "Let's go to Elizabeth's Pizza. I could use those breadsticks in my life."

I lean into the sweet sensation of her hand making circles on my back.

"Hey, Mom, do you want to decorate the tree?"

She groans. I guess she's not all the way back to being herself.

"This place deserves better than a naked tree stuffed into a bucket on the porch."

"I'm not sure it does. Plus, all the ornaments are in storage."

"Then we can make some. Remember those gingerbread men you did one year? Those would be adorable. And smell great."

"I just don't have the energy for all of that. Sorry, hun."

"Okay, whatever. I wasn't really in the mood anyway."

What does it all matter if I'm the only one who cares? I already put a lame Santa hat on top of Abies's crooked head, and that pretty much suits her...and us.

It's totally fine that my mom hates Christmas activities now. That's only the complete opposite of how she has ever acted before. But I can deal. I'm a big girl.

I don't want to continue looking at her face though.

I shut myself in the bedroom. Maybe while I'm feeling unmotivated to have any joy, I should do homework. When I open my computer, a wave of fatigue hits me. I might as well go ahead and end this downer day so I can get to my night with Miller sooner.

TWENTY-SIX

Peope are running low on Days till Christmas to send gifts to loved ones affordably, so we're slammed at work. I've grown moist hauling the onslaught of packages to the back. By the time Miller shows up, I'm praying I don't smell.

"Keep the oven on," Harry says in reference to a joke we started earlier in the day.

"Roast the beef," I joke back.

Miller stares at his shoes.

"Hold on a sec," I say, running to the kitchen to get my Christmas travel mug. I'm filling it with a new drink each morning until I sample the entire Starbucks specialty menu.

Miller nods to Harry before we leave. It's the most cordial thing I've seen him do to someone. Friend candidate alert!

I'd show some excitement if I wasn't so paranoid about my armpits.

"Do you mind if we stop by my apartment before we head to your place?" I ask. "I'd like to change out of these work clothes."

"Oh... Sure."

When we pull up to the apartment, Miller leans back in his seat. "I'll wait here while you change."

"Don't wait out here. It might take a minute and I'll feel terrible. Come inside so I can feed you cookies while you wait."

He gnaws his lip. Then he grabs a ball cap out of his glovebox and pulls it over his dark waves. "Okay."

The tattered Berkeley hat looks adorable on him. I fight the urge to latch onto his arm and parade him up the apartment stairwell.

He settles onto the couch with a plate of Mom's ginger snaps while I head to my room to change. I contemplate a shower but decide after a sniff that a fresh coat of deodorant can handle the job. It's not like he's getting anywhere close to any of the funky zones, especially not if they could be a little funky.

I pass my mom in the hallway.

"There's a guy in the living room, so be cool."

"Does this young man need food?"

"I already took care of that."

"Well, what do I do with him?"

"I don't know. Talk to him? He gets along with older people better anyway."

I push her into his line of sight and duck into my room. On to date clothes. I find some fancy panties, well, semi-fancy—they have polka dots at least. I switch into a bra that somewhat matches and top the improved undergarments with fitted black jeans and a chunky black sweater. I accessorize with gray booties and some dangly, silver earrings. I quickly run a flat iron over my front frizz and dot a little gloss on my lips. Does Miller like the taste of peppermint?

Not that it matters.

I'm taking a little too long, probably, but I decide to do up my eyes. A girl's whole soul is bottled in her eyes. They should be reflective—a road sign.

With a spritz of body spray, I'm complete. I feel like a million bucks.

I find mom scampering around the kitchen with a dish saying something about how ghastly shipping costs have become. So when I bring boys home, she turns into an unfiltered squirrel. Good to know. I take the plate from Miller and excuse him.

We run into Drew coming up the stairs outside. He's talking on the phone. "Adia just walked up. Call you later?" He waves at me. "Love you too. Bye, babe."

Oh, my gosh. Big brother's whipped.

"Welcome home!" I reach out for a squeeze. "Also, when did the L-word start happening?"

He grins. "Couple of weeks ago."

I love my brother in love. He's so sappy about it. He's the best and Claudia better recognize. "Wow. Good for you."

I turn to Miller who has scooted behind me. "Drew this is Miller. Miller this is my brother, well not by blood but by heart."

"Same difference," says Drew, mussing my hair. "Nice to meet you, man."

Miller stares at Drew's outstretched hand like it's going to bite.

"Hey," yells someone from down the walkway. It's the girl with the arm tattoo. Her eyes are wide, and she starts walking toward us.

"Shit..." Miller backs up, looking at us, then her, then us again. "I need to go."

He darts down the stairs, leaving me and Drew behind.

"Miller!" I jog after him.

At the bottom step, he swings around. His eyes are feral. "I can't do this, Adia. Leave me alone."

His harsh tone stops me in my tracks.

Miller escapes to his car. The tattoo girl blows past me. She catches Miller and knocks on his window until he rolls it down.

What's up with them? Miller claims he never dated her, but they clearly have some history. I strain, but not a single bit of their conversation reaches my ears.

"What was that about?" Drew asks, catching up to me.

After a brief exchange, Miller peels away. The girl gets in her mustang and drives away too.

"I feel like I might know your friend. What's his name again?"

"Miller Blaze."

"Nope. I definitely don't recognize that name. Sounds like a comic book hero."

It kind of does. I'd laugh if I weren't falling into a self-pity pit. All this primping, wasted. I sit down on the step with my chin in my hands.

"Well"—Drew squeezes my shoulder— "I hate to benefit from your misfortune, but this means we can move our pizza night up. What do you say?"

I know people say to enjoy every moment, but I've been looking forward to this date since I woke up at the butt crack of dawn. Doing anything else will just plain suck. I don't get it. Am I giving off a scent that repels fun things?

Or maybe it's this depressing apartment. It's rubbing off.

TWENTY-SEVEN

Mom tilts her seat back while we're driving to the restaurant. I temporarily stop gnawing my nail to observe her.

"You feeling okay, baby?" Cal asks.

"I'm fine," she says, massaging her temples with her good hand.

Cal pulls the car into a parking spot. "You two go on ahead. We'll catch up."

"Mom?"

"Go on, hun. I'm just a little dizzy. I won't be but a minute."

I follow my brother's cue and scoot out of the car around her reclined seat. Drew and I sit inside the entrance of Elizabeth's. The place gives my senses a big hug—cheesy dough, warm, thick air, the chatter of happy patrons. Tonight isn't an entirely lost cause.

"How's Claudia?"

"Great. She's down in Florida. I'm considering going for Christmas to surprise her."

"You're going to drive all that way for a surprise?"

"Well, yeah." He grins.

"Wow." Yet another casualty to this holiday. "I'm sure she'll be knocked off her feet."

"Hope so."

My folks come through the restaurant door with stretched smiles. "Let's get a table," Mom chirps.

We slide into our usual booth.

I stare at Mom.

She smiles without her eyes. Faker.

Before I can get out my thought, she says, "I get my stitches out tomorrow. After that I can start using my arm normally again."

"That's good news, Sammy," Drew says. "I'm glad you'll be able to work your magic in the kitchen again. I miss your biscuits."

I perk up. "Good point. You can make some cookies for the Twinkle Dash."

"Sure, hun. Which ones do you want?"

"Those reindeer M&M ones and some jelly tarts?"

"I can do that."

Cal rubs Mom's arm. "What does everyone want to eat?"

The mozzarella sticks arrive. Drew makes goofy comments about anything and everything in his visual frame of reference. I fill my consciousness with melty cheese.

Nothing can really get to you when you have fried mozzarella in your mouth. It just can't.

After I eat my portion of our appetizer too quickly, I look for another distraction. My eyes settle on the jukebox when Mom speaks.

"How's your schoolwork coming?"

Cal's head snaps to me. "Why do you still have schoolwork?"

"I got an extension on some of my assignments due to our family emergency."

"It's been two weeks. You should have had things tied up by now." He looks at Mom with big eyes. "Have we checked to make sure this is allowed?"

"I thought it was a bad idea for her to stay home in the first place, but she refused to listen."

"It's not a big deal," I say. "I'll take my exams in January, and I've just got this one paper to do."

"So your professors were totally fine with this?" Cal crosses his arms.

"Mostly." Except for two of them. But my chem lab teacher is a TA, so that hardly counts. I fiddle with the edge of the marinara bowl.

"College doesn't do training wheels, Ads. It's an institution for adults, and they expect you to act like one. If you screw this up, you're only hurting yourself."

"Since when do you care so much?"

Pain flits across his eyes.

I feel bad for saying it. I know Cal cares a lot. But right now, he doesn't get what I'm going through. I'm trying my best here, and I don't need the added pressure.

"Why don't you focus on what's up with Mom? She's the one with the broken arm. I guess no one else cares about that."

Both their faces pinch.

Is this a good time to bring up the fact that I'm also thinking about changing my major?

I stab the sauce with a fork.

"I think I got an A in probability this semester," Drew says.

Mom squeezes his arm. "That's incredible, hun. How'd you turn things around?"

Drew starts talking about study tactics. I zone him out. I'm over this day and this fake family dinner, where we're all pretending like everything is normal but it actually sucks.

I text Jemma and beg her to come save me.

I don't say anything to my family when she pulls up. I just walk out.

And they let it happen.

Jemma and I sit on her double bed, and she lets me vent. She braids my hair in the elaborate, soothing way that her mom taught her. It's heaven having my best friend close. I fall asleep wishing I could refresh this moment and do it over and over.

Why does time have to run out on good things?

TWENTY-EIGHT

Cal's packing his bags the next morning when I come home to get dressed for work. Mom is lying on the couch in an over-sized sweatshirt. She's looking at a book titled *It's Not Supposed to Be This Way*. I glance over her shoulder. Since when does she read nonfiction?

The same page is open when I come back into the living room dressed.

"You should try something lighter." I switch out her book for my latest issue of *People*.

"Sammy," says Cal from their bedroom, being super obvious. They clearly discussed something in private.

She shimmies into a sitting position. "Adia, have a seat." She pats the cushion beside her.

I plop down with a banana. "What's up?"

"Cal and I want to make sure you're taking your schoolwork seriously."

"Mom. I am."

"Good. Tell me exactly what's going on with your extensions."

"All but one of my professors is being cool." I leave out the TA who doesn't need mentioning.

"And what's the plan for the one who isn't?"

I roll my eyes. "I'm going to reach back out. I can handle this, Mom."

"You'll reach out today, and I want to know what the plan is by this evening."

"Okay. Fine."

"I don't want you to use me as an excuse to avoid your responsibilities."

I can't believe what I'm hearing. "I'm trying to take care of you. I was worried about you."

"I know, honey, and I appreciate it. But you don't seem all that thrilled about school. I don't want you giving up on it before you give it a real shot."

I've lost my appetite. I fling my banana peel on the coffee table and stand. "Whoever said I was giving up on anything?!"

Mom pets the couch. "You do that sometimes. When things are too hard. Like soccer...or that musical you tried out for."

"I didn't want to do those things."

"Well, I don't want college to be one of those things that you decide you don't want to do."

"This is ridiculous." I grab my purse and my mom's keys. "I'm going to work. Like the responsible human being I am."

Before she can argue, I slam the door behind me.

Miller was right: it *was* a smart idea to practice driving before I got a car.

His work truck is being loaded when I pull into the parking lot. I march past, planning to ignore him, but he isn't there. I check the parking lot for his car, and, sure enough, no sign of it.

Good. I can avoid one nuisance.

I don't need his weirdness.

But while I'm filling up my mug at the Keurig in the kitchen, my heart twinges. Miller's good to talk to, like Jemma. Maybe even better. I want to vent to him about my fight and watch him look at me like he can't understand why this is a big deal. Or say something totally practical about it all.

Or he could give me his really satisfying excuse for why he bailed.

Or maybe I just want breakfast. My stomach's grumbling.

After one of Rosa's blueberry muffins, I'm settled enough to problem solve. The moment I see Miller roll into the parking lot, I rush out the back before I can talk myself out of it.

"What's up with yesterday?"

His eyes crinkle with distress. He removes his beanie and runs his fingers through the shag.

I cross my arms.

He won't look at me. Why is he being so weird? I really need a friend, not a headcase.

"What is it? Are you with some other girl or something?"

"No, Adia. I just... I don't know if I can handle all of this."

"All what? I'm not expecting anything from you, Miller. Except for maybe that you not shut me out."

He opens the back of the truck and sticks a clipboard inside.

I grab his arm. "What's up with that girl?"

He flinches.

I huff but step back. "Well?"

"Nothing's up."

I wait for the truth.

"She's a terrible person."

"Bad enough to scare you away?"

"I don't know... It's complicated."

I fed the boy cookies, for heaven's sake. I need a more acceptable explanation. "I don't know about complicated, but it was definitely rude. *I'm* not a terrible person, and you ditched me."

He slams the loading door of his truck and walks to the cab.

"Hey, we're talking here."

"I need to work."

"Fine! Be a baby and leave." I throw my hands up.

He gets in his truck and drives away. I stomp back inside and bury myself in letter sorting. What has the world come to when the best thing in my life is a job?

TWENTY-NINE

I'm angry-organizing in the storage closet when Harry enters. I go about my shoving, not in the mood for banter. Something slips over my head.

I remove it and look. It's an elf hat with jingle bells. "Cute," I say, feeling touched but still miserable.

"Found it at the gas station and thought of you."

"That's cool."

"You doing okay?"

"I don't want to talk about it."

He leaves me to my moping.

Customers flood the store the entire day, which helps keep my mind off of my stupid life.

I'm exhausted by five o'clock and looking forward to a day off tomorrow. I want to wallow with the help of Netflix. And dollar-store cheese balls.

The door chimes while I'm sticking the last pile of packages in the back bins. I hustle to the front since Harry has already left.

Miller's standing there in his hoodie and messy hair, looking at his Chucks. I snatch the hat off my head. He flicks the bangs out of his eyes and turns his seafoam irises up to me.

"I'm an idiot."

I chew my lip. Do I want to play hardball? I don't want him to get all cagey again, so I'll be the bigger person and cut to the chase. "You can't keep blowing me off like this."

"I'm sorry. This is hard for me."

"Yeah. I get it. You're not a people person. Well, too bad. We're officially friends, so figure your mess out."

"Can I get a redo?"

My fidgeting makes the hat in my hand jingle quietly. I want to be merry. "Fine, but the buildup is real. You better be ready to impress."

His lips curl into an actual, real-life grin, and my heart nearly stops. They say you hear a bell when an angel gets wings. I'm hearing a symphony.

"This date is tailor-made for you."

Date. He said it. This isn't going to be some sneaky move where the guy puts in zero effort and expects to be paid richly for his wit and gelled hair. Miller's got a plan.

I call down from my cloud, "Do I need to bring anything for this event?"

"I've got it all covered."

"Okay then. I'll run home and meet you at your place in like an hour?"

"I'll text you the address."

I'm still floating when I get into my mom's car. My feet are in fact too light to function properly on the floor pedals. The crunch happens first. Then tires squeal while the car refuses to advance any farther due to the concrete-encased light pole in its path.

I scream and let go of everything. The car purrs like it has no idea one of its eyes just got squished.

"Okay. Okay."

Tears threaten. I knew something like this would happen. I should have trusted my instincts and avoided driving. I'm not ready.

I look up to see if anybody's witnessing this faux pas. Nope.

Breathe. Focus.

I put the Volvo into reverse, which I should have done in the first place, and back away from the light.

Something bangs against the asphalt. Cringing, I turn off the poor car.

A mechanical crime scene awaits. Glass bits cover the area of insult. Wires poke out around a flickering light. A metal appendage hangs down below the hood.

I bend over, feeling faint. Mom is going to kill me, or worse, ground me from all my Christmas fun.

My primal instincts surface. Is there any possible way to dig a hole and bury this? Right now, I have a situation. It only becomes a problem if I'm found out.

THIRTY

Target always saves the day. I shuffle down lower in my seat so nobody else in the store parking lot can see, and I change out of my UPS clothes. Deodorant and a new emerald-colored slouchy cardigan and dangly gold necklace freshen me up. Now I can avoid Mom's wrath and head straight to Miller's.

The autonomy of driving is a redeeming quality, I suppose.

Locking the broken car, I leave it to wait while I enjoy the exciting opportunity in front of me. I'm not letting this mishap get me in trouble *and* ruin my date.

I double-check the address Miller sent. This can't be his place. It's a house, for one thing. And, for another, holiday music is permeating through the walls.

After confirming, I knock.

Miller shakes his wet hair as he lets me through the door. He must have showered when he got home. Miller showering... Is it hot in here?

My date has on sweatpants and a faded green Monopoly t-shirt. His feet are bare. They're nice feet, the toes long and smooth, masculine but not macho. His second toe is shorter than the first, like I wish mine were. His toenails are well groomed. I might even consider touching those feet.

"Hey," he says.

I look up, smiling to cover up my momentary fixation. "Hey."

Harry Connick Jr. sings a tune I've heard before, on Mom's favorite Christmas album. It makes me all sorts of warm and fuzzy to hear that coming from Miller's sound system.

"I like your tunes."

"You can thank Apple Music. It's part of what I have planned for this evening."

I clap. "Are we doing Christmas music trivia?"

"I'm more original than that."

He leads me through the living room, which has one single couch, a large TV sitting on a modern-looking stand, and little else. No pictures and no decorations, unless you count gaming equipment. The only other furniture is a TV tray serving as an end table.

The next room we pass through has a dining table but seems to be more of an office. It has a wall-to-wall desk holding the prettiest computer I've ever seen. Its casing is clear and displays a glowing fan and some other parts with multicolored neon liquid running through them.

"How do you not have a phone when you're clearly very into technology?"

"If phones left you the hell alone, I'd like them too."

I roll my eyes at his back.

We stop in the kitchen. Nothing's out on the counters.

Where is he hiding all his stuff?

I check a cabinet out of curiosity. And another. Both empty.

"How long have you lived here?"

"What's it...six years, I guess."

He lifts the lid off a mini crockpot. A guy with a mini crockpot in his possession is kind of adorable, but the smell coming from it is the real pleasure. Orange and clove. If I was a bird, I'd nest in here.

"When do I get some of this?" I ask.

"Depends. Are you ready to start your challenge?"

"Challenge?"

"We're going to dip into some rarely experienced but often-referenced holiday foods and beverages, since, you know, you're kind of obsessed with Christmas. Your task is to guess what they are."

He gets me.

I reach for him with the intention of a giddy hug, but then I turn it into a dance move at the last minute. I don't know if I'm with the Miller who reached out for me, or if we're back to not appreciating physical contact. I elaborate on the happy dance to make it look intentional.

He shakes his head and fills two glasses with the nest-worthy liquid.

"Your first quiz."

I climb onto the kitchen counter and assess my drink, alternating between blowing on the steam and breathing in the goodness. It's kind of a marmalade color with brown specks of spice. Notes of apple rest beneath the orange and clove. "This test better have some sort of reward, because I've got enough schoolwork to deal with over break."

"What do you want?"

This. Is. My. Chance. "I want to throw a dinner party here!"

"No."

"Go big or go home."

"I am home, and that means I make the rules. No parties."

I droop.

"Is there any other prize you might like?"

Tipping the liquid to my lips, I consider. "I want to be able to ask you any question and you give me a whole, *detailed* answer."

He narrows his eyes, probably seeing right through my plot. "Fine. But if you lose, you have to do something for me."

"What?"

"I don't know yet."

"That's not exactly a fair agreement, since I don't know what I'm potentially getting myself into."

"You better not lose then, huh?"

Trusting my robust knowledge of all things Christmas, I nod. "Deal. This is wassail, by the way."

His jaw drops.

I do victory antlers, which he wrinkles his nose at. I get up in his face and do it more. He smells good, soapy.

"Bring it," I challenge.

"I will."

I take another sip. "My stepdad, Cal, would love this drink. He's an orange juice fanatic."

"What's the deal with your family? You have a stepdad and a stepbrother?"

"My mom got remarried when I was seven. The brother and stepdad were a package deal."

Miller nods. A lot.

"What?"

"Nothing. Do you and your stepbrother get along?"

"Yeah. Great. He's so much fun, and he always looks out for me. He's my favorite."

"Cool."

The noise he makes suggests he has more to say, but he turns his back to me instead. He pulls a platter from the fridge and peels the tinfoil back to reveal an array of colorful morsels. He separates the various items onto plates. I bring two into the dining room but turn right back around.

I cannot enjoy food if I'm staring at paperwork.

"What's with the mess in there?" I tease, considering the rest of his house is pristine.

"Yeah, sorry. I got carried away with something and didn't have time to pick up before you arrived."

Crawling back onto the kitchen counter, I cross my legs and settle in for my holiday food experience. "What were you working on?"

"It's nothing."

"You look nervous. What was it?"

"It doesn't matter."

"Just tell me."

He flashes his eyes at me. "I have this idea for a business."

"Oh?" Does Miller have a secret passion project?

"Don't look so giddy. It's no big thing. It's kind of stupid." He turns away from me and lingers over the sink with his emptied platter. "I want to design a company that allows people to drop off empty

154

product packages for refilling. I think I can program a machine that would sort the containers and prepare them for redistribution to manufacturers. It would allow us to recuperate tons of waste from common products, like ketchup and laundry detergent, and drastically reduce pollution."

He turns around to find me ogling him with my head in my hands. His eyes roll.

"Why is that stupid?" I ask.

"It's not a stupid *idea*. In fact, I like playing around with it. But it's not something I'll ever do anything with. It's just a way to waste time."

"Yeah. Why would you want to use your brilliance to help the world? That sounds extremely crazy."

"Just shut your mouth and eat your food." He joins me on the counter.

With my eyes closed, I hold out my hands. "What's up next?"

In drops a small, round object that has zero give, a nut. Is he looking at my mouth as I taste it? It has an unfamiliar flavor, kind of sweet but in a weird way. And furry. "It's not my favorite," I say. I hate it. I look around for a napkin, disappointed to see none.

"Any guesses?"

"Well, it's a nut." I push it down my throat and use my teeth to scrape the remnants off my tongue. The wassail helps.

"You're going to need to be more specific."

"The only nut I can think of in a Christmas song is a chestnut roasting on an open fire."

"Name the song."

"'The Christmas Song.' Nat King Cole."

"Correct."

He picks up his iPod, and after some thumbing the song starts playing on the speakers in the living room. It's a peppier version than the original.

"I wonder if chestnuts are the same thing as water chestnuts," I say. "I've never been a big fan of those either. Maybe they're better roasted."

"I have a fireplace. I've never used it, but I'm willing to try if you want."

The slightest hint of nutty slime still lingers in my mouth. "I think I'm good."

"Probably for the best. I don't actually have any firewood."

"Your neighbors do. I saw a big pile next to their house."

"I make a point not to ask my neighbors for things."

How does he survive?

Mrs. Karen once picked me up from dance when Mom was sick with the flu and I sprained my ankle. She took me to urgent care for x-rays and everything. Every spring, Mr. Bob gives us fresh vegetables from his garden. We look after their labradoodle, Pepper, anytime they travel. Or at least we did.

Life is much easier with a support system.

"It's weird you live in a neighborhood."

"It's what people do."

"Only some of them. I pictured you as more of a condo guy or something."

"I like my space. Tried an apartment when I first moved away from home. Hated the noise and people being right on top of you. I had some money saved from my tech job, so I decided to get my own place."

"You're very mature."

"What do you want to try next?"

"I obviously know what this is." I point to a bowl of popcorn in the center of the tray.

"But what song inspired that choice?"

"'Let It Snow.'" I smirk. He's so spilling the beans about his past tonight.

He starts a techno remix of the classic tune. "Would you like some popcorn?" he asks.

"Popcorn should only be eaten while watching movies. Got any good ones?"

"I have whatever you want, but let's finish our game before we start one."

"What's your favorite Christmas movie?"

"Am I supposed to have a favorite?"

156

"Definitely. Otherwise, you're at risk of being a Scrooge."

His face drops.

"Kidding," I reassure. "Scrooge doesn't host holiday food dates."

"True." He drums his fingers on the table. *Batman Returns.*

"Batman! How does that qualify?"

"It takes place at Christmastime. Haven't you seen it?"

I shake my head.

"You haven't had the Catwoman experience? This must be fixed. We'll save this popcorn for our after-dinner entertainment."

I don't have the heart to tell him I'm not into comic book movies. He looks—dare I say—excited.

"What's this?" I ask, pointing to two bowls filled with something brown that's topped with blobs of whipped cream.

He passes me a spoon from the tray. "You're three for three. You tell me."

I smell it first. The lovely aroma of brown sugar and cream intrigues my taste buds.

My spoon slides through the dessert. Miller's mouth moves along with mine as it slides over the utensil, as if he's the one tasting this bite. It's adorable how into this he is. It's maybe more than adorable. Dropping one leg over the side of the counter, I put on a little bit of a performance. I close my eyes to explore the food. The bite is spongy and dense in my mouth, like a bread pudding. It's very sweet. Surprisingly, it's too sweet for my stomach right now. Not sure that's ever happened before. I lick my lips. "Did you make this?"

He swallows. "Enlisted the help of Rosa."

I try not to make a big deal about that confession, but aw!

"Got any guesses?" He's smirking, so this must be an obscure one.

"Uh..." I say the only thing I think could possibly be it: "Figgy pudding from 'We Wish You a Merry Christmas'?"

"What?" He falls back on the counter.

I'm totally right. I love how it feels to surprise him.

When I help him up, our hands linger together. I bite my lip. God, I want him to kiss me. Not my shoulder this time either.

He drops his hand.

I shove him. "You don't know who you've gone up against, obviously. This girl knows her baked goods."

"You've made this before?"

"No, but there were only so many things it could be. I can't think of any other cakes mentioned in familiar Christmas songs, and this is cakey."

"But the song doesn't mention cake."

"Yeah, but cake and bread pudding are basically the same thing."

He waves his hands up and down in praise. "You've got two more to go," he says.

"This is fun."

"Good." His lips spread across his poetic face.

Heat floods through me.

"Next?"

I grimace at the slices of pumpkin pie, which I've been avoiding because they have "store-bought" written all over them. I am no longer hungry. Not for food.

But he's planned this thing for me. He *planned*.

I pick up a reddish-brown ball that looks like it has specks of nuts inside and a granulated sugar coating. I have no clue what I'm holding. I nibble.

It's got the fruity tartness of cranberry and cherry. The mild flavor of walnuts lightens the sweetness. And there's a note of chocolate. "Did you get these from a confectionery?"

"If that means a nice Latina lady who will hound you until you associate with her, then yes."

"They're tasty. I have no idea what they are, though." I shuffle through all the Christmas songs I know and come up with only one possibility, which I doubt is correct. "It tastes like gummy chocolate, so I'm going to go candy and cite Dolly's 'Hard Candy Christmas'?"

"I'm afraid that's wrong. These are sugarplums. I win."

"What! That's not in a Christmas song."

"Christmas poem. Same thing."

"Not hardly."

"Don't be a sore loser."

"That tasted nothing like plums. I feel cheated." I cross my arms.

"Oh, come on. I wasn't trying to be tricky. Want some more

wassail to make you feel better?"

I nod. When he brings it over, I pull him in for a selfie.

He tries to snatch the phone, but I predict it this time and dodge. "You cheated. The least you could do is let me take a photo of our date."

"Look." He blocks the screen as I come at him again with the camera. "I will let you take a photo as long as you swear not to post it anywhere."

Okay...

Did he just agree to a photo? Let the cataloging begin! "Why can't I post it?"

"I don't want to be involved in all that mess. It's invasive."

I suppose it can be. "I respect that. Now get over here and cheese it up."

He leans down with his adorable Innovise mug of wassail and tucks his arm around my waist. It's the closest we've been since the tree farm, and, well...I'm pretty sure the picture's going to be blurry.

A few scenes into *Batman Returns*, Miller's car starts to make sense. It's basically Bruce Wayne's, who also happens to be an intense tech genius. Hmm.

The popcorn disappears, leaving nothing left between me and another hour and a half of oddball action.

I excuse myself for more wassail...and the bathroom.

The movie is paused when I return.

"You're not that into this, are you?"

"No, it's good."

He folds his arms. "You don't have to pretend with me."

That's not what I was doing. Was it? "I didn't want to ruin your fun."

"I don't care about this. I wanted to do something fun with you. If you don't think this is fun, we can do something else."

"Oh."

"What's *your* favorite Christmas movie?"

"I imagine you'd be just as bored watching mine as I am watching this."

"So you *were* bored."

I scrunch my face.

"Try me. What movie?"

"Well, I've already watched my favorite."

"Which is?"

"The Holiday."

"My mom used to watch that movie every year. What do women like about it so much? Nothing really happens."

"You're talking crazy. A lot happens. Iris and Miles banter. They make music. The old man gets a new lease on life. Several people fall in love. Cameron proves that a car is no match for a solid high heel when it comes to chasing down your honey. It all just works for me."

He studies me.

"What?"

"You like the fluffed-up version of life better than reality, don't you?"

"What's that supposed to mean?"

"Nothing, just that you might be a little high-maintenance."

"Miller!" I'm annoyed by his dig, but also sort of touched by the way he's saying it, like he isn't judging me for it, just noticing.

"Tell me this: do you like the grand gestures in love stories, or do you think they're cheesy?"

I sit up straight. "Of course I love a grand gesture...not *all* of them. Some of them fall flat. It's all about how they're executed. Do they make sense for the story? Are they natural or forced? Are they original?"

"Give me an example."

"Well...let's go with an obvious one. *The Notebook*. Noah fixes up that house and includes the things that Allie wants even though they aren't together. He didn't do it for her, which would have been cheesy. He did it because of his inability to let go of her. It's so touching. Especially when he can't bring himself to sell the house." I sigh.

"You're definitely high-maintenance."

"And you're not?"

"Do I look like it?"

"Not on the surface. You've created a situation where it seems like you don't care about anything. You've carved anything you would have to care about out of your life."

"That's an exaggeration."

"No, it's not. Look at your job."

"I care about my job. I take it very seriously. I'm one of the best employees they have."

"Yeah, but it's routine." My voice is still teasing, but I'm having trouble staying casual. Miller cannot waste his potential. "You go in, drive your truck around all by yourself, and go home. You're not pushing yourself. You're probably some sort of computer genius based on what you've told me, but you're not using your gift. Why is that?"

"My talents are mine to use how I choose. They're not an obligation."

"If you could do anything in the world, what would you do?"

He shrugs.

"Come on. I know there's something. Everyone has something."

"I'd play video games."

"That's sad."

"What would you do?"

"I wish I knew, but we aren't talking about me. You're twenty-four and done with college. You spend every day mostly alone with that over-pensive brain of yours, so you can't tell me you don't have something that calls to you."

"I never went to college, actually."

"What?"

"Decided it wasn't worth it."

"My mom would say you're an idiot."

"I don't care what your mom thinks."

I shut my mouth.

He starts flipping through TV apps. We've apparently moved past the portion of the evening where we have fun.

"I'm gonna go."

"Wait. Why?"

"Well, for one thing, you don't want me here, and for another, you convinced me I should be driving, and now I've wrecked my mom's car and I need to figure out what the heck to do about it."

I grab my coat and purse from the dining room and get out my mom's keys. Miller follows me wordlessly. This night is not ending the way I had hoped.

How did I hope? Conversation so good it goes all night. Brand-new experiences. Palpable connection. A transcendent daybreak kiss. Or something like that.

Maybe I am high-maintenance.

I suck in a breath and walk past him.

"You're it," he says.

I stop. "I'm what, Miller?"

"You're what calls to me, okay?" He yanks at his hair, leaving it in a big hump.

The air in the room has changed—every molecule is charged and brushing across my consciousness. The weight of it weakens me. I sit.

Miller looks down at me with his cavernous eyes. They hold the same devastation they had when I told him about Charlie. He's about to confess something. I drop my eyes to the floor.

"I hate this," he says. He collapses beside me on the couch and holds his head in his hands.

I reach out to him, setting my hand not quite on his leg but right at the cusp of it. Can we just be people that touch each other already?

He looks up at the blank TV screen, dragging his hands across his thighs.

Come on, boy. You can do this.

I touch him. It's a light pawing at his legs. He scoots away.

Ugh. What the heck am I doing here? I'm smarter than this.

I grab my purse and head for the door. My hand is on the knob when I hear that intense voice again.

"I don't know what's happening to me, and I hate it... I hate that you make me want to do things like go to Christmas tree farms and plan corny dates just so that I can convince you to be around my pathetic ass."

I drop the handle.

"I hate that I regularly pull into restaurant parking lots while I'm working to try and connect to Wi-Fi so I can see if you've texted me."

The springs of the couch creak, getting released from their load.

"I hate that if I don't get to put my hands all over you soon I'll only feel like half a human." His voice is close enough to feel on my skin. "I already knew deep down that I haven't been okay for a long time, but since I met you, I feel how broken I am. I physically feel it."

The rush of his hand swiping through the air to thump his chest rustles my hair. His closeness crawls over my skin.

I touch my own aching chest. Should I turn around? Can I move?

"I don't want to need anyone, especially not a girlfriend. But dammit...I need you."

Whoa.

Does Miller want to be with me? Like, *be* with me, be with me? I'm in college three hours away. How would that even work? This is ridiculous. Crazy. But...

The pull.

I sense him only inches from me. My arms fill with goosebumps, which I try to rub away.

His fingers stop me, curling around mine.

"Say something," he whispers.

"I..." *need you too.* I can't say it. It feels too, well, needy.

He squeezes my hand. I snake my fingers into his. This is definitely palpable.

"Dammit," he grumbles.

My body swings around and slams against the door. Miller's mouth takes over my consciousness. It pauses mere centimeters from my own. Spicy orange breath brushes against my lips. He holds my face between his hands. One thumb trails across my bottom lip.

Boy, do I hope my breath is okay. People aren't meant to share air this close. They either find a comfortable distance apart, or they connect their faces. The in-between feels messy. Slippery.

Am I on the edge of a coast or a canyon?

His forehead presses against mine. "This is a bad idea."

Right now, I don't care about ideas—good, bad, crazy, anything. There is something in me that must be satisfied.

I press my mouth against his.

For a moment he simply holds me there, his soft lips squished under mine. A weak shield.

Then his mouth moves, and I see why this was a bad idea. He enters the soft, sensitive part of me just beyond what the outside world can touch. The bond disassociates me from everything else. I am no longer body or heart or mind. I'm electric current—aggressive, all-consuming current. And I'm hooked.

Part of me will never be able to walk away from this high.

Other parts of me fight to get closer to him: my arms, my legs, my mouth. And it hurts. Feeling so drawn to someone that it rips out of you.

I'm pinned against the door by his kisses. The soft cotton of his t-shirt skims across my belly as my body lifts. I anchor myself to his hips with my thighs. I can't stop my affection. My lips swell from all the friction.

My whole body does. I start to want things....

Things I am a little terrified to want again. But the apprehension in my counterpart's expression neutralizes my own.

He rakes his fingers across my butt, pulling me tighter against him, and I go a little floppy. How does one maintain muscle function when not breathing?

"I'm going to pay for this," he mumbles against my mouth.

I moan as the anguish in his words strikes the ache where my heart used to be.

I grab his head and kiss him in the most reassuring way I can, loading it with all the need I couldn't speak about before. I'm here, whatever the cost.

When I pull back, he folds his arms around me and drops his head into the nook of my shoulder—forevermore his spot. He holds me. Just holds me. It's so different from my last romantic encounter that tears well in my eyes. I hope he won't look up anytime soon.

"What did you say about your car before?" His words get muffled by my skin.

Do we have to switch from this thing we're doing to that? I like this better.

He sets me on my feet. I beat my tears into submission and smile when he finally looks at me. "I introduced the front headlight to an unfriendly light pole."

"That's not good."

"It's fine. Cars are fixable. I'm going to try and hide it from my mom until I can get it into a shop. She doesn't need that stress."

"Will she not need to drive it anywhere?"

"I'm going to stall her. I have a whole thing planned. It's my day off tomorrow, so I'm going to convince her to decorate Abies with me and make homemade gifts for whoever is on her Christmas list. She loves that sort of thing. I'm sure I can make a whole day of it."

"Want me to take the car somewhere while you distract her?"

"You have work."

"I can manage it."

"Really?" My voice cracks.

"Sure. Let me take you home. Leave the car to me."

I have an ally. The tears sneak up into my eyelids again. I hug his neck. My nose lingers near the woodsy scent of his shirt a little too long, because he places a small peck on my ear. It's like a trigger.

I dissolve into current again.

A few minutes later, he comes up for air.

"Damn." He backs away from me. "Uh, I'm going to be a gentleman and go pack you a goody bag."

I wander through his house, his actually full-sized, very adult house. I picture myself living here with him. It'd definitely beat my tiny dorm room that has been overrun by my roommate and her Vinyasa posse.

I'd exchange Miller's treadmill and weights for a bed in the guest room. I'd add curtains to all the windows. We could make an event out of painting over all the beige. There's a huge wall in the hall for photos. We could have plants. Miller would love plants.

I'm fondling a door frame when he finds me.

"What's up?" He eyeballs me.

I probably have the stupidest look on my face. "Nothing."

Not anything at all.

I take the container of food and excuse myself from his presence before he can ask any more questions.

THIRTY-ONE

Instead of tossing and turning all night, I sleep like a person who's got things under control.

In the morning, I guard Mom's bedroom while scouring Pinterest for ideas on cheap DIY ornaments. A post about t-shirt ribbons inspires me. This is going to be a classy tree, but vintage classy—nice on a budget.

Before waking the guest of this party, I assemble the gingerbread dough. My hands cramp from kneading, but the smell is well worth the effort.

I arm myself with coffee and leftover figgy pudding and enter her room. "Morning sunshine."

She rolls over and rubs her eyes. "How long have you been up?"

"Six-thirty. I was too excited to sleep. I've got plans for us today."

She sits up. "What do you have there?"

"Coffee with hazelnut creamer, and this"—I do a Vanna White move—"is figgy pudding. Miller made it for me."

"How late were you out with him?"

"I don't know. Like eleven?"

"What did y'all do?"

I try not to think about everything we did, since my thoughts usually etch themselves all over my face. "It was the cutest thing. He set up this date where we sampled a bunch of random Christmas foods that you've never actually tried, like from songs. Roasted chestnuts are disgusting, by the way."

"You seem like you had a nice time." For some reason, her eyebrows pinch together. If this is one of those judgy mom things, where she assumes his character based on his job, I don't want to hear it.

"Anyway, clear your schedule. We're decorating our poor little Christmas tree today and our wreath. And then I thought we could tackle Christmas gifts for anyone left on your list. We'll put a Christmas movie on in the background, of course."

"Hun..."

"I don't want to hear any arguments. Eat up. Get dressed. I'll see you in the kitchen." I leave her nursing her coffee.

My mom joins me ten minutes later, still in her pj's, which is perfect. A cozy girls' day!

"I've rolled out the dough. We just need to cut out the gingerbread men and make a hole at the top for the ribbon."

"Smells good."

Drew's still asleep, so I don't turn on the TV. We work in the quiet. I cut the shapes and pass them to her for holes. She finds a stirring spoon with a round handle to make her job quicker. Before we've filled the sheet pan all the way, she sits. I scoot the tray over to her.

"How are you feeling today?" I ask.

"Just fine."

"Something on your mind? You seem quiet."

"No. It's just early."

The baked gingerbread men turn out adorable. I find some fishing line in a junk drawer, and we string them up. Four dozen get scattered among the branches.

"I found the cutest link for these ribbons. They look like the ones you'd see tied on the branches of Christmas trees from the twenties. You make them out of old sheets. And I found another link for citrus garland. I mean, hello, where has that been all our lives, right?"

My mom checks the clock. "I've got to get ready to go out."

"Can't you stay? It would really mean a lot if we could spend the day together."

"It's not something I can miss. It shouldn't take too long, though. Maybe we could go to lunch after."

"If we don't finish, we'll never get around to it again. Christmas is three weeks away. We have to decorate our tree!"

"I promise we'll do it tonight."

"This is my one day off, and I was really hoping we could spend it together."

She inhales.

I'm screwed if she doesn't cave, but also, this hurts. She cares about some gathering with her new friends more than she cares about spending quality time with her daughter, whom she never sees.

"It's rude to cancel on these things at the last minute."

"God, Mom, whatever."

I storm toward my room until I remember it's occupied. Balcony it is. I slam the front door and squeeze the railing. My eyes well with tears.

What do I do?

It's freezing out here in a camisole, so avoidance is not an option. When some lady walks out her front door into the breezeway, I blush and race back inside.

"Apartments are the worst!"

I twist my arms over my chest, wishing I could scream. But no. We are fraternizing with a bunch of strangers now.

My phone dings.

Miller: Car's dropped off. Said they can have it done by tomorrow and will text you when it's ready. Repairs are going to set you back about $500
Adia: K thanks

My lucky day. It's going to cost almost all of the money I'll bring home from my new job to fix this problem.

What will I do about school? There's no way I'm getting stuck here with my mom, who has no room left for me in her life.

My stepbrother walks out of our shared sleeping quarters with drowsy eyes. He sits beside me at the counter and pushes a huge stack of dirty dishes my direction.

I growl.

"Adia, will you calm down, please?" Mom says.

"Yum. What's in this stuff?" Drew asks.

I snatch the figgy pudding from him. "That wasn't for you."

He holds up his hands.

"Drew's going to have to drive you to your meeting, Mom. I left your car at Miller's house."

"You left it with him?" she says in an unnecessarily high pitch. She and my brother exchange a look.

"What was that?"

"Well, I need my car, for one thing. I said you could bring it to work, not gallivant all over the place in it. Why would you leave it at his house?"

"I was tired," I lie. "Miller was nice enough to offer me a ride home."

"Well, I guess since you were tired, I'll need to have Drew drive me over to this boy's house to get the car you left behind."

Uh… "I don't have the keys, and Miller's working today. Maybe you should just skip your thing."

"I have to go to my thing!"

My arms fly into the air. Drew scoots back into our bedroom.

"And I don't like it at all that you left my car with this boy. I'm not sure I trust him."

"Why would you, after he helped me save your life?"

"That's a little dramatic."

"You just don't like that he's a delivery boy!"

"It's just that you barely know him, Adia. And you're in college now. You don't need to be getting attached to some local."

I scowl.

"Also, your brother got creeped out."

"Drew said something bad about Miller?"

"Yes. We both feel like something's off about that boy, Adia."

"How so?"

"He's not exactly Mr. Friendly. Drew said when they met he wouldn't shake his hand, and then he left. I will not tolerate rude behavior in this house."

"It's an apartment."

"You think I don't know that?"

I throw the bedroom door open. "You told Mom my boyfriend's a creep!"

"Your boyfriend?" He scrunches his face. "Adia."

"Save it. I don't want your opinion right now."

Drew pinches his lips together.

Is Miller my boyfriend? Do I want him to be?

I think I do. He's the one bright spot in this whole crappy holiday, but everyone seems to be against him. Against me.

The bathroom I try to escape to smells like it has something evil breeding in the toilet. I gag.

"Sorry," Drew calls.

I stomp back into my occupied bedroom and cast myself onto the bed.

"Don't get all pouty, Ads. We're just speaking up because we love you."

Where can a girl get some freaking privacy?

I throw my pillow over my head and growl. There isn't room for me in this apartment. There isn't anything for me here.

I'm done trying.

I pack my bags.

THIRTY-TWO

J emma pulls into her driveway and pops the trunk. I pull out my duffel.

"So why does Drew think Miller's a creep?" she asks.

I wave at Mrs. Sanyal as we walk into Jemma's room. My face hits her bed pillows. They smell like baby powder. They smell like her.

"He got a bad vibe."

"What did Miller say about the whole thing?"

"He blew it off."

"Mm. What do you think?"

"Well, Miller's kind of a weird person, for sure. Very withdrawn. But he's also incredibly sincere. I don't know… I see a different side of him than he lets other people see."

"You still deserve an explanation."

"I know. I've got to figure out a way to get him to open up."

"You could say, 'Miller, I want to know why you're weird about people or we can't be together.' See if that works."

"Ha ha. It's not that easy."

"Okay."

She's skeptical. I wish Miller could be himself around everyone. I curl up into a ball.

Jemma lies down next to me and rubs my back. "You want to turn on Hallmark and zone out on real life for a while?"

I roll over to face her. "Actually, I'm in the mood for something dark and dysfunctional."

"Praise be to this day! Are you finally going to watch *Evil Genius* with me?"

"No way. I need fiction…and preferably nothing about murder, please."

"You said dark."

"I mean like people with interpersonal problems or something, not like heads blowing off."

"Boo."

Jemma puts on Netflix and starts scrolling. "Okay, I heard this was great." She selects a show called *Atypical*, about a teenager with autism spectrum disorder and his family drama.

Perfect.

I don't even blink until season one ends and Jemma pauses the screen on the first episode of season two. "We've got about an hour before we need to start getting ready."

"For what?"

"My sisters want to meet up at the hookah lounge downtown and then hang out at Jess's condo for a little while."

"Are Hailey and Viv coming?"

"Hailey's not answering her phone, and Viv's going out with some guy from State that came to see her."

"They've been busy every time I try to hang out with them," I mumble.

Outside, blackness is making its march across the sky, matching the feeling swelling in my chest. The one-on-one hours I have left with my BFF are dwindling.

"I'm hungry," Jemma says. "Do you want anything?"

"No thanks."

"I'll bring extra in case you change your mind."

I won't. No room for food between all these knots. I stare up at the ceiling, aching to be in a place where it doesn't feel like I'm about to lose everything. I get out my phone to see if Miller's still working.

Miller's not home when we get there, but I tell Jemma not to wait. Her sisters are expecting her in fifteen minutes, and I don't want to mess up their plans. They probably want all the time they can get with their absentee family member—like normal relatives.

It's unfortunately cold with the blades of wind gusting around the porch, and my coat doesn't keep me warm long. I break into my duffel, doubling up on socks and using another pair as mittens. Is underwear an appropriate headcover in a family neighborhood? I opt for a sweater turban.

I try to read *People* on my phone, but the teeth-chattering gets too aggressive for me to see the small font. I'm forced to move around. Doing jumping jacks proves to be challenging with my joints near rigor mortis. On the third jump, my legs refuse to come back to center. Miller pulls up for a nice view of me trying to pull my lower half back together and instead tumbling onto my face.

"What are you doing out here in the cold?"

"Waiting for you." I stumble to my feet, pulling the sweater off my face.

"I told you I could come get you."

"Jemma needed to be somewhere, so…"

"You're shivering."

My sock hand ends up in his hand as he drags me inside.

He looks around and frowns. "Wait here."

He comes back with a giant navy blue comforter that has frayed edges. After wrapping it around my shoulders, he rubs my arms. My body convulsions don't stop. Most of me is ice.

"Let me run you a shower."

He leads me through his bedroom, past his bed that's missing its comforter, and into the master bath. It's decked out in floral wallpaper. Miller tests the water until it's ready, then grabs me a towel and excuses himself.

I figure out the source of his woodsy smell. It's the bar of soap in his shower. It's actually the only thing in his shower. Without conditioner, I may never get a brush through my hair again, but I wet it anyway, desperately wanting to end the body convulsions. The steamy downpour works wonders on me outside and in.

When I pull back the shower curtain, I find my bag waiting, which is good since I wouldn't have had the nerve to go out in a towel to seek it out. What would Miller think of me roaming his house half-naked? What would he do? He was already pretty close to seeing me naked when he brought this bag in here. Did that do to him what thinking about it is doing to me?

On go gray leggings and a baggy Avery University tee. The clothes are chilly and unpleasant, but I'm glad to be in something fresh.

Miller's waiting for me in the kitchen next to a steaming mug of what my nose concludes is a medium roast coffee.

"Milk?" he asks.

"Yes please."

He pours some into my cup and passes it to me along with a bag of sugar.

"None for you?"

"I'm not a coffee drinker."

"But you have coffee?" I look around, realizing there isn't a pot anywhere.

"I ran to the gas station across the street and filled up a cup. I hope it isn't terrible."

It's not the best, but I savor every sip of it.

"So... What's with the duffel bag?"

"My mom and I had a fight."

"About the car?"

"Sort of..."

"So where are you going?"

"Here, maybe?"

He rakes a hand through his hair. I love his hair. He shouldn't hide it under a hat so much.

"I'm sorry to throw this on you. I just... My mom's forgotten how to be a mom, and until I figure out how to accept that, it's better for both of us if I keep my distance."

He turns on the sink and starts washing the one dirty dish.

My stomach tangles around itself. Have I overstepped? We're

hardly a couple. Of course I shouldn't be asking to stay over. Should I call Jemma to come back?

I start filling the silence with words. "Look, I'm sorry. I'm dumb. This is too soon, isn't it? I can stay with—"

A fork tumbles from his hand, clattering against the plate in the sink. He swings around so fast it startles me. He scoops me in by my face and overtakes my mouth. Holy man muscles. The last hint of outdoor chill disintegrates.

I fight him for position, each of us tugging at the other, trying to move closer. He lifts me onto the counter and presses against me while kisses trail down my neck. My legs reflexively clench around him.

"I'm really glad you're here," he breathes, and then he holds my face still to plant a kiss so deep it's as if he's sealing the entirety of his emotion under this connection. For me, it does the opposite. Every type of thing my body was designed to feel bursts forth. It's unsafe. My urges may never come back to baseline.

"Come on."

I watch in a stupor as Miller steps back and leaves the room. I was not done here. I fill up a glass of water and drink it sip by sip until every drop is coursing through my system.

"You coming?" Miller asks, sticking his head back through the doorway. "I'm taking you out to dinner."

My nonhormonal urges poke up out of hiding and greet this proposition. "I could eat."

"Where do you keep your shampoo?" I ask, wrangling my clump of hair into a messy bun as we enter the dive.

"It's that bar in there. It's soap and shampoo."

"How economical." This guy's extreme. I'm going to have to run out and get hair products if I stay with him for long. My wild mane would turn soap into a single-use product.

A young black guy with a ponytail that puts mine to shame greets Miller fondly and leads us to a dark back corner. A wave of yeasty steam welcomes us to our table, which is right beside the kitchen.

"Should I tell Kobe to whip up a double portion of your usual?" the waiter asks.

Miller turns to me. "Do you like eggplant?"

"I, uh, don't know." I really don't want to find out.

"She's a burger girl," he says.

Amen.

"Gotcha," says the waiter in a tone of surprise. "Coming right up."

Is it weird to eat burgers here or something? Do I care? My stomach is in no condition to be trying some food that literally has plant in the name.

"So you're on a first-name basis with the chef here?"

"Yeah. It's the closest place around, so I come a good bit."

"And you always get the same thing?"

"Mostly. When you're a pescatarian, you take what you can get. Kobe makes this amazing vegetable piroshki. He bakes this Italian stuffing into a sticky bun and serves it hot. You're probably going to wish you had one. Piroshkis are the real deal here."

"Hold up. Pescatarian?"

"Fish is the only animal I eat."

"Yeah. But why?"

"It's better."

"That's a matter of opinion."

"Have you tried it?"

"I can't live in a world without bacon."

He shakes his head with a grin.

How did I end up so fond of this eccentric human?

He might have good taste in restaurants, though. This one has that understated confidence that comes from making such good food that you don't really need to attend to basic upkeep. It's not just the buns that are sticky.

But if these piroshki delicacies have anything to do with the divine smell, I *have* missed out. "Do they have meat buns too?"

"All kinds."

"Well, I would have ordered one if I'd known."

"We can come back again."

Oh, can we? Maybe I won't need Jemma to rescue me after all. Which means I better get busy proving my mom wrong. I need answers.

"Miller..."

He looks at me with his all-encompassing eyes, and for the first time tonight, I notice it. A longing.

I wonder where I'll sleep tonight. Will Miller sleep with me? Is he a cuddler? What does he wear to sleep?

Shoot. *Focus, Adia. You need to find out why the guy you're into avoids people.*

Oh, lord. How do I ask that?

"Tell me about your worldview."

"I like the world. That's why I try to protect it."

I laugh. Why is his deal so hard to discuss?

I guess Miller still feels like a stranger to me. But the kind of stranger you know how good it feels to kiss. Like a new album you've only listened to once but are certain will eventually stitch itself deep into the fibers of your soul. That kind of stranger.

"Why are you...so standoffish?"

His eyes bulge. "What the hell is that supposed to mean?"

"No. I just meant like..."

"Like, you have a problem with who I am?"

"No. I... I was just wondering if something happened to you, or if you have, like, a condition and that's why you—"

"Holy shit, Adia. Where is this coming from?" He scoots away from my hand as I try to reach for his. *Crap, crap, crap.*

"I don't know what I'm trying to say. Look, it's nothing." I reach for him again, but he's totally closed off. I pull my chair over and sit knee-to-knee with him. I should have gone with Jemma's approach. "I'm sorry I asked that. It was weird."

"Where did that come from, Adia? Damn."

"I don't know."

"That's a lie." His chair skids back as he stands up.

"I want to know exactly why you left my apartment in such a hurry the other day," I blurt.

He stops.

"My brother thought you were acting really shady. He thinks you're a creep."

"Are you kidding me? He called me that?"

"I mean, I think he's being unfair. It's why I left. It's why I'm here with you. Please sit down."

His jaw tenses and relaxes for several seconds in a row. Then he turns his rattling irises on me. "This is why you need a place to stay? *I'm* why?"

"I mean, that was the final straw, but things have been crumbling ever since I got home. I don't fit anymore." My voice cracks.

Miller drags his hands all the way down his face. Then, he sits.

I breathe again.

Our waiter comes back with two succulent-looking plates. My stomach does a cheer flip. I scoot back to my side of the table.

"I don't mind that you're different, you know. But I do want to understand you. I get the feeling that you've been withholding something from me that keeps making you pull away. If you aren't ready to talk about your past, that's your choice. I can't make you. But I'm in this with you. I'm not going to disappear the moment I hear something I don't like. I see you, Miller. I don't think you're a creep. I think you're a really good person."

He sits staring at the table with his arms crossed. The lines slowly disappear from his forehead.

My stomach begs until I stuff the meat patty into my mouth. It hits every good note. Juicy, cheesy, a hint of char. I lick the ketchup off the corner of my mouth and focus on my fries while I wait for Miller to say something. He'll feel better when he gets whatever it is off his chest, just like I have. At least then he could eat those sticky buns he hyped.

"What are you thinking?"

When he grumbles and rubs his temple, I deflate, busying myself with constructing a little French fry house.

His voice startles me. "You know how I told you I got beat up when I was seventeen?"

"Yeah. You got hospitalized."

He nods. "I broke two ribs. One punctured my lung. I couldn't breathe because it filled up with blood. You can't even imagine how that feels." His eyes slip closed.

I slip my fingers into his clenched palm and squeeze. I hate that he's reliving this pain, but I need to hear it. It's him, and I want a share.

"Your brother was one of them."

"One of…your attackers?"

He gives me a face that says as much. My mouth goes dry.

"Are you sure?"

"I remember that scar. The one on his hand. I remember every single thing about that hand. All their hands. After a while, it was all I could see. Hands and shoes."

Drew's scar runs across the entire top of his left hand. He got it in a bike accident when he was six. I always thought of it as a smiley face that almost seemed on purpose since it's so fitting for him.

"Why did he do it?"

"Well…I think he was just backing up his buddy who had it out for me."

I hide behind my hands and stare at my lap. It's like I've been punched. How could my playful big brother who I adore be the guy in Miller's story? My image of him shatters around me, leaving jagged shards where a bond once was. A tear streaks down my cheek.

My last safety blanket. Gone.

"Want to get this stuff to go?" Miller asks.

I nod at my food.

"You okay?"

"I need some air."

I rush out into the cool night. My skin cries as I drag my back down the brick wall and fold myself into a ball.

Dang it, Drew. How could you be that guy? You're supposed to be my champion, my role model. What do I do with this?

Miller catches my fist, which has been hitting the sidewalk without me realizing.

"Hey. It's okay."

"My brother's an assailant." Tears spill.

"He did that once. It's in the past. I'm sure he's a great brother."

"Don't defend him. He almost committed murder."

"Not on purpose."

"Sort of on purpose." I get up and pace. "I don't know if I should yell at him or report him or…did you ever press charges?"

"Adia." Miller stops me and grabs the sides of my face, his thumb running softly across my cheeks. "I'm okay. You don't need to do anything about this. It's way back in the past, and I want it left there."

"I mean, dang, every time you look at me, you probably think of him."

"That's not what looking at you does to me. Trust me." He clings to my shoulders as his eyes search mine. Then he places a thunderclap of a kiss on my lips and hugs me to his chest.

Eyes closed, I soak in the sound of his softly thumping heart. He runs his fingers up and down my back. My focus turns to new things. Tingles. Heat. The toxicity of his embrace.

I need it more than I want, the comfort of someone paying attention to me.

His hands stop moving and spread over my shoulder blades, effectively fastening me to him. "Can we get out of here?" His words tickle my ear. "You owe me a prize from the other night."

I nod.

The entirety of my insides flip. This prize better involve more kissing.

THIRTY-THREE

M iller plops a controller into my hand.

So...no kissing.

"You're about to have the most fun you've ever had in front of a screen."

Judging from his last attempt at good screen action, I have my doubts. "What are you forcing on me here?"

"An out of body experience." He hops up and turns off the living room lights.

"Can I get a blanket? I'm a little chilly." Also, I don't do entertainment without a cozy cover. It's unhealthy.

"Let me grab my comforter while I turn off the rest of the lights."

"Is that the only blanket you own?"

"It's all I need."

The whole house goes dark except for my breathing...and his footsteps.

And the buzz of the gaming system. Miller plops back down onto the thinly padded couch and grabs his controller.

I tuck us both into the gargantuan comforter.

A set of hands holding some sort of parcel appears on the TV screen. We're in a cockpit in the air. The nighttime haze suggests some mystery about to unfold. Then we crash into a body of water and a light tower rises out of the storm. I have not pressed a single button on my controller.

"Is this a video game or a movie?"

"A little of each." Miller winks, and I melt into my britches. If gaming makes him playful, then let's play.

We travel down the mysterious tower, and at the bottom a video screen welcomes us to an underwater utopia. It's intriguing, with fancy signs and posh buildings that are all covered in seaweed and crustaceans. This splendid, decaying world resonates in my soul. A giant whale drifts past. The music turns dark.

"Am I going to need a night light after this?"

"Nah. I'll be here to keep you safe." He runs his hand along my thigh, expecting me to still be able to play. My body floods with heat. Luckily, all I'm required to do at this point is press the forward button.

"Ahhh!" During my embarrassing scream, I jump against Miller's arm. "What is that she-creature, and why is she coming after me?"

Miller chuckles. "There are mutants down here. You better focus if we're going to survive."

"Sir, yes sir."

My mind concentrates on the game, but my body keeps tabs on every brush across it. Cuddled together, Miller and I frolic through a land of mutants.

It's midnight before I even realize time has been passing.

A big, painful yawn takes over my face.

"Let's give it up," Miller says.

He rolls up the controllers. My fatigue doesn't quite cool the heat that's built up between our closely situated bodies. I don't want any of this to end. "I want to know where they took the little sisters. We're so close."

"We're not that close, trust me." He comes over to the couch and offers me a lift to my feet. "Take my bed, okay? I don't trust you out here with the Xbox."

Another yawn tries to pull the edges of my jaw apart. Maybe sleep is best. I check my phone for the time and get bombarded by dozens of texts from my mom. "What time did they say my mom's car would be ready tomorrow?"

"They said they'd call, but maybe early afternoon."

"I should be off by then. I'm not allowed to work more than thirty hours this week because of part-time restrictions, so Rosa wants me to leave early tomorrow and Friday. Do you get a lunch break?"

"If I want. Why?"

"I know I've asked a lot of you already, but could you drop me off at the repair shop at lunch? I'll wait on the car and bring it to my mom as soon as it's done. Her texts are getting increasingly irritable."

"You could be waiting for hours. Why don't I pick you up from your shift when you're done, and you can ride around with me until they text about the car?"

"You're trying to get me to do your work again, aren't you?"

"Nah. You don't have to do a thing but sit there and look pretty."

"You better let me do something. What do you think I am, a bum?"

"You are homeless." His lips curve upward into a definite symbol of positivity. It's glorious. I make this boy happy. My work here can be done. I get up, wrapping Miller's comforter around me, and turn toward the bedroom.

"Miller…"

"Yeah?"

"What are you going to use to sleep with?"

"I've got a pillow here." He points to a flimsy lumbar pillow that matches the orange and brown Seventies pattern on the couch.

"I think your pillow needs a pillow. And what about for a blanket?"

"I don't get cold."

"I have never heard of anyone in history who slept well without some sort of cover. Why don't we share the bed? Come on."

"Not a good idea."

"Miller, come on. I'm squatting at your place. The least you can do is let me share the bed with you."

He folds his arms.

"I'll feel terrible. I won't be able to sleep knowing you're out here tossing and turning because I took the only blanket you own."

His shoulders slump.

"Please."

I really don't want to put him out, but also, snuggling could be nice. My eyes work him over.

He takes a deep breath and follows me to his room.

We stand side-by-side brushing our teeth, and I try to keep him from seeing me. I'm like an ogre with bubbles dripping down my chin, while he's over there with his wooden toothbrush neatly going tooth by tooth.

"I have to pee," I tell him.

He quickly disappears.

I find him in the bed as far to one edge as a person can get without tumbling off.

"I don't bite."

"That's more than I deserve to know."

I turn out the light and crawl into my side. It's normal for me to hear another person breathing in the dark. But the way I feel about Miller's breathing is nothing familiar. My skin prickles. Millions of microscopic threads are being drawn through it and tugged side-ways...toward Miller. My hands feel empty.

"Miller?"

"Yeah?"

"Can I see your scars? From when my brother hurt you, I mean."

Silence.

"I want to see what you have to carry with you."

The sheets ruffle. A lamp clicks on, and there he is, shirtless.

His frame is narrow but wonderfully taut, with a veined chisel that comes from years of heavy lifting. He shifts away from the lamp to face me, and the full picture comes into view. Across his left upper chest runs a thick, peach-colored scar. A few smaller scars are scattered over his abdomen. He slips back into bed.

He points to the smallest ones. "This is where they put the ports after surgery. That's where they cut me open to drain the blood in my lung," he says about the big one.

"May I touch them?"

He closes his eyes and nods.

The rib cage scar feels lumpy and firm, and it burrows around his side almost to his back. As I trace the track, I notice another sizable scar on his inner arm.

"It's from the surgery to reset my fracture," he explains, his eyelids fluttering to the stroke of my finger.

I kiss each mark. He tenses up the whole time.

"Are there any more?"

"Not if you're going to kiss them."

"Why?"

"Because..." he whispers.

I break out the puppy dog eyes.

He surrenders his palm, where a crooked white mark runs against the natural skin lines.

"What did that?"

"A rock. My hand got caught between it and someone's foot."

"Poor hand."

My lips linger over the scar, and his breath seems to disappear entirely until a small "Adia" escapes the threshold of his lungs.

I come to the plea.

He curls me into him and absorbs me with his arms before placing his mouth on mine. He handles me like something he must touch carefully, or it will sting.

But I have different ideas. I kiss him like I'm leaving in a few short weeks and we don't have time to waste. I kiss him like I want to stay.

Staying would be much easier than the alternative. Easier than facing all the campus trolls. It would be much better than being alone again.

I don't want to think about everything else. I just want this.

My kisses get rougher.

He matches my vigor.

We're a tangle of mouths and limbs. He flips me onto my back.

I flinch against the gut-wrenching memory of the last time I was in this position.

No. That guy will not control me anymore. I follow my desire, slipping my fingers inside the waist of Miller's sweatpants.

He jerks back. Traps my hand. "Adia, please."

"Don't you want this?"

"That's not the issue."

"Okay." I try to advance my hand, but he holds it hostage.

"I want to be a good guy."

"You are. Why would you say it like that?"

"Good guys don't let things go too far."

Were we going too far? What is too far?

"Oh." I take in an armful of the comforter and hug it.

Miller caresses a tendril of hair on my forehead. "Will you let me hold you while you fall asleep?" With a wave of his strength, he shifts us and tucks his body against mine. "Don't turn around. Just lie here with me. Would that be okay?"

"Sure." Let me just get my ovaries to stop sending aggressive signals.

He absorbs me. While we lie there, I think of all I've just learned about his body...and how much I like it.

"Do you think bad people can make themselves into good people?" he asks, pulling my wandering brain back into focus.

"Bad people are good people. They're the same people."

"So you think it's possible?"

"I don't think it's either-or. There's bad and good in everyone."

"No."

"Yes. No one's perfect."

"I'm not talking about snowy white. I'm talking about people falling into one category or the other."

"Categories are cruel. We all have two sides. We all need help sometimes, and we all screw up. If you think some people don't and that's what you expect for yourself, then you're being unfair, and *that's* bad."

His chest rises and falls in unison with mine. A soothing synchronization. I let it rock me while he disappears into his overactive mind. The only other person I've had this level of comfort with is my best friend. But unlike Jemma, having Miller's arms around me feels more than comfy. I feel complete.

"I want you to meet Jemma. I have to make sure you pass the best friend test if I'm going to continue living with you."

"I see."

"How about I cook dinner tomorrow, and we invite her over?" Baby steps.

He takes a deep breath into my neck. *Come on, Miller.*

"Okay," he says.

"Yeah?"

"Yeah."

"Could I invite one more person too? So Jemma doesn't feel like a third wheel? I can take care of everything."

He squeezes me tighter and nuzzles into my hair. "If you insist, I'll allow it."

I respond with my own squeeze. We hold each other silently, breathing in unison. Every part of me feels warm and fuzzy—some warmer than others, but I stay still like he requested. It's powerful, the restraint.

I want to stay awake to keep enjoying my nest of boy, but my eyes grow heavy.

When I wake up in the middle of a nightmare involving Santa, packing tape, and my linguistics paper, I reach for him. He isn't in the bed anymore.

THIRTY-FOUR

I linger somewhere between the front office and the break room, watching for customers with my iPhone at my ear. A small coffee stain on my snazzy teal polo doesn't budge with my spit treatment. I'll have to do laundry at Miller's. Hopefully he has detergent like a normal person.

"Should I bring something?" Jemma asks.

"Nope, nothing. Just yourself. I've got the rest covered. I'm making homemade ravioli."

"Breaking out all the stops for this guy, huh?"

"I want tonight to be awesome."

"Well, I'll be there, so…"

"You're the best. See you at seven."

When I hang up, Harry pokes me. "Am I invited to your party?"

I was hoping he'd react like this. It's why I strategically called Jemma from work. "It's a small dinner party, but I can set a place for you if you're interested."

"I can't pass up homemade ravioli."

"No, you really can't. It's a family recipe, and it's the bomb." I've never made it by myself, but I've got to get used to doing that now. I've helped my mom make it tons of times. I've got this.

Favorite coffee mug in hand, I greet the customer walking through the door.

~

We're in the middle of a rush when Miller shows up to get me.

"Almost ready," I tell him, handing a customer four books of stamps.

Miller grabs the stack of packages on the counter and takes them to the back for processing. He passes Harry, who's returning from the back with a customer's mail.

"Hey, man," Harry says. "Thanks for jumping in."

"It's fine."

Though it's tough to decipher so few syllables, I'm thinking this is guy code for "let's be best friends."

I'm over my time limit by twenty minutes, but I don't want to bail on Harry with a store full of customers. They really need to hire someone full-time, but, lucky for me, seasonal employees are only allowed part-time status to simplify paperwork. I'm not trying to sacrifice my whole holiday for a paycheck. Even if I do need the money.

"Go on," Harry urges. "Rosa will be back at one. I've got this."

"Yeah, okay. Sorry I can't stay."

"No probs. Just take this to the back for me before you go," he says, sticking a packing label to my face.

"See you later," I chuckle. "I'll text you."

"Hit me up, girl."

On my way to the kitchen, I get out my phone to send Harry the address. There's a missed call from my brother. How do I talk to him now?

I ignore it.

Miller has taken care of a whole pile of packages that were building up in the back.

"I'm so sorry I made you wait. I'm sure you have better things to do than my work."

"I figure you'll return the favor. You ready to head out?"

"Sure am."

"You may want to…" He points at the shipping label on my face.

"You sure? I was thinking it looked cool. You know, on-brand."

"I see."

He's not smiling. Is he mad?

A few hairs ditch me for the sticker when I remove it. I toss it in the trash can beside the back door.

We are no less than a few feet from the building when he turns to me with his serious face. Oh, dear.

"I know I shouldn't do this here, but I can't help it."

His mouth crushes mine.

"You are super sexy when you work."

I didn't even know Miller was capable of uttering such salacious words. I like what kissing does to him.

Miller and I make a great team. He teaches me how to locate the packages we need for each stop. I grab and pass; he distributes and verifies. We make record time.

At one door, he surprises me by knocking and disappearing inside.

A little kid runs through the yard. He dives forward, rolling across the grass while making some sort of plane sound. It's a pretty slick move. I chuckle.

Miller takes several minutes to return.

"What was that about?" I ask.

"Mrs. Libby lives here. She's blind and gets a lot of stuff delivered since she can't drive. That's her grandson." He points at the little guy who's now sitting in a sandbox, crashing two toy cars against each other. "She takes care of him during the daytime while his dad works. I like to check in on her and make sure there's nothing she needs."

Well, that makes me want to be a better person and, also, to grab his neck and take a selfie and post my guy for the world to see. Would that be so much to ask?

"I told my mom you're my boyfriend."

"Yeah?"

"Yeah."

"Is that what you want?"

"Is it what you want?"

"I think it's more important that you decide. You're the one who's going to be affected by a relationship."

"You won't be affected?"

"You know what I mean. You're in college. You've got the whole world ahead of you. You don't even know what you want to be yet."

"You sound like you've given up on yourself."

"I haven't given up on anything. I'm just in a different place than you are."

"Not really. You've still got everything at your fingertips too. You're twenty-four, dude, and your brain is so big."

He shakes his head. "Listen, I'm okay with where I'm at and what I'm doing. I'm not looking for more. But if you want that... If you want some guy with big aspirations who wants fancy things and a big lifestyle, then let's not do this. I'm not that guy."

"Does this have to be some grand decision about what I want for my life?" I like how I feel when I'm with Miller, and that's enough for me right now.

"I don't want to get hurt."

Neither do I. But the future is too big to figure out all at once. Can't we just focus on the now?

I try to give him a goofy face, but he won't look at me. He stares at the road, rubbing his chin up and down. Why does he have to be so serious?

"I don't need fancy things to be happy," I say.

"Okay...good." He finally turns to me, his eyes slippery and desperate. "Because I think that in order to be whatever version of happy is possible for me, I need *you*."

This hits me like a thousand arrows. It's so honest...and sad.

My grin fades. Do I love this guy?

"You're really sweet. Like maybe the sweetest guy I've ever met."

Miller presses the brakes as his eyes shutter closed. The muscles in his face tighten up around my words like he's wrestling them to stay put in his consciousness.

Something inside of me fundamentally shifts as I stare at this unsettled, overthinking, overserious, old-fashioned boy.

Until now, I've carried around this girlish fantasy about love. I'd find a perfect Prince Charming and we'd kiss, and the rest of life would fade to blissful black. But now, here, with a very real, very imperfect guy who's gutting me with his expression, I'm sprung into a colorful array of possibilities. Love isn't a magical formula. It's a messy thing. An involuntary thing. It's me being real and a boy who sticks around. It's flaws and misunderstandings that don't divide. It's us being better people together.

"Be my boyfriend, okay?"

When he kisses me this time, it's with conviction. He finally believes in us. I grab his shirt in my fists and return his zeal.

A horn bleats behind us at the same time my phone dings, successfully breaking us apart.

"The car's ready," I say.

Time to pay up and face my mom. My stomach twists.

Miller takes my hand as he puts the truck back into drive.

THIRTY-FIVE

The cute little stuffed ravioli are pressed and drying on the counter when I get a text from Viv. I'm relieved it's not my mom, whom I avoided this afternoon by leaving her car key at the front desk of the apartment complex.

> Vivianne: Heard Harry Rau is coming to your boy toy's place tonight. I want in.

Extra guests—especially of the Viv variety—could put Miller over the edge, but it might also be preferable to the whole thing feeling like a double date. The more the attention can be spread out, the better. I risk it and send her the address.

I should have expected the follow-up text from Hailey. She and our longtime guy friend Reed get added to the guest list. How nice of them to finally acknowledge my presence, but whatever. It's good timing. I'm going to have to get creative with seating though.

Except that all the creativity in the world won't materialize nonexistent chairs.

My boy seriously has the bare minimum a person can have and get by. It's almost impressive. His desk shares a chair with the dining room set. He only has one single charger, for his iPod, which he keeps unplugged and tucked away in his nightstand drawer. He doesn't have paper towels, so who knows what cleaning looks like. It definitely happens, because all the surfaces in this place are spick-and-span, but it can't be easy.

The neighbor tilts her head in confusion when she finds me on her doorstep. She's got an easygoing way about her. Her hair is cut close to her scalp and has a slight grayish tint to the little corkscrew curls. She has dark brown skin and wire-rimmed glasses.

"This is going to sound crazy, but I'm dating your neighbor, Miller, and I'm wondering if you have a folding table and chairs I could borrow for a dinner party. He's got four chairs in his entire house."

"Who?"

"Who what?"

"Who's Miller?"

"Your neighbor right there." I point to his house.

"I've never seen the person who lives there. I always wondered. Stopped by a few times years ago, but no one ever answered. Figured he or she must be either shy or very private."

"Private. But I'm trying to help with that. Hence the dinner party. Do you have a table I could borrow by chance?"

"You know, I think I do. Come on in."

We find a four-top in the garage. The lady, Shana, pulls off a cobweb. "Sorry, it's a little dusty."

"This will do just fine. Thank you."

"Tell Miller if he ever needs anything he shouldn't hesitate to stop by. When I'm not working, I'm around here most of the time."

"That's nice. I'll let him know."

"I think it's an awful shame how much people keep to themselves now. We've really lost our value for community over the years, with the internet and all."

"It's not got anything to do with that for Miller. He's just very guarded. He doesn't want to need people, I think. You should stop by sometime and meet him. He really is a sweet guy. He could use a good neighbor."

"Perhaps I will."

Jemma arrives first, and I put her to work babysitting the sauce.

After using some sheets to cover the tables, I place some of the leftover herbs from the meal into glasses as centerpieces. Miller had some nice napkins hidden in a drawer, so I fold them into knots and place them on the plates around the table. It's a simple display, but it works.

"Look who's turning into her mom," Jemma says from the kitchen.

"Eyes on the carbonara, woman."

Vivienne comes through the front door whispering about Harry.

"He's not here yet."

"Then where are the cocktails? This is an adult dinner party, right?"

I point her toward the kitchen, where I'm chilling the bottles of wine I talked Miller into purchasing.

What would my Italian spread be without a touch of vino?

Hailey and Reed follow her in, sucking in the tantalizing smells of flour, fresh tomato, and basil.

"I'm going to eat my own tongue if I can't have some of that gluten soon," Reed says as they follow me through the dining room to join the others.

"Wow, girl," Hailey says. "This is so adult. Cute."

"Oh, my god, you dyed your hair," Viv says to Hailey when we get to the kitchen.

"I thought I'd go darker for the holidays. Is it weird?"

"If you like it, then it's great," Jemma says.

"What does that mean? Do you think it's bad?"

Jemma makes a face at me.

I say, "It's really fun, Hailey. You could pull off any hairstyle." She could. She's got a great bone structure.

She smiles and sits at the table

"Hey, Viv. How have you been?" Reed asks, his eyes heavy on her.

Jemma eyes me again. We have a lot to dissect later.

We both feel super bad for poor Reed. He's pined for Viv since middle school, and I guess the feelings didn't totally fade in college.

She loves him too. That's the kicker. In high school, he was her shoulder to cry on, her hand to hold, her listening ear. Anything she needed. The problem is, Viv loves a lot of other guys too, and for very different parts of their bodies.

I wonder if Viv and Reed have kept in touch now that they're so far apart.

"How's California, Jem?" Reed asks.

"Not good enough, apparently, since she's leaving it for a year to live in London," I say.

"It's not a whole year, and actually California is a dream. I love the easygoing vibe out there."

"That's cool. How about you, Adia? Are you enjoying Avery?"

"It's okay."

"Don't worry. My brother hated his first year there. It probably had something to do with the fact that his roommate was a pothead who ended up getting expelled, but anyway, he eventually found his footing. Made some great friends and all that. He's a senior, and he couldn't be happier. He's thinking about staying there when he graduates."

"I heard His Divine Hunkiness Jason Derulo did a concert on your campus," adds Viv, "so if you aren't enjoying it, that's on you."

He did come for a concert. I spent that night in the library, crouched over my chem book, but I saw pictures of it, and several girls, all over Douche Face's Instagram the next day.

I fish out the second batch of ravioli and place it into the one large dish I could find in Miller's cabinets. It's supposed to be a mixing bowl, but whatever. I cover it back up with tinfoil. Now it's just a matter of keeping things warm until all the guests arrive.

"Helloooo," comes a voice from the front of the house.

Harry stands in the living room, holding two liquor bottles in the air. His eyes look red. "Who's ready to party, bitches?!"

"Oh," I say, taking them from him. "You didn't have to bring anything."

"I don't go anywhere without party favors. You look hot." He winks at me.

I guess I'm pulling off the overalls dress and turtleneck look I copied from Pinterest. Or maybe Harry's too used to seeing me in a polo and khakis.

I introduce him to my friends.

"Hell yeah. Is that Jack Daniel's?" Viv takes one of the bottles from me.

She's not shy about poking through the cabinets.

I decline when she tries to hand me a glass. Miller will have a hard enough time at this event without me getting rowdy.

Reed opens the other bottle and pours a round. Viv and Harry clink glasses.

Hailey pushes off the counter. "I almost forgot. I brought you something." She opens her purse and pulls out a fancy candle that smells like pine trees.

"Thanks, girl."

So fun. Miller should be here to see our host gift. Where is he?

Harry sits beside Hailey at the table, a glass of Jack in hand.

Hailey tucks a strand of her newly auburn hair behind her ear. "You played lacrosse, right?"

"Sure did. Number thirty-three, baby. State champs. What, what!" He tosses back his glass and refills. I better get some food into him before the second glass has a chance to join the first. How will Miller and Harry become friends if Harry's incoherent?

I start pulling stuff out of the fridge. "Olives, anyone?"

Finally, the knob on the back door rustles. Miller walks in looking a little pale and holding a bouquet of wildflowers. They are red and yellow and will perfect my table setting. I die.

Then I resurrect and add the flowers to the centerpiece.

"Thanks. How was the rest of your route?"

"Good." He takes in the crowd.

"We've had a few extra drop-ins for dinner. You know Harry from work. This is Jemma, Hailey, Viv, and Reed. We all went to high school together."

Miller's hands are buried in his pockets, so he can't dole out physical greetings. He bobs his head and says a cool "hey."

"I'm glad you're here," I whisper and then peck him on the cheek. "Let's eat!"

Harry points at the random computer in Miller's dining room and says, "Hey man, that's a sweet COTS."

"Thanks." Miller walks over to admire it with Harry.

"Which processor do you have?" Harry asks.

"Intel. Are you in the market?"

"I've thought about making one, but I haven't gotten around to it yet."

"Cool."

"Do you use it for gaming?"

Miller nods. "I just installed an RTX 2080 Ti GPU, so the graphics are sick."

"Damn." Harry pets the computer.

Yay! Common ground. I try not to grin.

We all spread out around the neighbor's square table and Miller's round one, which I've joined together as best I could.

"Nice table," Miller comments.

"Thank you. I met a lovely neighbor of yours today."

"How long have you lived here?" Jemma asks.

"Six years."

Harry pours another shot of whiskey. "Wow, dude. How old are you?"

"Twenty-four."

"Crazy, man. I can barely afford my apartment."

Miller doesn't respond, not with his mouth or his face.

I distribute my ravioli among the plates. They've gotten a little cold, but the warm sauce should help.

"Renting a house isn't that much more than an apartment if you have roommates," Reed says.

"Depending on where you live," Jemma points out. "The cost of living in Greensboro isn't too bad."

Harry looks around. "If I lived here, I'd throw parties all the time. This place is huge...and empty. You could fit so many people."

I poke Miller, but he doesn't respond.

"Looks amazing, Adia," says Viv. "Is this a family recipe?"

"Sure is."

"Damn, girl. I'm impressed that you pulled something like this off. I only know how to make Chef Boyardee, the microwave version."

I pass around the sauce. "Try it before you get too excited. It's my first shot at it by myself."

Hailey picks at her salad and doesn't go anywhere near the carbs. I wonder if she's spiraling again. Miller watches Harry finish his shot of whiskey and sloppily suck down a ravioli. Viv takes a bite, wipes off the sauce, and tries again. Not the best reaction, but also not the worst.

I give it a taste. Salt shrivels the skin on my tongue. I must have gotten the measurement wrong. "Ugh, you guys. It's way too salty. Put your forks down immediately."

"I think it's fine," says Harry, slurping down another bite.

"Thank you for making this nice meal for us," Miller adds, refusing to relinquish his fork. He eats everything on his plate while I get the girls and Reed extra salad and rolls.

Reed takes the two rolls Hailey offers him with a smile. "Too bad you didn't bring your cello, Hails. You could have put on a performance for us."

"It's clunky, or else I would have. I could use more practice."

Viv flicks a piece of salad at her. "That's baloney. You're great and you know it."

Miller picks up the piece of salad and wipes up the puddle of dressing with his napkin.

Viv raises an eyebrow.

"I'll take a concert later," Reed says. "I love hearing you play."

Hailey's cheeks redden.

Are they flirting? Weird.

Harry stands up and rubs his belly. "I'm full. Who's ready to dance?"

Viv jumps up. "Let's do it, baby."

Jemma sips a bit more of her wine and shrugs. "I'll give it a go."

I look at Miller with an apology in my eyes.

He looks back at me, expressionless. "I'll set up some music."

"Sweet system," Harry says, checking out Miller's electronics. "Is that surround?"

"Yep." Miller presses a button and a chime roars over the room as the receiver turns on.

"Dope." Harry picks up the Xbox remote and scans the games. "Do you have Dance Dance Revolution, bro?"

"I could get something close."

"Hell yeah. Let's do it. That shit is bananas."

Miller shows us all how to download the *Just Dance* app on our phones and connect to his TV.

In no time, Harry is showing off his impressive coordination. Viv and Hailey get up there with him and work their bodies to Lady Gaga. It's an attractive sight. Hailey is soft and lovely. Viv is wild and seductive. Harry is the steamy Asian version of Justin Timberlake.

Miller keeps the songs flowing.

"Do you have any Disney?" asks Jemma. She passes me her wineglass.

Miller finds "One Jump Ahead" from Aladdin, and my best friend rehashes her epic elementary school talent show performance. I die.

I'm surprised to see her step into the limelight. Look at her go.

"Dance with me?" I ask Miller when it's my turn.

"I'll watch." He winks—thank god. He must not be miserable.

"I got you, girl," Harry says, shimmying over to me. His drink sloshes onto my sweater.

I get pulled by the force that is Harry into the dance while Miller gets a rag to wipe the floor.

I'm in stitches by the time it's done. Something about trying to do these outlandish moves and the exertion sends me into giggles. I collapse. Harry lies on my stomach. I roll over, not comfortable with the contact.

Viv pulls him back to his feet. They begin a dance following the steps, but they end up just grinding on each other.

Reed and Hailey are sitting on the floor in a deep discussion. They seem to have gotten close since both going off to schools in Boston.

I sit next to Miller and Jemma on the couch. "This is weird, huh?"

"The Disney dance was definitely the highlight," Miller comments with a straight face.

"I'm a natural," Jemma replies.

"Obviously," says Miller.

I pass Jemma back her wine. She nods me toward Reed and Hailey, who are now connected by their faces. Whoa. I'm way out of the loop. Maybe Reed *has* moved on from his infatuation with Vivianne. Good for him. Hails is still a handful, but at least she's low-key about it.

Jemma says, "Did Hailey eat anything, or is it all alcohol in her belly?"

"I didn't see her take more than two bites."

Viv stops dancing mid gyration, drains the glass in her hand, and walks over to the kissing couple.

"Hey. What are you doing? You don't even like her."

Oh boy. Viv doesn't like to share, even things that aren't really hers.

Reed looks up, eyes huge, and clenches his jaw. "Vivi, don't."

"What is this?" Viv hisses.

"I'm just— I care about her, Vivi."

"That's cute. Can't you go bark up some other tree? Keep it out of the family for once."

"We're not family. We've never *been* family. We're friends, and I'm allowed to have feelings."

"No you're not. Not about her."

Viv throws her empty drink at Hailey's feet. I jump at the sound. Glass pieces skid across the floor.

"Okay, party's over." Miller yanks the front door open and points at his yard.

I touch his arm, but he doesn't budge.

Reed walks out first.

"Hey, wait," Viv calls. "I need a ride."

Hailey stands in her way. "When are you going to stop stringing him along?"

Viv slaps her across her delicate pink cheek. I run over to Hailey, who collapses into a sobbing heap on the floor, all over the glass.

"Out!" Miller yells.

"You're a real stick-in-the-mud," Viv says, turning to Miller.

"And you're a real treat," he says back. "Now get out."

That was a little harsh. My cheeks burn.

Viv's eyes get big and incredulous. I can only imagine what she'll say about him. She prefers docile guys.

"Call me tomorrow," Jemma says to me, smirking.

Viv follows her, calling out that she needs a ride.

Harry offers Miller a fist bump. "Sweet place, man."

Miller limps into the gesture. We'll work on that. Fortunately for us, Miller will have another shot at male bonding this weekend at the UPS holiday party.

I turn to our remaining guest, who's slumped over on the couch. I kneel beside Hailey and move her hair out of her face. A line of mascara runs from her eyelid to her nostril.

Miller walks out of the room.

"I really like him," she cries. "He's not hers. Why does she have to be such a bitch sometimes?"

"She's complicated. You know this."

"She sucks." More tears spill out.

"Let me take you home." I look up at Miller, who has returned with a broom.

He nods, drenching me with his eyes. "Call me later."

Why do I want to abandon my distraught friend with the bleeding leg for a boy? Why do I want to abandon everything for this boy?

THIRTY-SIX

W hy Goodwill is such a draw for me, I can't say for sure. Maybe I love giving new life to old things. Maybe I like dusty mothball smell. Maybe I'm just super cheap.

"I'll entertain anything that's neon or can transform into leg warmers."

Jemma gives me the thumbs-up and starts scouring the racks with fierceness in her eyes.

This is why we are friends.

"Holy baby cow," I say, flashing her the enormous, hot-pink hoop earrings I'm holding on the sides of my head. "These will definitely go with big hair."

"And check this out." She parts the stack of clothes in her hand to reveal an actual flipping tracksuit.

"No. Way." I snatch it and run my fingers across the fabric. "Do you hear that? It whoops. Can you imagine what it'll be like when I break into a full sprint?"

"I can only dream of that sight."

"Where's the dressing room?"

I slo-mo run up and down the aisle enough times to make Jemma hide from me.

After I've changed and packed my enthusiasm back inside my

heart, I find Jemma in the book section. She has an armful of novels, and knowing her, she'll probably finish them all before her trip.

"What's Miller wearing to this shindig?" she asks.

"I don't know. The Breakfast Club bad boy thing could really suit him. We'll be adorable together. I should pick up a few things for him here, in case his stash of random clothing with costume potential is running low. We could find some gloves to cut up and make fingerless, and find a jacket with some texture. That would only cost, like, six dollars."

Jemma accompanies me to the men's section. She says, "Last night was interesting."

"Yeah. It seems Reed has a thing for girls in our friend group. You better watch out."

"Are Reed and Hailey a thing now?"

"Pretty much. She told me last night they've been dating for a month. I think he's the only thing keeping her sane this semester. She's putting all kinds of pressure on herself with music school. She wants to get first chair in the orchestra by next year. The girl's wearing herself thin."

"She definitely looks it. She's skin and bones. Did you ask her about any of that?"

I grab a super-soft plaid flannel and pass it to my friend. "This is totally you."

She runs her hands along the fabric, smiling.

"Hails dodged the question," I continue, "but I know she's not eating. I hate her being so far away. I want to look out for her."

"Well, you can't, so let it go. It's Reed's mantle now."

She sounds just like Miller with the fancy words. I want so badly to ask her what she thinks about him, but I don't want her to think I need her opinion. I decide to beat around it. "It's crazy that Miller has his own place, isn't it?"

"I don't know. He's older. Makes sense."

"Really? I don't see myself owning a house by then."

"Yeah, but you also still have to bum rides everywhere."

I stick my tongue out at her.

"He's kind of a serious guy," she says.

Is that a good thing or a bad thing? What does she *mean?*

"Not exactly the kind of guy I pictured you dating."

"Who'd you picture?"

"The student body president or something."

Do they even have those in college? And what am I doing to come across so stuck up?

She pats my back. "I didn't mean that as a bad thing. It's just that you're all about curating this adorable little life. You join all the clubs and plan all the activities. I figured you'd end up with a guy who's into all the social scene stuff too. You know, the beloved couple that campaigns for mayor or does major charity work or whatever."

"I tried the Mr. It guy a few months ago, remember? Look how that turned out."

"You tried the narcissistic baseball star thing. That's different."

"How?"

"I don't think you care about finding a guy who's impressive to everyone else. I just thought you'd end up with someone more social than Miller. You love parties and spending time with people. I don't see that for him."

"He did it last night."

"Did he, though?"

"He said he had a good time." I start ripping through the clothes. There's nothing that would be cute. Dang it.

"Okay, look." She stops my frantic hands. "He's a fine guy. I just think things are moving a little fast. You've known him for all of a month, and now you're shacking up together. That's not like you."

"Do you have a problem with me, or with Miller?"

"Chicklet, I don't have a problem. I'm just looking out for you."

"Well, worry about someone else, okay? I'm fine."

Jemma doesn't like my boyfriend.

I've lost my shop-etite.

"Let's get this stuff and go," I grumble.

I wish I hadn't left Goodwill without something for Miller. A badass leather jacket might have made him more agreeable right about now.

"I've never gone before. Why would I start now?"

"Uh, because you have a date?" I display myself.

He surprises me with a kiss. "Stay home with me."

"But it's Eighties themed! There are very few times in my life when I will have an excuse to channel Madonna, and I'm not about to miss my chance." I vogue around him. "Does this not speak to you?"

He shakes his head. "I don't know why you're convinced that I like torturing myself."

I keep dancing. "Come on. Eighties music. It's like one step from techno. You'll be right at home."

"No."

"There's going to be Twister. Could be interesting." I grope his chest. If getting handsy won't convince him, I'm sunk.

"I'll go buy it right now. We can play here. What do you think I have all this space for?"

I giggle. "When you see me in my tracksuit, you'll change your mind."

He plops down on his couch and turns on the TV.

I leave the jacket zipper almost all the way undone over a tight tank and go the extra mile with bright pink lipstick and lots of hair spray. I look pretty boss, which better be enough to convince my boyfriend to give this a try. I really don't want to go by myself.

Not that I'm dependent. I don't ever have a problem enjoying myself solo at social gatherings, especially if there are awesome things planned like karaoke. But I want to share this with him.

My tracksuit swishes as I kneel down and block his view of some monster war game. "Hey there." I wink.

He fights a smile.

"Will you please go with me to this thing? I want you to be there. It won't be the same if you're not."

His face twists all up. "I'm sorry, Adia. I really can't."

I huff and return to the bedroom for my stuff.

Going solo to a party is one thing. Going solo when your boyfriend is somewhere else voluntarily is entirely another. It's like putting out cookies with no milk. It's depressing.

Do I really want an antisocial boyfriend?

I text out an SOS.

"Well, I'm going. See you later, I guess."

He nods. He freaking nods.

I shiver on the porch stoop waiting for Harry to arrive.

THIRTY-SEVEN

The party decorations look so fantastic it almost makes me smile. Someone transformed this warehouse into a rocking bash using posters, streamers, and strobe lights. The mixture of classic red and green with fluorescent pink, blue, and yellow somehow works. It's like putting clothes on a puppy. It sounds like it should be tacky, but instead the adorableness multiplies.

Harry brings me a Solo cup of wine, but I don't feel comfortable underage drinking in front of my employers. Or having any fun at all, really. I skip the *Pretty in Pink* table, which is too bubbly for my mood, and park myself with E.T. to watch everyone else enjoy themselves.

But Whitney won't have it. Her vocal power gets up into my funk and summons me. This is why I love the Eighties. You can't stay upset when engulfed in the decade's soundtrack. I abandon my cup and grab Rosa, who seems equally moved by the song. We take the karaoke stage and sing at the top of our lungs about wanting to dance with somebody while acting out all the lines—another plus of Eighties music.

Harry joins me on stage on my next go-round. We kill "(I've Had) The Time of My Life." He puts his arm around me as we belt it. I should take his arm off, but I don't, because this is how I wanted tonight to go. Different guy, same idea.

We bow to the crowd's cheers and spot a new conquest: life-sized Pac-Man.

Harry tosses back his cocktail so he can put on his Pac-Man head-piece. Geared up, we take our place at the start of the blow-up arena. Four volunteers suit up in ghost headpieces. The foghorn sends us scrambling for pom-pom balls. I dart one direction while Harry goes the other. My windbreaker gets its full glory as I sprint away from Thomas, one of the older UPS drivers from our store. I hide behind an inflatable wall. Harry whizzes past me. He's still rocking some lacrosse skills. We load our masks with the little balls at an impressive rate.

A cherry-patterned beach ball sails past my head. It's worth twenty-five bonus points. I pounce. Blue ghost jumps out from behind a blow-up tree and startles me. I abandon my prize and scream at the top of my lungs. My thighs whip across each other as I race for an exit. Who knew how useful my aerodynamic ensemble would turn out to be?

Harry pops out of the maze a few seconds later with the cherry ball in hand. I scream again and high five him.

The judges tally our points, and we slide into first place on the leaderboard. Harry lifts me into his arms and runs a victory lap around the warehouse past several classic posters, including New Kids on the Block and Duran Duran. Neon lights flash around us. Music blares. My chest gets sore from cackling.

I look around feeling dizzyingly happy...and then painfully sad.

What's Miller's favorite Eighties band? And what would he think of the crunk moves his manager is pulling out on the dance floor? Or the freaking life-sized video games? This is a once-in-a-lifetime experi-ence we could have shared.

I make Harry put me down and excuse myself. A fresh look at my killer style tempers my gloom. I should keep costumes on hand for down days back at school. It would beat the type of notoriety I have currently.

Back outside, I lean against a wall and watch. Where am I right now? What is this life? I don't know these people.

But...who are my people?

I don't know, but I'd rather watch the *Gremlins* movie that just started than continue my pity party. I don't want to sit by myself and watch, but Harry's back at the bar. I find Rosa working on a trivia card at a table decorated with my kind of prop: candy.

"What do you think number seven is?" she asks. "The prize is a Polaroid camera. My daughter Camila would love that."

"Jawbreaker, maybe."

"Oh, I get it. Mouth-crusher. I was thinking more literally, like some sort of bubble gum." She scribbles down the answer. "What about Crazy Biscuits, though? I was thinking maybe Kit Kat bars, but that might be a stretch. What other cookie-type candies are there?"

"Cookies 'N' Creme bars?"

After we've made our guesses, we go to the movie area. I chew on my cuticle as I watch the little fur-balls start misbehaving.

"Miller would have really enjoyed this," I mumble.

"How's he doing?"

"I don't know. He refused to come tonight."

Rosa pulls my hand from my mouth. "Miller has an extreme form of social anxiety. I don't expect a scene like this would be something he could handle."

"Why do you think he has so much trouble?"

"I really don't know. He keeps all that to himself."

"He did get beat up when he was seventeen. He ended up in the hospital. I think that has something to do with it."

"He told you that?"

"Yeah."

"Wow. It's good he's opening up to someone. I think you've been very good for him, missy."

The hole in my chest where I'm storing all my resentment squeezes in a little. I haven't really been considering Miller's point of view. I don't want to push him so far that I become another reason why he walls himself off from people.

But if he never changes, how will we work?

"Adia," barks Harry over the loudspeaker. "Come up here with me, girl. I've got a performance I want to do."

Everyone looks around wondering who the guy on the stage is summoning.

I hide in my hands.

"I need you. Come on. Adia."

"I don't think he's going to stop," Rosa says.

"Adia!"

Someone in the crowd starts a chant of my name.

I stand and throw my hands up to the applause of the whole warehouse. I guess I'm about to perform for the entire company with my word-slurring co-worker. This should be good.

"There's my lady. DJ Stank, play us some 'Hungry Eyes.'" He drapes himself over the microphone stand. "We're about to do a dirty dance."

The guy who's been put in charge of music furrows his brow at Harry but still flicks through the playlist on his iPad.

I step up on the stage. "Do you know the steps to this dance? Because I surely don't."

"Nah, we're gonna wing it. I got you. Just follow me and work these hips."

He grips them and pulls me close.

My cheeks burn.

The drums and chimes that introduce the iconic song play over the room. We're really doing this.

Harry moves us forward and back in what might be considered a sort of rumba. As the singer talks about lust, Harry spins me. Before I can acknowledge my dizziness, he sweeps me into a dip. People all around egg him on with whistles and hollers.

He whips me up and goes back to the rumba steps. The boy has no problem leading a girl through some sexy moves. My missteps don't phase him. After he dizzies me with another few spins, I grab onto him.

"I want you," he mumbles into my ear.

I'm too confused to react. On the one hand, this whirling is exhilarating. On the other, Harry is sloppy drunk. Instead of saturating seafoam irises, the ones looking at me—or trying to—are bloodshot. Not exactly my idea of romantic. I laugh him off.

He turns me around and lifts my arm above our heads exactly how Swayze does it in the movie, finger graze along the chest and all.

I jump away. "Do you try this on all your girls?"

"Are you my girl?"

"Not what I meant."

He clutches my hips to finish the routine. The next time he pulls me in, his lips dive-bomb mine. I turn away at the last minute when I realize what he's doing. This is too much.

I laugh to the crowd upon hearing some oohs. Harry tries to turn me back toward his face, and the embarrassment of this happening so publicly overwhelms me. I shove him and run for the edge of the stage.

He mumbles, "Come on. Come back, Jingle Bell."

Then the mic squeals and amplifies a terrible crashing sound. I turn back in time to see Harry tumble off the stage and headbutt some unsuspecting dude in the face. Harry's hefty body drops like a noodle, getting splattered on the way down by blood from his victim's insulted nose. It is not the kind of party confetti I'd hoped to see.

And if Harry can't respect boundaries, my friendship match is going to be a bust too.

THIRTY-EIGHT

Professor Frume twirls me around a warehouse until I'm sick, while my phone rings and rings on my desk. Music surrounds us. It gets louder and louder. I'm so dizzy. I stumble for the phone, but I can't focus. The ringing. The music. The spinning. My hands press against my ears. I can't stop the chaos.

"Morning, sleepyhead."

The dream fades. My eyes pop open and Miller's hovering over me with my Christmas tree mug. Christmas music is playing from the speakers in the living room.

My shirt collar is wet and stuck to my neck. I slide into a sitting position and check the time.

Ten o'clock.

So much for getting up early and working on my linguistics paper.

I have three missed calls. One from Jemma, one from Drew, and one from Mom. The whole ditch-Adia crew. I put my phone back down.

"How long have you been up?" I ask.

"A couple hours. Here's an apology drink."

He places my Christmas tumbler into my hands, and I inhale a creamy cocoa bean aroma deep into my not-fully-emerged consciousness. "This isn't BP grade, is it?"

"The Drowsy Poet's finest. I'm sorry about last night."

"You are?"

He nods.

"About not going to the party?"

"No. That I'm very glad about. But I'm sorry I let you down. I really want to be the kind of boyfriend you want me to be. I don't want to give you a reason to question us."

Hope glimmers in my heart. "Are you ever going to be able to take me out to things?"

"I want to take you with me today to do this thing I do. It's even Christmassy."

I pinch down a smile.

"I can't promise I'll be able to take you to parties, though, so if that's a deal-breaker..." His face knots up. "I know I'm hard."

Poor thing. My heart smacks my face into releasing the withheld smile. "At least you didn't drunkenly stumble off a stage and destroy a coworker's face in front of your boss," I say.

"Did that happen?"

I nod. I don't want to mention who it was, because that could lead to other questions.

"I'm not sure if I'm sorry to have missed that."

"You're not. Trust me. It was very sad and concerning. I'm sorry too, by the way."

"Really?"

"I was being very focused on myself. I can see how a big, elaborate party like that wouldn't be your scene, and I tried to bully you into going."

"You were hard to resist." I gulp at the way his eyes sweep over me. He shakes his head. "You had me considering doing one of the things I hate most in the world."

"Big parties are on your list of top worst things? What about genocide, rape, child pornography, cancer...dental cleanings...cats?"

He sits beside me and kisses my neck. "Cats are a case-by-case basis for me, unlike parties, which pretty much all make me want to jump off a cliff."

"You're crazy."

"You're cute when you argue."

"Oh, you like when I diplomate?"

He kisses my ear. "Do you mean deliberate?"

"Shut up. Words are not my forte."

He kisses my jaw. What is this game we're playing? "What is your forte? Besides party-going, that is."

"Right now? Nothing. In high school, I guess I was good at history. I really liked AP Psych too."

He finally gets to my mouth, and I'm eager. I set down the non-gas-station coffee that he made a special trip to get for me and drape my arms over him. We fall back onto the mattress in a tangle. He keeps up his traveling kisses, going first to my nose and then my eyes.

"You know what I think you'd be good at?" he says, lying beside me and drawing circles along my belly.

I perk up. I would love to know what unsolicited observations he's made about me. "What?"

"PR."

"Really? Why?"

"Because you're good at looking out for people."

This is by far the most wonderful thing a guy has ever said to me. I dive into another kiss. Do I really need a boy to go out with when this one is so nice to stay in with?

Another text from Mom sits on my phone screen like a rock in my stomach. I contemplate how to respond. *I'm not coming home because you're pretending to be happy when you're not…. Because I wasn't enough to make you happy… Because you don't care about our traditions anymore, and I'm not ready to lose them…*

I hold back with a simple "I'll stop by later."

"So do you want to do this thing with me?" Miller asks.

"We just had a fight about how I didn't like not doing something with you. So, yeah. I do."

"Good."

After I get dressed, we get into the Batmobile. He drives me to the warehouse I was just at last night.

"Are you trying to redo the party?" I ask. "Because I think I'm over it."

"Uh, no. This place also happens to be where I make a living. We're here to pick something up."

I watch him casually stroll across the lot. He has a humble way about him, how his head dips and his hands hide away. He's got on faded jeans today. The hood of his old sweatshirt sticks halfway out of his khaki jacket. I need to take him shopping.

He returns to the truck with a handful of packages.

"Are you trying to make us both work on your day off?"

"Sort of, but not how you think. This is off-the-clock stuff."

He shows me the top of a package, where there's a big yellow label with a pointing finger and the message "return to sender."

"For whatever reason, these didn't make it to their destinations. Who knows what's in them, but if, say, some kid was waiting on a toy from his pop and it never came... I dig around on the internet to try and track down the intended recipients and get their packages to them before Christmas."

"That's...really cool." Miller puts me to shame at this elf thing.

"It's Rosa's deal, really. She roped me into it because she knows nothing about computers. I don't know...I kind of like it, though. I guess it's my way of getting into the Christmas spirit. Plus, Rosa makes me peanut butter balls as a reward."

"Do you figure out where these people are most of the time?"

"Yeah. I've got mad skills."

We take the packages to the retail store. Miller unlocks the building, which is closed on Sundays. He has to shove the door open because it sticks.

I look around to see if any cops are in the process of jumping out from behind a bush to arrest us.

"Why do we have to do this here?" I ask.

"I need access to some databases on the store computer. Don't worry. It's Rosa-approved."

Sure enough, inside we find a box of homemade candy and a note from Rosa.

Miller,

Hope you had a good Saturday night. We missed you at the party. Leave any packages that aren't local in a stack here, and I'll make sure they get to the right truck.

Thank you,

Rosa

Miller slides the treats over to me. My tongue savors the rich flavors, a light and fresh version of a Reese's cup. I can see why they're such good motivation.

I spread out the packages. There are five medium-sized boxes, a small heavy one, and an envelope. "What do you think's in these?"

"Presents, probably."

"Yeah, but what kind? Take Hillary Wilkinson, for instance. Do you think this box is a pair of slippers or some deeply romantic mementos from a long-lost lover?"

"We'll never know."

"It probably doesn't even matter. It's really the thought itself that counts. The Halloween care package my mom sent to my dorm back in October was the single bright spot in my semester. I ate every last crumb of her chocolate oatmeal cookies even though they arrived crumbly and stale, and I decked out my dorm room with dollar-store decorations that Adrienne absolutely hated."

I guess Mom hadn't given up on me at that point.

These packages could be desperately needed bright spots.

And Miller's making it happen. He can act like this disengaged guy all he wants, but I'm on to him.

"Gotcha," he says after a few minutes. "Write this down."

I add Hillary's correct address to a fresh label.

While I'm feasting on the sight of an adorable guy doing good deeds, my phone buzzes in my pocket.

I find a notification for an email from the counseling office at Avery.

Dear Miss Bell,

It has been brought to our attention that you have received a grade of Incomplete for all five of your classes this semester. Unfortunately, you did not go through the proper channels to have any sort of family leave or final exam extension approved. Your status with our institution is in jeopardy, and we would appreciate your contacting our office as soon as possible to discuss how to resolve this matter.

Regards,

Cathleen Crawley

Dean of Students

Oh, boy.

Should I call now?

It sounds like an unpleasant experience waiting to happen.

I'll call first thing tomorrow. Surely it will be fine. Institutions make exceptions for these types of things, and I'm new to college life. How was I to know there were "proper channels" for family emergencies? A good talk will clear this all up.

My phone buzzes again.

Jemma: Leaving for the airport tomorrow afternoon. Are we doing something before I go?

What is this, bad news hour?

"What's wrong?" Miller asks.

"Nothing."

"Want to talk about it instead of chewing off the tip of your finger?"

I pick the less complex situation. "Jemma leaves tomorrow."

"So I suppose you'll be planning some fancy Adia-style send-off."

"Jemma's not really into big events in her honor."

"So there are two of us in existence?"

My two favorite people are both party poopers. The irony.

"I'll think of something fitting." Heck, I can appreciate the act of just showing up these days. I text Jemma, telling her to count me in on any and all evening plans.

Miller finds all seven correct addresses.

"Now I know who to come to if I lose track of someone important."

"I've learned a few tricks over the years. Want to put on your Christmas hat and help me deliver the two local ones?"

"Want to put it on for me?"

His brows lift at my tone.

From under the counter, I pluck the elf hat Harry gave me—which I had stashed away for Christmas week—and pass it to Miller.

He shakes his head. "Of course you have an actual hat."

While he reaches over my crown, I sneak attack his lips. Watching him do nice things has me feeling all sorts of affectionate. I back him against the counter and snake my fingers through his shag.

The jingle bells flutter to the ground.

Miller keeps my lips occupied while also dragging his hand down my thigh. My body lifts. We shift, and I'm planted on the countertop. I wrap all my limbs around him.

"I want you," he mumbles.

"Yeah."

His shirt flies off. I'm not sure who is responsible.

His lips return to place. My body moves from counter to floor. He presses against me, blanketing me with himself. I cling to his muscled back. It's very ripply and boy-like. Holy holly balls—I'm touching a boy's naked back. At my workplace! I'm definitely getting taken off the nice list.

"You make me want to do all kinds of things I think I shouldn't do," he whispers.

The only proper way to respond to someone who says this is to devour them, right? I try my best.

We move against each other. Miller's hand slips to my waist. Fingers sneak past clothing barriers. I freeze. Not because I'm thinking about anything rational, like if this is a good idea. I've just lost the ability to function for a moment.

Miller backs away. "Sorry. Too far?"

"No. I…"

Miller peels himself from my body and grabs his shirt. "That was…whoa."

It was. I can't stay in control around this boy, especially not when he's spreading holiday cheer. It's like being near pie all the time.

Once I'm steady enough, I stand.

Miller has already gathered our packages onto his shoulder. "Ho ho ho," he says.

"Miller, if I didn't know any better, I'd say you have a Christmas tradition."

I lay a big smooch on his cheek.

My phone dings.

Mom: Come home immediately. Need to talk to you NOW

While I'm holding my phone, I snap a photo of Miller.

He rolls his eyes.

I tidy up our mess.

My phone dings again. These contraptions *are* intrusive.

Mom: Just received call from school. If you're not here in next half hour, I'm coming to that boy's house. Jemma gave me address

Jemma will be hearing from me about this BFF-code violation.

"I think you'd better drop me off at my parents' apartment," I tell Miller. "It seems I'm due for a fight with my mom."

Miller picks up the jingly green accessory that's lying on the floor all innocently. "Maybe bring the hat."

THIRTY-NINE

W̲e park in front of the apartment, and Miller turns to me.
"Do you... I could go in with you, if you need support. I
know how these things can be."

Is it appropriate to say yes? Mom would love that. "Best I do this
alone, but thanks."

I leave the hat on the dashboard.

A gingerbread man lies broken on my parents' living room floor.
All the others face a similar fate, clinging to the edges of Abies's now
drooping branches. I check her stand. Bone dry.

Stepping over the cookie carcass, I poke my head into the hallway.
"I'm here," I announce.

"Well great," says my mom from the bedroom.

She doesn't usually get this attitude with me, but then again,
nothing she's done lately is characteristic. She walks into the living
room with her arms crossed. Mine are already there. We do a crossed-
arm stare down.

I don't know who this woman is anymore. I don't know what this
life is. This claustrophobic room. This tension. This feeling like I'm
dreaming and I know it's a dream, because everything is familiar but
warped.

"What the heck are you thinking? Putting your education in jeopardy, seriously?"

This again? When are people going to start acknowledging that this isn't my fault? I was *trying to help.*

"Don't roll your eyes at me, young lady."

"What do you want me to say?"

"I want you to explain to me why you're being so thoughtless. I mean, my gracious. Academic probation! I cannot deal with this right now." She clutches her head.

"I'm taking care of it, Mom."

"The heck you are. Do you know how embarrassing it was getting a phone call from the dean telling me you haven't taken any of your final exams and that two of your professors have complained? You told me you had worked things out. You quit school without getting permission? You're not allowed to make decisions like that unilaterally. You acted without thinking."

"I was thinking about you!"

Her finger jabs into my sternum. "Don't blame this on me. You wanted an excuse to escape your responsibilities."

She thinks I stayed because I wanted to? Because I'm selfish? My eyes burn with hot tears. "Why would I want to stay in this stupid apartment? I hate it here!"

"Well boo-hoo. I'm so sorry your life isn't perfect right now."

"You're my mom. You're supposed to be sorry."

"I'm done babying you. I did that for too long, and you never learned how to grow up."

"Don't worry, Mom. You can call it quits. I don't need anything else from you."

Me and my tree are out of here. I duck between the branches and try to get a good hold.

"Sure. Run off to that weird boyfriend of yours and pretend like that will make everything go away."

"He's weird in a good way!" I let go of the sticky bark and give her a glare.

"Well, I think he's an odd choice, and your brother agrees."

"Maybe you should take Drew down off of his pedestal. News

flash: He isn't perfect either. He's done some really crappy things." I try a different angle on Abies.

"Adia, what in the world are you doing to that tree?"

"Oh, you mean this one that you let shrivel up? I'm taking it some-place where people give a crap about it."

"Good! It's the ugliest tree I've ever seen. It was depressing me."

"Fine!"

I get behind it and push the stand toward the door. My progress is stopped abruptly by the threshold between the living room and doorway.

My mom stands there scowling.

I rotate the giant stand over the metal lip.

"I'm calling Dean Crawley tomorrow," Mom says. "I'll tell her you'll get your linguistics paper written and turned in right away, since it was that professor who made the most fuss. Can you finish it tonight?"

"Jemma's leaving tomorrow for Europe. It's our last chance to hang out." Jemma has been my other half since early middle school. Mom gets it.

"I am sorry your friend is leaving, but this is your future. You need to adjust your priorities."

Or she's completely lost all ability to understand me.

"I can't do it tonight!"

"There's only a week until Christmas. I'll try to work out a few more days, but you better work your butt off. Capeesh?"

"I don't know. I'll try."

"You'll get this done, or I'll—"

"You'll what, Mom? What control do you have over my life anymore? You've gotten me out of the house, and you're not helping me pay for anything."

Mom holds her hand to her forehead.

I grab the doorknob.

"Adia," she snaps. "Just don't be stupid. Get it done. And as for the other four classes, I will be bringing you back to school right after the new year so you can sit for those exams, if the professors agree to that. Who knows if they'll be willing to take time away from their families to fix *your* problem. I hope you know how inconsiderate this was."

Inconsiderate? I guess I'm going to die on my sword here. So be it. I shove the tree out the door, its branches scraping the frame and scattering brown needles all over the place.

"Good grief, Adia!"

"Sorry I'm such a disappointment!" I slam the door before she can continue her badgering.

The metal stand grinds against the concrete. We halt at the elevator and wait for the doors to open. I am treated to our disturbing reflection, me with no access to real shampoo and Abies in the midst of a dry spell. We look like the aftermath of a lightning strike.

I kick the door.

It opens. I shove Abies inside, but she clings to where she came from with vigor. We tussle. The doors slide together, ding, and reopen.

"Get in here," I grumble, but her downcast tip refuses to fit within the threshold. Another ding and reappearance of floor three. I grope. I yank. But I'm far too out-limbed by my counterpart.

I drag her back onto the walkway.

"We'll do this the hard way then."

We get to the edge of the stairs. I look down. Only roughly fifty steps, and we'll be scot-free. Piece of cake. I'll just...

Or I could...

Maybe if...

I position myself in front of Abies with my back to the descent. I step first, then tip her stand over the edge and tug. Only when I realize her full weight bearing down on me do I conclude that my plan was ill-conceived. Several gingerbread men jump ship. I stumble toward certain death, Abies forcing me along bouncily.

My feet scramble to stay ahead of us, and they make it down five steps before missing one. This won't end well. I careen.

Right into a pair of arms. A hand catches Abies, stopping us both in our tracks.

"Need a little help?" Miller asks.

"Yes," I grumble. "I'm trying to save the tree, but she's being a pest."

"Here." He lifts the tree by its stand and starts skipping down steps like he's holding a houseplant.

I should be impressed...or grateful, but it's hard in this mood. I slink along behind him.

He doesn't see the tattoo chick scowling at us from down the hall. I make sure she knows I do. I'm not trying to play. If she wants drama, she best move along to some other, more sensitive girl.

I'm about done with problems.

FORTY

The sight of Miller's yard lifts my spirits. I like grass. And a little distance between neighbors. And mailboxes. And not needing an elevator to move about my residence.

Miller loosens the bungee cords attaching Abies to the back of his car. "On the count of three, we lift together. Ready?"

I curl my palms around Abies's neck.

"Get to the grass."

She loses more needles as we go. We ease her onto the lawn.

"What now?" I say.

Miller shrugs.

I consult Google.

"Okay, okay. We should trim back her stump. That might give her a chance to start drinking again."

"Her?"

"Yeah, Abies. She's a she."

"Adia."

"What?"

"I think you might not want to get too attached."

"Stop that. Stop whatever you're doing and help me fix her. We need a saw."

"No can do."

"For real?"

He shrugs.

"Can you go ask a neighbor?"

He grumbles.

"Miller, come on. She's dying. We got her into this situation, now it's up to us to help her."

"She's going to die either way."

"Not yet she's not," I growl. I stomp toward Shana's house.

By the time she answers, I've managed to calm down enough to be polite. "Um, hello again. I'm back to ask another favor. Sorry."

She smiles. "That's no problem. What is it you need?"

"Some sort of saw. We're trying to trim the bottom of a Christmas tree."

"My husband handles that stuff. Let me get him. Come on in."

Ten minutes later, I'm back at Abies's side with reinforcements. Shana's husband Ed fires up the motor on his chainsaw. Miller holds Abies still while the machine slides through her stump.

"Want me to trim back a few of these lower limbs so you can get it back in that stand easier?"

"Please. And maybe a few of the brown areas, if that's not too much trouble."

"Absolutely."

Ed shapes her up a bit. I could hug him. He tips his fedora to us and heads back home.

"That wasn't so hard, was it? And now look at her. She's almost decent again." I pat Abies, knocking away a handful of brittle greenery.

"Almost."

I punch his shoulder even though he's not wrong.

Google, what else you got?

"This arborist website says you can feed the tree aspirin. It acts like a growth hormone," I announce. "Maybe that will help."

"Why not? We humans probably won't need those."

We situate Abies in the living room with a stand full of medicated water. Miller grimaces at her.

"Nothing a little accessorizing can't fix," I say. I cover her stand with a white towel and adjust her gingerbread ornaments. "She needs something nice on top."

Miller squints his eyes. "Maybe that'll help. There's a little hardware shop up the street that might have something, and I'd enjoy the exercise. Want to check it out?"

I can spare a little money for this. There are still a couple weeks to earn the rest of what I need for next semester's tuition. And I'll get a job back at school to take care of the deficit from my Black Friday tragedy. It'll all work out. Most likely.

Instead of dwelling on how depressing that sounds, I focus on my first home improvement purchase with my boyfriend. Aw! I practically drag him out the door.

Miller reaches into my pocket and takes my hand. I weave my gloved fingers between his and snuggle close to his body for warmth. I can see the general appeal of boyfriends. They're cozy. Big portable heaters.

"So what happened back there?" Miller asks.

"I wanted to give her a chance. I get that it might be a lost cause, but I don't care."

"Not the tree. I mean with your mom."

"Oh, you mean the woman who thinks I'm a selfish drain on her time?"

"Why would she think that? You don't even live there."

"She's mad at me for getting put on academic probation."

"What?"

"Yeah. She got a call from the dean's office. Apparently I didn't go through the proper channels to get my leave approved, and a couple of the teachers were jerks about it." I roll my eyes and then rub the one that has started itching. Allergies are the worst.

"That's not good."

"It's fine. My mom's working it all out. She expects me to whip out a paper over the next few days, though. I just don't get why everyone isn't more understanding. My mom broke her arm and needed me."

"You mean broken bones in immediate family members don't work as excuses?"

"It was worse than that. You know it was."

"What kind of paper do you need to write?"

"Something about linguistics. I'm not really sure. I don't think I even understand the class well enough to pick a topic."

"Stop rubbing," he scolds.

My eyes are so itchy. I stick my tongue out at him.

He says, "Linguistics…that's the study of language, right?"

"That seems like an oversimplification, but I guess so."

"Are there any requirements for the essay?"

"It has to be ten to fifteen pages, double-spaced. Let's call it ten."

"I meant subject-wise."

"It's wide-open, which is the problem. It can be about anything we touched on during the semester."

The door of the shop dings a merry greeting on our way through. The place smells strongly of cinnamon. I hold tight to Miller's guiding hand and close my eyes so that I can fully transport to the inside of a Cinnabon.

"You've got to pick a topic that gets your juices flowing."

"I don't think that exists"—sneeze—"when it comes to speech patterns."

He follows me to the Christmas section. I touch everything, because shopping by feel has the highest success rate.

"When you think about the way people talk, what does it make you wonder about?"

"I don't know…how people don't do it enough anymore. Computers are so much easier."

"Do you think computer talk is different from actual talk?"

"Well, usually it's one-sided, except for texting."

"And what are the consequences of that?"

"I don't know."

"Could that become a topic?"

"Maybe." I run my fingers across the scarlet tulle in my hand. I've never seen something with a bow on it that wasn't adorable. "How about this?"

"It's big."

Another sneeze. "That's the point."

"Then a bow it is." Miller turns for the cash registers.

"What about the rest of her? Look at all this tinsel."

"Your eyes look really red."

I blink. They are quite itchy.

"You look pretty miserable. Do you think maybe we need to get rid of the tree?"

"Don't you say that. We are not trashing Abies. I will keep myself medicated and I'll be fine."

"You can't live on Benadryl. You're not supposed to drive while taking it, for one thing."

"Then it's a good thing I work at the same place as my boyfriend."

"Adia, a decrepit tree is not worth upsetting your immune system for."

"I can't have Christmas without a Christmas tree."

"Then we can get one of those artificial ones."

"Don't insult me."

He shakes his head.

My phone vibrates in my pocket. It's Drew. Voicemail can handle that one. "Let's finish picking out her outfit."

Miller follows me from bay to bay and then carries my armful of tree trappings to the front of the store. When I try to pay, he blocks me and swipes his card. He may not have a high-society job, but his generosity with his income is definitely another boyfriend perk.

"Would it help you if I looked up some topics for your paper and sent you a file of ideas?"

"Why would you want to do that?"

"I don't. But I don't want my girl on academic probation either."

My phone dings.

Drew: Sammy's really upset. What happened between you two?

Ignore.

I turn to Miller. "I'll look at them if you send them. Sure."

"Great. That's what I'm going to do while you're dressing up our tree."

"Hey, wait."

"Nope. I draw the line at tree resuscitation and an hour-long shopping trip. That's as far as my decorating patience extends."

I push out my lower lip.

"I'll also help you stick the ribbon on top."

"And the lights? Please? I don't have much time before Jemma's thing."

"Abies isn't going anywhere."

"Fine, the bow and the top layer of lights."

"Just the bow. And moral support." He traps me inside a string of garland and tugs me in. "Lots of moral support."

He may not be totally into Christmas, but at least he's encouraging. And very kissable.

I chew on my ballpoint pen and try not to think about how Jemma's plane is taking off down the runway at this exact moment. She's going to get addicted to seeing the world, and I'll never really have her around again. I'll become her boring friend.

The pen cap flicks me in the lip. I throw it.

No one around me appreciates the outburst.

It would be a lot easier to concentrate on linguistics if it wasn't so mind-numbing.

Something presses against my eyes and they go blind. I pull hands away and find Miller standing behind me. "What are you doing here?" I hug him around the neck.

He sets my coffee mug next to me. "Picked it up at your favorite place."

"You did, did you?" I take a sip of creamy cinnamon latte. "It's good you turned up, because I have something I want to show you."

"You do?"

"Yes. It's that way." I point to a tall row of bookshelves.

"Oh, really?"

Grabbing his hand, I lead him to the most private corner I can find. This feels untoward, which makes it all the more irresistible. My heart is pounding when I finally push him up against the stacks.

To my delight, he doesn't waste any time questioning it. His two hands travel opposite directions, one up and one down, locking me in place. My knee knocks a few books off the shelf as it latches to him.

This moment feels different from the others. Less controlled, like if we weren't in this library, things might move past our previous threshold. And the thought doesn't bring on its normal shame. I want intimacy with him, a guy who is present and giving. I want him to repair my damage.

I detach my lips from him and stroke his face. "You mean so much to me," I whisper.

He scoops me up into a hug that nearly lifts my feet from the floor.

Yes, definitely. I want more with this boy. I want it all.

I don't want to leave him in two weeks.

"How's the paper coming?" Miller asks, setting me back on solid ground.

I flutter over my thoughts until I find one that answers his question. "I just wrote three entire paragraphs that don't have a readily identifiable first language."

He chuckles.

I drop my head into his chest. "I don't know how I'm going to dump out ten pages of this gibberish."

"I don't know how I'm going to leave you here and finish my job, so we've both got obstacles."

"I want to make you dinner."

"I want to eat your dinner." He nips at my bottom lip. "Can it be a late-ish one? The truck's packed."

"I'll have a snack. What time should I shoot for?"

"Eight-thirty?"

"How does stir-fry sound?"

"Best idea I've heard all day." He picks up the fallen books and replaces them. "I like seeing you crouched over books, being all studious."

"I'll be here all week."

"When do you need a ride back to my place?"

"It's beautiful out, and it's only a few blocks. I'll walk it. You've got a lot to do."

"Miss Bell, am I rubbing off on you?" He kisses my cheek and disappears.

I grin. My man's getting the best homemade stir-fry he's ever experienced. I sit with my back against the bookshelf and skim my phone for recipes.

I leave behind a haze of candle smoke and go into Miller's bedroom. The lacy panties come off with the rest of my ensemble, because I like sleep. I replace them with comfy boy-short underwear and sweatpants. It crosses my mind to snag a shirt from Miller's dirty clothes bin, but I don't want his smell to make me sad.

He didn't show for dinner.

It isn't his fault.

I'm sad anyway.

I brush my teeth and get into bed.

The term paper should have been more of a priority. Now the next few days are going to be miserable. Between writing and working, I won't properly see Miller for a whole week. And not too long after that, I leave....

The back door squeaks open and thumps shut.

I hear rustling for a while and then the bang of porcelain against a counter. He's found the plate I wrapped up for him. One of us gets to enjoy the meal, at least.

The next thing I'm aware of is arms wrapping around me.

"Thank you for dinner," Miller whispers.

My sleepy brain groans. "Mmm."

"I'm sorry I didn't get home in time to enjoy it with you."

"It's okay."

"I missed you." He places a tender kiss on my neck. "Can we have a makeup dinner?"

I roll over to face him, inspired by an idea. "Will you come with me to my grandparents' house on E Dubs?"

"On what?"

"E Dubs. Christmas Double Eve. It's the day my mom's family traditionally celebrates the holiday together, because Christmas Eve night used to be taken up by mass and an early bedtime. Anyway, we do an amazing dinner called La Vigilia, which is even pescatarian. I know it's probably a lot, but I could really use you there when I face my mom again. Will you come with me?"

"Adia...I wish I could. It's the busiest day of the year for me."

"You can't even get away for a little bit? A couple hours?"

"I really can't."

"You can't, or you won't? Be honest. You wouldn't come anyway."

He backs up. "What's that supposed to mean?"

"I have to beg and plead you to do anything social. It's exhausting."

"I have a job to do."

I roll over and block him out. I know I'm being dramatic, but I can't help it. I really want Miller to come. I want to watch him experience his first baked *spigola*...and *panettone*...I want a chance to finally enjoy the mistletoe Nonna hangs every year...I want to show my mom why she's wrong about him.

Miller has to be there for this stuff. He just does.

"Look," Miller says, "it wouldn't be my first choice of things to do with my little bit of free time, but I'd like to go for you. I just really can't. I'm already worried about getting done in time to help you set up for the Twinkle Dash that night."

My pillow receives most of my grumble.

He touches my shoulder. "I'll have more time after the twenty-sixth. We can do whatever you want after that. We could go out somewhere fancy, or invite your friends over here again, or hang out with every single living member of your family at the same time. Anything."

"Dancing?"

"Even dancing."

Well then. "Okay. Let's do all of that."

"Whatever you want. Seriously. I've never cared about not having any time off for Christmas until you came along. Now, I'm basically miserable at work. So thanks for that."

I reach my hand back and he takes it, tugging me. I flip over and use my leg to scoop him close. My body heat rises. I'm groggy from lying in the dark for so long, and it's a strange sensation, almost like finishing that last part of a good dream when you wake up in the morning.

His mouth finds mine. My hands find his shirt and wander beneath it.

"I'm gross from work. Let me shower and come back."

My body flushes at the tickle of his words against my earlobe. I find it hard to let go. He stuns me with a luscious full body press, lips included, then slips from my grip.

I do my best to keep my eyes open, but distanced from Miller's sizzle, I fade fast. All I can think about as I lose the battle is that I've got one week to enjoy my guy. One good and proper week.

I'm not ready to go back.

FORTY-ONE

Mr. Gentry storms past the line of twelve people and slams his fist on the counter.

Harry focuses his attention on the transaction he's doing for another guest.

"I've been in here three different times, and I won't be made to wait any longer. Where is my package?"

Expecting this behavior, I pull out the box that I took it upon myself to track and fetch off the truck.

He snatches it out of my hand without so much as a thank you.

I have so many questions. He must really be going through some stuff to behave that way in public.

"Thanks," Rosa says in her mad dash to the back.

"Not a problem."

"When this all slows down, I have something I'd like to talk to you about. Don't leave before we chat, okay?"

I nod.

I hate when that statement comes without any explanation. She didn't even leave a little hint. Is it about a customer? Some mistake I unwittingly made? Miller?

Is someone else going to come out against me and Miller?

Harry turns to me while a customer searches for something on her phone. "That party was hype, right?"

"I'm surprised you remember it." I hand the lady her credit card back.

"Well, I do. Sort of...Rosa told me."

The door dings again as more customers crowd the store. "Can we discuss this later?"

"You seem off. Are you mad at me?"

I am mad...or, more like, humiliated. But how do I say that to Harry's face? That's awkward. "No, Harry. It's all good."

He nods and starts to walk off while I ask the next customer about her package. Then he comes back to the counter and tells the lady to give him one more second. He sets down all the boxes he's holding and pulls me behind them.

"Look, I like being around you. I know I'm a screwup right now, but I'd like it if we could stay friends."

"Yeah, Harry. We can be friends." I try to go back to the job I'm supposed to be doing, not wanting to add any extra talking points to the Rosa conference.

Harry catches my arm. "Wait. I... If you ever need anything, or just want to, uh, kick back, I'm here."

"Got it."

"Excuse me," says the lady at the back of the line.

"Sorry!" I say and jump back on the register.

Harry grabs the packages and leaves with a wistful stare on his face. It's the first time he's ever been the slightest bit serious around me, and it's more than a little unsettling, like watching an animal stand stock still in the middle of a busy highway. Is this a cry for help?

I need to find a way to spend some one-on-one time with him before I go back to school.

The day stretches to its seam as people continue to flood the place with last-minute holiday packages. By the time I approach Rosa in the small kitchen, I'm sweating.

"You had something you needed to talk to me about?"

She pulls out a sandwich from the refrigerator and makes a face. The green dots of mold are visible from over here in the doorway.

"Yes, I did."

The food nails the wall to the left of the trash can.

"Good try, boss." I finish the job.

"Thanks." She sits and pats the chair beside her.

Oh, lord. It's serious.

"If this is about Miller, I'd rather not hear it."

"What?" She looks at me like I've grown a second head.

"Never mind. What were you saying?'

Smiling, she begins again. "This has nothing to do with Miller. Though I love him dearly, you know way more about that boy than I ever will. What I wanted to talk to you about is your job here."

Gulp.

"You've done amazing work temping for Jane. Unfortunately, she has decided not to come back from maternity leave. These things tend to happen with new moms. It's quite a life change, and sometimes they realize they have to navigate the unfamiliar path a different way. Anyhow, there's a position open, and I know you're a student, but I wanted to offer it to you first. I'd be crazy if I didn't at least ask. You've gone above and beyond what we've asked of you. You're great with customers. You recognize and meet my needs before they're even mentioned. And your attitude makes the workday so very pleasant. So, if you want a full-time job here, as a manager, it's yours."

Wow. "That is not at all what I was expecting you to say. Um…"

"Take some time, darling. Think about what you want. Just let me know by New Year's Eve."

"Okay."

Hugging her is unconventional, but it feels like exactly the right thing. I love my boss. For a first job, I think I hit the jackpot.

"I've had the best time here. Thank you for taking me in."

"The pleasure is all mine."

Would I want to do this as my career?

It would beat linguistics papers. Plus, making my own money instead of draining it from my parents would sure help them out.

And there's Miller…

But college is what you're supposed to do at my age.

Ugh.

Why does life have to be so complicated? Even with good things happening it all feels a lot like chaos. Do they have coaches for life? I need someone to tell me how to play this game.

∼

I don't see Miller out front at the end of my shift, so I sit on the curb to play with my phone. I hear a vehicle approach, but it's a cute little black car and not Miller's big brown truck.

People has a fun spread of celebrity holiday fireplace displays. My mind wanders to Miller's fireplace, which is currently the dumping ground for hanging clothes.

"Hey, pretty girl with the phone complex."

I look toward Miller's teasing voice. He's getting out of the little black car.

"Where's your work truck?"

"About that… Can you give me a ride somewhere?"

"I'm confused. My ride is here to get a ride?"

"Exactly."

I look nervously at the unfamiliar black vehicle. "Whose car are you making me drive? You do recall my fender bender last week, right?"

"About that. I would suggest trying to avoid any future parking lot wrecks in your new car."

"Excuse me?"

"I'm confident it's within your control not to wreck when moving at a speed of less than ten miles per hour."

"Shut up. You know I'm talking about the fact that you just said *my* car?"

He tucks his hands into his pockets and shrugs. To his feet, he says, "I'm giving you your Christmas present a little early. Do you like it?"

"My Christmas present! A car?"

He shrugs again. "I figured you'd need one if you're going to come back and visit me."

"I need to sit."

"How about sitting in the driver's seat," he says, ushering me to the...Honda.

Miller got me a little black Honda for Christmas. OH MY GOODNESS. I do my best to temper my elation. Squeals are nice in theory, but I've seen enough rom-coms to know that they aren't actually all that becoming.

He says, "It's a rescue. About five years old, so you don't have to worry so much about dinging it up. Since it's a hybrid, it gets good gas mileage, and it has a great safety record."

I survey the inside. "It's so cute."

"And it's cute. I told the lady I definitely needed a cute one."

I giggle and take a seat behind the wheel. I can't believe my boyfriend bought me a car. This is mega post-able. Not that I'm going to. But I know it's worthy. Sigh.

She drives like a dream, all zippy and smooth. She needs a name. Something classic, since she is. Black Beauty.

I drop Miller off at the CarMax dealership where he gets back in his UPS truck to continue his shift...which he took precious time away from to BUY ME A CAR.

I don't even know what to say.

All I know is that I'm going to have to think of a stellar Christmas gift for Miller that also happens to be way less expensive than his present. Lord help me. Or baby Jesus. Anyone capable of miracles.

FORTY-TWO

W hy is it that whenever you need life to run smoothly, everything goes to hell?

I don't escape work until a quarter after one, which means I have no time to finalize my paper before La Vigilia. I'll have to squeeze it in tomorrow, along with making Miller's gift, since I'm in the poorhouse and can't buy anything. Plus, there's the Twinkle Dash at dawn.

Ugh.

"Hey mom," I say into the message. "I'm running late. Harry called out, and I couldn't leave Rosa alone with all those frazzled customers. Boy, are people worked up about getting stuff on time. We must've had a dozen conversations about how we can't control when packages arrive at our store. This one lady tried to come across the counter to look for herself, I kid you not. Anyway, tell everyone I'm on my way. See you in thirty, as long as I don't get lost."

Aunt Stella, the middle of Mom's three younger sisters, and her longtime partner Opal bought a roomy house out on a farm and wanted to host La Vigilia this year. I manage to keep all four wheels on the windy back roads and find the place on the first try.

My aunt scoops me through the door and into a hug. I love her nose ring. While I'm admiring it, something moves in the corner of my eye. The something snorts, and I jump half a mile.

"What is that?"

"Sebastian? He's a rescued potbelly. The family who originally bought him didn't expect him to get so big...or grow tusks. They let him loose on a nearby farm and the owners brought him into Opal's office."

"How is Opal?"

"Fine, actually. She's gone into cooking overdrive to keep herself busy. We're definitely glad you're here to buffer all the crazy."

Is there going to be some crazy?

I tell her, "I'm happy to be here too."

She shows off the house as we walk. It's the most adorable place. It was built in the Twenties, so it's a little bit falling apart, but also has oodles of character. Pops of Aunt Stella's hand-painted animal art grace the walls. In the kitchen, she and Opal have accentuated the original untreated hardwood floors with teal cabinets and a pueblo-style ceramic backsplash. Family photos with all their animals are prominently displayed on the mantel. I love how personal it all feels.

How fun it must have been to buy a house and make it all senti-mental and unique.

We find Opal pulling a bowl of dough out of the refrigerator.

"Welcome, Adia. Help yourself to a drink. I've got to get these veggies in the oven before the bread."

"Do you have any of your sweet tea made?"

"Two pitchers."

Aunt Stella grabs glasses.

Opal says, "Better finish it off before your parents show. Wouldn't want to give them any more room to comment on how we've become hillbillies."

Aunt Stella raises a glass to Opal. "Here's to family and all their opinions."

They clink their cups.

Whose opinions?

While they enjoy their inside joke, I set my purse on a cute little bench and pull out my Secret Santa gift. I sneak it under the tree, feeling all fancy. It's my first year bringing my own present and exchanging with the adults.

"Can you deliver this to the men?" Aunt Stella asks when I return. She hands me an elegant charcuterie spread.

Uncle Tony and Uncle Lou briefly look up from the football game to accept the tray.

"Where are Mom and Cal?" I ask when I'm back in the kitchen.

"No sign of them yet."

"What the heck?"

I get Mom's voicemail again. I dial Cal.

"Hey, baby."

"Hey. Mom's not answering her phone. Where are you guys?"

"I'm headed back from Missouri. Should be home a little after midnight."

"Well, where's Mom then?"

"At... She had an appointment of some sort this afternoon. Where are you?"

My voice raises. "Uh, at Aunt Stella's, for our family Christmas thing, which we do on this day every year."

"I didn't realize you had those plans, baby. I'll give her a call."

"Can you remind her I need cookies for the Twinkle Dash too?"

"Will do."

I hang up confused. I can't believe Mom scheduled something else for today. What is going on?

"Are they headed over?"

I shrug. "Cal thinks Mom has some kind of appointment today. I'm not sure if she's going to show."

"Oh, well... I'm sure it was important."

It or *them*? If I find out she stood us up for her friends, I'll be crushed. "Really? More important than La Vigilia?"

"Sometimes missing these things is necessary. Life evolves, you know. Traditions don't last forever."

"But some traditions should be protected. How often do we all get to see each other?"

Aunt Stella runs her fingers through my hair and kisses my temple. It reminds me of how lovely it feels when Mom does it.

"Hand me some dough," I say.

I need something to smash.

Everyone draws a number to see what order the gifts get opened. We start with the little cousins, which now amounts to only five people. They tear through their offerings in a matter of minutes, then get shooed to the side so we adults can enjoy our round.

Erika, my only girl cousin on Mom's side, goes first and pulls a movie trivia board game out of her Santa bag.

"Yay," she says with zero enthusiasm, and then out of the side of her mouth adds, "Pretty sure this is the gift Aunt Liza gave to Aunt Tina last year."

A strategic move on Aunt Tina's part, considering Aunt Liza couldn't come.

My nonna goes next. Her gift is in a tiny box with a huge bow. It takes her several minutes to get the bow disassembled. She lifts an ornament out of the box and examines it.

"Oh, my heavens," she exclaims. "Is this true?"

"Is what true, hun?" No-no, my grandpa, asks. "Fill the rest of us in, please."

"Congratulations!" Nonna wraps Aunt Stella into a hug.

No-no grabs the ornament out of her hand while she goes to caress Opal's face.

"They're expecting, Dante. We're going to be grandparents again."

Tears fill Aunt Stella's eyes.

"How did this all work?" No-no asks. His voice lacks a certain joy, and it makes everyone else drop their celebratory praises.

"We got a donor, Dad, obviously."

"Who's the mother?"

"Does it matter?"

"Well, no. I just wanted to know if you were passing on any of your amazing talents, is all."

I cringe. Was it *his* opinions Aunt Stella was bemoaning earlier?

"Can you not do this?" she asks.

"I think it's a reasonable question."

"But does it have to be the first thing you bring up?"

"I'm guessing Stella's the one pregnant," Uncle Tony says. "E-m-o-t-i-o-n-a-l."

My aunt stands and winds back her arm, which is holding a wrapped box. It goes flying at Uncle Tony's head. He deflects, and it hits Nonna square on the neck.

She squeaks.

"This was supposed to be a special announcement!" She glares at Uncle Tony on her march out of the room. "Sorry, Mom. That wasn't intended for you."

Opal sits as still as a statue with a smile smeared across her face. She could use that bread dough right about now.

I move from my spot across the room and sit beside her. "I'm beyond excited for you two," I whisper. "You'll make the most fun moms."

We embrace.

"Thank you for the wonderful news, Opal." My nonna smiles big, like this can mask all of her husband's insensitivity.

"Dad, you're next," Cousin Erika says.

Uncle Tony unwraps the novel *Educated* and passes it to his daughter. "You need this more than I do."

Erika puts her middle finger up behind his back. It's weird to see. I would never do something like that to my parents. Or, at least, I don't think I would....

Aunt Tina, the second oldest daughter behind Mom, goes next. She has her youngest, Jacob, open the package. It's a crocheted picture of two young children laughing.

"How adorable. It's homemade," says Opal.

Nonna reaches for the gift. "I want a look."

I beam as it gets passed around. It's so personal and thoughtful. By far the best gift opened yet. And it probably seems like I worked on it for months.

Nonna confirms my suspicions by saying, "I just love this. Such a sweet memento."

"You can keep it, Mom, if you love it that much. Crochet is a little out of style anyway."

Well, gee, Aunt Tina, so sorry to cramp your style with my thoughtfulness.

"No, I couldn't. It's an homage to your babies."

Erika bumps me. "Your turn."

The thrill of opening a wrapped gift soothes the sting on my pride. My finger slides beneath the paper. I imagine all the possibilities. Will this token of someone's affection make me feel seen and special? Will I treasure it forever?

I unveil my surprise. It's a book titled *Get Out of Your Own Way*.

A self-help book? Is this how people see me? "This looks...interesting. I haven't ever heard of it."

"It's a great book for finding motivation," No-no says.

Guess I know who thinks I'm not good enough.

Opal goes to get Aunt Stella when it's her turn.

She comes back still scowling and quickly rips open her box. Inside is a multicolored crocheted hat. My mom must have brought over her contribution at some point. It has her written all over it.

I hope she made me the exact same one.

"Someone must be hurting for money with all this homemade junk," cracks Uncle Tony. He snatches the hat from Aunt Stella. "Seriously, this crocheted crap is just sad."

Uncle Tony is way more irritating than I ever noticed before. "I actually think homemade gifts are touching," I say.

"And everything's not all about money," Aunt Stella snaps, taking her gift back. "Look where all your money has landed you. Mr. Big Shot who has spawned three hellions—not you, Erika—and lost the best thing that ever happened to him. Maybe you should worry about your marriage problems and stop picking on the rest of us."

"Just because you've become Suzy Puritan doesn't mean you need to ruin the fun for the rest of the family. You're as miserable as Tighty Tina now."

"Lou," Aunt Tina hisses to her husband.

Aunt Stella balls her fists. "You've always been miserable, so—"

"Darlings, can we all get along?" Nonna says.

"Oh, I'm miserable?" Uncle Tony yells. "The whole lot of you have no sense of humor. You're all drama queens, and I hate being a part of this damn family. The only tolerable one of you didn't bother to show up, and I don't blame her one bit."

Uncle Lou finally crumbles under the pressure of his wife's gaze. "I think you need to take it easy on your sisters, man. Maybe apologize."

"That's a start," agrees Aunt Stella. "And I think it would be best if you stop joining us for family get-togethers until you learn how to be less obnoxious."

"Now, honey," squeaks Nonna, looking at Aunt Stella.

Uncle Tony leaps to his feet. "Fine by me. Because I'm done coming around. This family is exasperating." He begins pointing at his family members one by one. "Stuck-up. Weirdo. You try too hard. Uptight. You're a coward who wants to bone your neighbor and won't use your balls to do it."

I grab my spinning head. Why are my loved ones being like this?

Uncle Tony moves his finger from Uncle Lou but Aunt Tina's horrified eyes stay fixed on her husband.

Aunt Stella does us all a favor and slaps a five-fingered imprint across her brother's cheek.

Aunt Tina leaves first. She says nothing while she dresses her two confused boys in their overcoats and hats and gloves. She gathers her bag and walks out the front door, pushing Uncle Lou back inside when he attempts to follow.

He falls to his knees, and the rest of us exchange desperate glances. Does anyone come back from telling their brother-in-law they want to cheat on their wife?

The oven is the only thing that speaks, beeping to inform us that the *panettone* is ready for those of us who still have an appetite, which is no one.

Opal takes it out and sets it on the counter. She stays there staring down at the tile.

No-no hovers over the fireplace with his back to everyone.

"Don't go," Nonna pleads to her only son, blocking Uncle Tony. "We need to stay here and find a way to get along. How about we all put our numbers back in? We can shuffle them, and when we pick a number, we each find something nice to say about that person."

"I have nothing good to say, Ma." He throws his beer can at the fire and storms out yelling at his "little turds" to meet him in the car.

"I think everyone should go," Aunt Stella says, a tear trickling down her cheek.

I don't take anything with me when I leave.

Maybe Miller's right about parties. And family.

I don't know if it's my evidently nutso family or the strain of trying so hard not to veer off into the death trap of trees, but I am *done*. I scream my way to the side of the road, halting on a gravel shoulder.

Okay, let's take stock.

The holidays have been a big pile of stink.

School stinks.

Driving stinks.

My mom stinks.

Everybody stinks.

Except for one person, and I'll have to leave him in about ten days, which stinks.

So, basically, my life is dog poop. No, cat poop.

I'm content wallowing in my tears and self-pity for a good fifteen minutes, up until a car speeds by so close it shakes mine.

This isn't safe. I need to deal.

How do I shovel all the stink out of my life?

Do I already know the answer?

Yes. I have for days.

Only, it seems crazy.

But you know what else is crazy? Rolling around in filth just because that's what you're surrounded by.

FORTY-THREE

M iller's house is dark and silent when I go inside. The sweet vanilla smell of the sugar cookies I baked early this morning hangs in the air.

I find a note on the dining room table.

I hope you had a great time with your family. I'll see you at the race. Bring your jingly hat. —M

I can do him one better. I pull out my computer and begin strategizing. The more I fiddle, the easier the dots are to connect. This all makes perfect sense. My finger hovers over the send button.

My heart races. Should I think this over first?

No. This is never going to feel good. It's poop shoveling.

I hold my breath. *Click.*

Holy big fat dairy cow.

I can't sit on this. I need to talk to Miller now.

I pull up my texts and send him one.

He doesn't respond.

Adia: You need a phone. I really want to talk to you

Five minutes later my phone dings.

Miller: We're talking now. What's up?
Adia: Too long for a text. How much more work do you have?
Miller: I can take a break if it's important
Adia: Can you meet me at your place for a minute?
Miller: What time?
Adia: ASAP
Miller: Be there in thirty

I tornado through the kitchen in search of something for dinner. We will both need fuel to stay up late tonight setting up the Twinkle Dash, which starts just before daybreak. And it has to be yummy fuel. I want the moment when my entire life pivoted to be memorable.

Miller has canned tomatoes, an onion, pinto beans, and rice. I drop in on Shana and acquire some spices that I use to whip up some easy veggie chili. It's Mom's go-to last-minute meal.

I use the candle Hailey gave us last week to create some ambiance.

Big question: Do I need the lacy panties?

Miller shows up to a shadowy rendezvous. "Is this a date?" he asks.

I smile. He kisses it.

"I probably should feel guilty about ditching work for this, but you're pretty cute."

"Come join me."

He sits down and sniffs the peppery aroma coming from inside his bowl.

"How was your thing with your family?"

"Could've been better. Mom didn't show."

"That sucks."

"Yeah."

Miller gulps down his water. "Did you have a nice time with the rest of your relatives?"

"Not really."

"Oh?"

"I've decided I don't like spending time around large groups of adults, especially if they're related to each other."

He chuckles.

"It's not funny. It's depressing."

"What went wrong?"

"Everything. The gathering ended in male tears and my aunt kicking everyone out."

"Ouch."

"It is what it is." I don't even feel bitter right now. Just relieved… excited. "Are you going to eat?" I ask him.

Miller nods and takes a big bite. "Wow. This is tasty. Less salty than I would have expected. Did *you* make it?"

"Hey now. I'm a good cook, I'll have you know. But we're going to have to beef up the pantry and kitchen supplies if I'm going to stay here. I had to borrow a few things from the neighbors again."

"I think we can manage for a week."

"What if I don't want to manage for only a week?"

He narrows those beautiful irises.

"I want to stay."

"You have school."

"What if I quit for a while?"

"Don't tempt me. You can't quit school. That's stupid."

"You did it."

"That was different."

"Just because we have different reasons doesn't mean this isn't right for me. Rosa offered me a full-time job at the store. As a manager."

"You can work for the rest of your life. Right now, you should be in school."

"I'll go online. I can't afford room and board back at school anyway. I could stay here with you, if you'll let me, and work while I earn a degree…and we can be together."

He sits with his fingers tugging on his bottom lip and studies me.

"I was miserable at school. I'm happy here. Don't tell me I have to be miserable."

He looks away. I want to touch him, but I can't intrude. I need to know he's on board with this first.

"This isn't a good idea..."

His head drops into his hands.

I start to fidget, wishing I hadn't been so quick to email the dean. If Miller won't have me, I don't know where I'll go. I can't go back to my parents'. It's too much to deal with. Too small. Too different from how things used to be. It would make me feel like I was taking a step backward, not the step forward I want to take with Miller.

"Damn, I want you to stay. But..." Miller places his hand on mine and closes his eyes. The contact makes my heart tremble. I gather up every bit of my self-restraint and wait. "Do you remember me telling you I wouldn't risk kissing you unless it was out of my control?"

Uh, yeah. It was only the most confusing thing anyone's ever said to me. I nod.

"That wasn't really right. What I didn't want to risk was wanting you to want me. *Needing* you to want me. Who would?" Miller falls to his knees in front of me. "Do you really want to stay with me?"

"Yes," I whisper.

"Adia, please..."

I won't survive this boy. Miller does not do this. He does not utter words that even resemble needs. He definitely doesn't beg. With the way he's looking at me, I want to give him everything I have to give.

He drops his face into my lap. "Don't leave me. Don't ever leave."

A smile spreads from one of my ears to the other. "I already resigned from school."

He yanks me off of my chair and wraps me up. We hold each other tight in sweet relief. We're in this together now. Our bodies stay tangled on the floor, arms full, hearts full, for several blossoming minutes.

"Your clothing management may need to be adjusted," Miller teases.

"I'm going to need some drawer space then."

"Deal."

"And I'm decorating for Christmas."

"We have a tree. What more could we need?"

"Is that a serious question?"

He shakes his head. "Just don't move any of my stuff, and I think I can handle it."

"What stuff? You have stuff?"

"A little bit." He pulls me in for a kiss and then checks his watch. "Well, roommate, I hate to say it, but I've got to get back to it."

I fall into his chest and check his watch too. All my fuzzy feelings disappear with the realization that I'm behind on Twinkle Dash tasks. I jump up. "I've got to make red and green icing. Do you want a few sugar cookies for the road?"

He gobbles two down while I look for some Tupperware to hold all the others.

"Do you have a big container?"

"I do not."

"I'll add that to the list of immediate enhancements I need to make to our place."

Our place. Whoa.

"You better save some money for online classes. We can't have two uneducated bums under one roof. I need a sugar mama."

"Oh, I've got sugar." I open the icing jar and dot some on his nose with my finger. He growls and swipes at it. When I reach out to drag his hand away, he sneaks a finger of icing and smears it from one of my cheeks to the other.

I squeal and try to rub it on him.

He blocks me with another finger of sugar goo. My eyes get sticky.

"You stinker!"

I take a whole fist full and cover his face.

"What the heck?" he scolds. "I have to work. Now I'm gross."

I lick him. I do. I lick sugar right off of his face.

It's delicious.

He licks me back.

Then our mouths share the tastiness. He grabs my head, smearing icing across my neck. We sticky kiss all over each other. Nothing's ever tasted sweeter.

～

When Miller leaves, I start over with the frosting. My feet practically dance across the kitchen. This is the first time I've felt truly unburdened since I left for school.

And all it took was quitting.

Once my cookie toppings are a beautiful green and red, I seal them up and pack them into the car along with my other Twinkle Dash supplies. Then, I dedicate the last couple of hours before I need to be at the race to decking the halls. Oh, the joy!

If Abies is going to live here, she needs a pretty view. I clear all the clothes off the fireplace and take a quick trip to the hardware store before it closes to get decorations. The display turns out very tasteful, and also understated—for Miller. I lean heavily on green garland and string lights. Using some tools I find in a closet, I manage to secure a wreath over the fireplace. We may not want to slam any doors, but otherwise it looks pretty darn good. My last touch is the cutest little wooden elf placed front and center on the mantel.

The daylight dwindles. I turn off the overhead lighting and sit by my twinkling tree.

In this quiet moment, my chest bursts with that feeling I always get in the hours leading up to the big day. The glow. My soul beams out in a thousand different directions, all of them touching some kind of delight: the Twinkle Dash, candlelit mass, carolers, sleigh bells, luminaries, festive sweaters, boxes and bows, family time, way too much food, baby Jesus... It's why I'm so crazy about Christmas.

The alarm on my phone tinkles. 9:00 p.m.

Let the festivities begin.

FORTY-FOUR

M y car swerves into the parking lot of my parents' apartment. I
don't actually have time to deal with my mom right now, but
I need her cookies. A quick I'm-here-but-in-a-hurry text should do the
trick in case she tries to engage.

I tackle the stairs two at a time. My thighs scream at me in a good
way. It's the one thing I'll miss about apartment living: the built-in
exercise.

The door swings open midway through my pounding.

"Hey, honey," Mom says.

"Cookies?"

"They're right over here."

She walks to the counter and picks up a holiday Tupperware
container. Reindeer-printed tissue paper obstructs the view of the
cookies within, but I have every confidence they will be as beautiful
and delicious as always.

"Thanks for making these. I've gotta run."

"I'm sorry I was harsh the other day. I think I was feeling guilty,
and I took it out on you."

"Can we talk about this later?"

"Are we going to see you tomorrow?"

"I don't know. I might have plans."

"I'd love to see you for at least a little bit."

I look her dead in the face. "Maybe you could just hang out with your friends like usual."

"Adia, what's gotten into you? Why are you so angry all the time?"

"I'm not angry." I reach for the door. "I'm freaked out. I don't recognize anything about my life anymore. And I've got to go."

I slam the door and race back to the parking lot.

"Hey," says a voice I don't recognize.

I turn to find the girl that knows Miller coming down the walkway toward me. She gets close enough for me to see that the tattoo on her arm is a bird. Somehow, despite the stark black ink stained across her pale skin, the tattoo looks delicate...and hip. The strawberry hair color's fake, though. Mealy blond roots deflect the lamplight.

"You're Hunter's friend, right?" she asks.

"Hunter?"

"Hunter Johnson. The UPS guy."

"You mean Miller?"

"His name is Hunter. I would know. He's my brother."

"Maybe you're talking about someone else."

"Tallish, skinny guy. Green eyes. Way too serious, has a people problem."

Probably him.

"You're his sister?"

"Yeah. Robin. And I'm not surprised Hunter lied about his name. He's such an asshole."

"I'm sorry?"

"Yeah, my brother's an asshole. Have you not figured that out yet?"

"I don't think we know the same person. Miller's closed off, but he has a good heart."

"That's ironic. He verbally harasses women, and somehow, *he's* the victim? Real cute."

"What are you talking about?"

"You might want to look up your boyfriend. You'll see what kind of person Hunter is. Oh, and be careful about confronting him. When I did that, he ditched me and my mom and left us to fend for ourselves, with no jobs and no money. I lost everything because of that selfish asshole. He's bad news, and I didn't feel right about seeing you guys together and not saying something."

"Okay." I swallow hard.

I turn before she can see me get whatever version of upset I'm about to become. I get into the car that an apparently lying schmuck bought for me, then slam the door and scavenge Google for any information on Hunter Johnson.

A bunch of unrelated stuff comes up, so I add in our hometown. Several news articles appear.

Technology Savant Put on Temporary Leave after Sexually Explicit Comment...

Uncovered Twitter Post Puts Grimsley Student in Increasingly Hot Water...

High School Standout Retaliates to Scathing Online Comments...

Mother Urges Hothead Son to Publicly Apologize...

Cyber Hothead Hospitalized after Insensitive Remarks Lead to Backlash...

I click on the first article. A younger, cleaner-cut image of Miller appears. Only he's Hunter, an apparent sexist. I skim. He was overheard at a meeting telling a coworker that he "bet Tracy would fork your dongle." Tracy reported the comment to her boss, stating she didn't think the situation merited legal action but wanted to speak out against that kind of workplace behavior. Hunter argued that his comment was taken out of context and was meant as a programming joke. He was put on temporary leave while his company explored the issue.

Okay. That doesn't sound terrible. Cracking sexual jokes seems like an odd move for Miller, but then again, he's also going by a fake name.

The next article explains that Hunter was ultimately fired after a tweet he sent a few years before the sexual harassment incident was brought to light by a classmate. The tweet read: *"Does anyone else feel like we should petition our new science teacher to come to school in a gold bikini?"*, and it was linked to a photoshopped image of his teacher's face on Princess Leia's body.

I don't care for that move at all. It feels a little close to home.

When Hunter was questioned about the offense, he went on record saying that the classmate who dredged it up was "a little bitch who was just trying to start something for personal gain." That went viral. Hunter lashed out against all the hate and shaming he received and got himself labeled the "Cyber Hothead." He got fired and lost a scholarship to Berkeley over the whole thing.

Wow. That's a lot to take in. This Hunter person sounds…insensitive. And a bit hostile. And maybe like he doesn't know the proper way to treat women. Which is upsetting, considering I'm dating him. Or an alter ego of his.

So, I guess I can add deception to his list of flaws.

A bucket of ice fills my lungs.

I toggle over the article about the physical attack. Do I want to go there right now? My stomach clenches at the thought of my brother being involved, but there's more to the story—a story Miller withheld.

How could he hide all this from me? At the very least, I should know his actual, real freaking name!

I squeeze the steering wheel and take a deep breath.

This is not happening to me. This is not happening *right now*.

I'm supposed to be reinventing a Christmas memory. I'm supposed to be getting past the fact that my family is done with me by doing my favorite Christmas festivity with my new boyfriend. I'm supposed to be basking in the Christmas glow.

Screw this information.

I will not have another holiday event ruined.

The Twinkle Dash *will* be perfect, and I *will* enjoy myself.

FORTY-FIVE

The balls are freaking beautiful. Dang it. My eyes prick with tears, which I aggressively shove away. The Voyer family directs me onto a side street designated for volunteer parking. I cruise through a crowd of bodies, all the Twinkle Dash committee members, plus numerous other neighbors.

I hope nobody recognizes me. I'm not ready to socialize.

A news station van pulls in right after me.

Ducking behind my giant check, I walk toward the volunteer station.

"Adia!" Director Jen hands off orange traffic cones to a neighbor wearing one of the bright yellow volunteer shirts and comes rushing over to me. She takes my shield. "Glad you're here. There is a whole team of volunteers setting up the lights at the finish line. Where's your tech guy?"

My stomach churns. "He should be on his way."

"Send him over ASAP. Also, I set up two folding tables for the cookie booth, and several people have dropped off their cookies already. Follow the lights toward the finish line, and you'll find the tables beside the finishers' tent."

Rubber tube lights track the race route along the street. That's a smart new addition. Director Jen doesn't mess around.

I'm draping the candy cane striped tablecloth over my station when I get a text from Miller, or whoever he is, that he's arrived. My chest tightens. On my deep inhale, the scent of brown sugar and chocolate fills my senses.

Focus on the cookies.

The boy formerly known as Miller struts up the street rolling a crate of equipment. He's also clutching something in his palm.

As he gets closer, I find it more and more imperative that I focus on the cookie display.

"Nice evening for an outdoor shindig," he says, pulling his jacket collar around his neck as the icy wind forces its way around our bodies. "Where's your hat?"

"Forgot it."

A small box wrapped in newspaper appears in front of me.

I push it aside. "Thanks. I need to get this done, and they're looking for you at the light display."

"Open it."

That would disrupt my efforts to not look at him. "Mil— Uh, they really need you over there."

"Do I get any more sugar first?" A glance reveals him wearing a big smile.

It's not contagious. All of a sudden, he's got a sense of humor?

I'm starting to feel like I want to throw this table at him, but that would ruin all the cookies. I take another breath filled with sweet smells. Pasting on a smile, I bend over the table to kiss my lying boyfriend on the cheek. "That's all you get. Now go away. The musical display is waiting."

"Who's in charge?" He comes around next to me and peeks in my cookie tin.

I scoot away. "You?"

"Okay. Is something wrong?"

"Nope."

"I like you in spandex," he whispers, flitting his eyebrows at my light bulb leggings.

I draw forth another fake smile. "Thanks."

His hands go into his pockets.

"What?" I ask.

"I'm waiting for you to tell me what's going on before I go do your bidding."

"Nothing's going on."

"Can you please not lie to me? I don't like that."

That makes two of us. "It's a social norm. If I want to ignore something while I try to enjoy the thing I'm currently doing, that's my prerogative. You would get it if you ever interacted with people."

He grimaces.

I can feel my cool crumbling. "I don't want to talk right now. Can you just go fix the lights?"

"Did I do something?"

I bite my lip. The tears are building, and if he makes them come out, I will...I will...probably growl a little, in my throat, quietly. There are a lot of people I know here.

"You're obviously really upset about something, and the last time we talked, we decided to move in together. Are you having second thoughts? Is that what this is? Because I'll be okay. I mean, it'll hurt like hell, but I want what's right for you...."

I step away from his touch.

"Can we go somewhere and talk about whatever this is?" he asks.

"I said I don't want to talk about it. I want to stay here at my cookie booth and make it look really cute and have a great time." One tear slips out. "Can you just go away?" While he stands there nodding at me with disgust on his face, I grab a three-tiered serving tray from a bag.

"You want me to leave, I'll leave." He grabs his equipment and turns in the direction of his car.

"Miller!" I stomp a divot into the crunchy lawn. He will not ruin this. "Or is it Hunter?" I snap. "When were you going to tell me about the sexual harassment charges? Or the cyber aggression?"

His arms drop to his sides. He turns back to me with his head bent toward the ground. "I...I'm not that guy."

"Your sister would argue otherwise."

"Hell no. Adia, stay away from my sister."

"Why, Miller? Why didn't you tell me who she was? That's a weird thing to do."

He crouches and clutches his head in his hands.

"Were you feeling guilty for abandoning her or something?"

He rubs his hands across his face.

"I saw the news articles."

"That wasn't about me."

"So you're not Hunter Johnson?"

"No. Yes. But I was never the guy they made me out to be."

People are starting to look, probably wondering why a grown man is wallowing on the ground. "Can you stand up, please?"

I wait.

He rises with glossy eyes.

"You made me think my brother beat you up for no reason." I know what my next words will do to him, but I'm too angry to stop them. "You made me turn on my family for a lie."

His head falls into his chest. With his eyes closed and his voice strained, he whispers, "I didn't tell you everything that happened because I didn't want it to ever be a part of your thought process about me. Once a lie gets out there, it stains."

I don't want to hear his clever rationale. I can't have this argument right now, not while I'm trying to stack these cookies like a fancy Christmas tree.

He walks up to the table and leans toward me. "I'm not a bad guy. And I can't have everyone telling me that I am anymore. I'm done with all of that."

"You still should have told me. I deserve to know what your deal is."

"You do." He spreads out his arms. "This is me. The aimless UPS driver. The guy who can't really understand a lot of people. Who probably spends way too much time playing video games and overthinking things. But recently I found someone who makes me feel like something else. Something good. And I really need you to stop avoiding eye contact like I'm some criminal and come talk to me about all this."

"This isn't a good time."

"Well, gee. I wouldn't want our relationship to ruin your *good time*.

You enjoy your fun run. I'll be somewhere else, punching myself in the face."

"What about the lights?"

"The lights can go screw themselves."

"Can you just get over yourself and do this one thing for me?"

He starts marching away.

"You jerk!"

Several neighbors look over at me, including Mr. Bob.

I giggle. "Just kidding."

Miller throws a thumbs-up behind his back.

"Catch you later!"

"Yeah. You just let me know when it's convenient for you to deal with me."

The cookie containers under the table make for a nice excuse to take cover. I cling to a batch of peanut butter blossoms and regroup.

Don't think about the humiliation. Don't think about where you're going to sleep tonight. Don't think about how bad it hurts that Miller just bailed on you. Focus on the problem you can solve.

The lights.

Who do I know that might be good with technology and would answer their phone this late?

"Heyo," Harry answers.

"Hey. This is Adia."

"Hot mama. What're you getting into tonight?"

This was a terrible idea. "Are you out and about?"

"Just kicking it at a friend's. Why?"

"I'm in a bit of a bind. You're good with gadgets, right?"

"I'm good with *gadgets*, yeah."

Oh, lord. "Great. I'm wondering if you might be able to give me a hand."

"I'm your guy, baby. Where you at?"

I'll have to worry about the consequences of this Hail Mary later. The kids need this.

FORTY-SIX

Harry swerves onto Sunset Boulevard and jerks to a stop somewhat in a parking space. I meet him at his car.

"What do you need, boo?" He flashes his incandescent teeth.

"I need you to help us program some lights to music."

"That ain't no thing. Where do we go?" He hops out of his car. His eyes drop to my blinking necklace. "You're looking pretty wild."

"Hey." I snap in his face. "Focus. What do we need to make this happen?"

"Let me check it out and see."

We trek over to the Murrays' yard.

Harry sings "Jingle Bells" at the top of his lungs and high fives random people as we go. "That's a damn Santa." He points as we approach the massive wire display of the jolly man himself.

It's hard to see in the dark, but I can make out elves, reindeer, and presents, all awaiting illumination and animation. The theme seems to be the North Pole. The finish line arch has candy cane striped posts and everything.

My cookie table coordinates perfectly.

We confer with Director Jen, who wants a set playlist of songs to synchronize with the movement of the lights. It seems like a pretty big undertaking for the few hours we have until the start of the race at daybreak, but there's a big team of volunteers working on it, so we'll be okay. I hope.

Harry walks away to examine the light hookups. Director Jen finishes giving me instructions on what needs to happen with the display. When I catch up to Harry, he's bent over some cords.

"If I've got a computer and a receiver, I can make it work." He flops over onto his back to gaze upward.

"Where can we get those things fast?" I ask.

"Look how tall this damn thing looks from down here." His eyes go glazed.

"Earth to Harry. A computer?"

He rolls over. And then does a couple more rolls. Then he stumbles to his feet. "We can use mine. My place is about ten minutes from here."

I'm starting to doubt I'll get any sleep before the race. Why do I like party planning, again? "Let's go then."

Upon further examination of Harry's gait, I decide to drive.

I turn the air conditioning on full blast to keep from nodding off while I wait in the driveway for Harry to get the equipment. The car clock ticks from 2:23 a.m. to 2:43 a.m. Should I go in after him?

I pop open the door just as he emerges with his arms full of stuff. He loudly loads my trunk, and I pray that the hardware will still be viable when we get back to the race site. A real winner I'll be if the light display doesn't happen.

Harry flumps into the passenger seat. He forgets to lock up, but I back out without mentioning it. We don't have time to waste.

"How much have you had to drink tonight?" I ask.

"I've hardly had any, and it's been a few hours since my last one. I'm fine."

Twenty minutes later, we pull up next to the barricade surrounding the Murrays' driveway. I push Harry over to the light display and get him working. Then I send a text to Director Jen that the process is underway. She shoots back a curt "hurry."

Harry's brain may not be all there, but his hands know what to do. They begin hooking plugs together and pressing buttons. He doesn't attempt to give direction to anyone else, other than singing at them to have a holly jolly Christmas, so I try to coordinate efforts as he goes. Display by display, things start clicking into motion.

I keep an eye on things from afar while I go back and finish styling my cookie booth.

When all the lights come on at once, the volunteers cheer. I sprint over to congratulate Harry.

One hour until go-time....

Harry holds up a flask, which I didn't know he had, to the cheers. He empties it.

"Is the music part ready?" I ask.

"Cool your britches. She'll get there." Harry presses a bunch of buttons and music bursts from the loudspeaker. We all grab our ears until the piercing sound dies, along with the lights.

And we're back at square one. Harry curses and stumbles over to some plugs.

Director Jen announces over the walkie-talkie that racers have already started to assemble.

I watch Harry tinker, and stagger, feeling hotter by the minute. At least I've got enough adrenaline pumping to not be the least bit tired.

He continues to fiddle.

Time shortens.

Harry tries the receiver again. The displays don't respond.

Director Jen comes over to check on the progress. Mr. Bob gives her an encouraging—embellished—report.

"Well, we're all ready," she says. "It's now or never with the lights."

"Harry, what's the deal?" I ask.

His eyes don't focus. If they can't find my face, how in the world will they solve a technical conundrum?

My sweat glands pour. "Mr. Bob," I plead.

Three neighborhood men join Mr. Bob at the controls.

"Adia, are we a go?" demands Director Jen. I'm beginning to really dislike the sound of her voice.

Mr. Bob shakes his head at me with a discouraging shrug.

"Adia!"

"Okay. Go!"

The course is three miles long. We have about twenty minutes to solve this problem.

The countdown crackles over the walkie-talkie, followed by a static squeal as the racers cheer their way into motion.

My former neighbor fiddles with the computer. Fourteen minutes...

He strikes the "on" button.

Again, nothing happens. The men confer and try a few new things.

Harry stumbles over a cord and falls. "Keep pressing go," he mumbles to me. "I'll check all these connections until everything moves so good you get knocked up."

I think I heard that right.

He wanders off, still talking to himself.

I take over the computer. Ten minutes...

I press and press and press...

The first runner bounces toward us about ten houses away.

Come on.

Click...click...

Come on.

More racers crest the final hill.

We have no music at all as the first one passes the finish line. My sense of failure squeezes its arms around my chest. The Twinkle Dash has never been a disappointment before. And it's all my fault.

Why did I ever think I could be the manager of something?

Two more participants cross over in dim silence. Someone points them toward the finishers' tent. I hope our cookies will be yummy enough to make up for this anticlimax.

Click...click...click, click, click, click.

CRAP.

A least twenty people have finished now. Their faces reflect not amusement but confusion as they cross the dark and solemn finish line.

A bulkier group appears up the road now.

Where is Harry? I wander into the darkness. I'm traversing through cords when a burst of movement threatens my skull. The lights are alive!

I dodge the elf's swinging hammer as angels hum in my ears. Well, not angels, but the angelic voices of Pentatonix. Let there be light and Christmas music and—*oh, dear holy blessed mother of the almighty*—a twenty-two-year-old spraying down the lighted Rudolph with his urine, his nether region entirely exposed...to the children.

∽

He doesn't put *it* away himself. I have to push him behind a bush.

"Harry, what the hell? You're in public. There are children here!"

"Shit. Did someone see me?"

"Yeah. They did. A good fifty someones. You have serious issues."

He turns to me, preparing to smooth talk.

I bury my eyes. "Cover up!"

While he rearranges things, I talk.

"Here's the deal. You're going to go that way through the backyard and across three more until you hit a giant oak tree. Turn right and take those backyards all the way out of the neighborhood. Do not let anyone spot you. Wait for me at the church at the end of Poplar Street. I'll take you home whenever I can slip away."

"I don't want to sit there and wait. I can drive myself." For someone who is so clearly wasted, he can talk pretty decently. I wonder how accustomed he is to this state of mind.

"The heck you can. If you go back toward the race, they'll likely have you arrested. Forget your car."

"I'm fine."

"Harry, don't take this the wrong way, but you need help."

"I know." He gets a big cheesy grin on his face. "Wanna help me?"

"I am helping you, idiot. Now go."

I scoot around the bushes and return to my booth. Two racers are arguing over the cookie choices. I get out a container of chocolate chip, which appeases them. "Hey!" I say to a boy who snags five in each hand. "Save some for the rest of us."

Director Jen marches toward me, wearing a scowl so intense I almost take cover. Her finger stops a centimeter from my nose. "Did you invite an inebriated young man to help with this event? This *family* event?"

My head falls. "I didn't know he was drunk when I asked him."

"Well, isn't that wonderful. It's all anyone's talking about, including the news crew. They'll probably broadcast this debauchery instead of our fundraising success, and this event will become the laughingstock of the greater Triad. Your little stunt may shut us down for good."

Tears prick my eyes. "I'm so sorry."

"A lot of good that does. I'm so humiliated." She scoffs as she leaves.

I'm developing a talent for making people do that, it seems.

"Is there any punch?" a young participant asks.

I even forgot punch.

This was supposed to be the pinnacle of my time back home, a golden opportunity to volunteer at an event that brought me so much joy as a kid. But I burned it down, just like I did the pies on Thanksgiving.

I'm worthless.

I want to go…somewhere. Away.

But I'm stuck until the race ends.

Lighted Santa waves at me. I prop myself up against a nearby fence to stare blankly into the jubilee that mocks me.

FORTY-SEVEN

By seven in the morning, the race crowd has broken up and my booth is no longer essential. I gather my things, leave the extra cookies on a paper plate, and sneak out the back way to deal with Harry. I find him passed out on a bench outside the church. With a lot of poking and dragging, I manage to get him to my car, and then to his apartment.

I get back in my car bone tired.

Where do I go from here? I refuse to crawl back to my parents. I'm pissed at Miller. Jemma's gone. I quit school. I would feel super uncomfortable staying by myself at a hotel. All I have is this charity car.

I stare at the fog my breath creates on the windshield. Nothing beyond this Honda is clear. My entire life is a giant blur. Merry almost Christmas to me.

My car seat buzzes as it reclines. Once I'm as flat as I can get, I curl up into a ball. My eyes eagerly close out the world.

The sound of tapping on glass shoves me back to reality.

A fresh-faced Harry nods his chin at me. I open the window, almost falling back asleep as it moves down.

"Girl, if you needed a place to crash you should have told me. You know you're welcome here."

"It's fine. The car was super comfortable." I stretch the crick in my back and sit up.

"Why are you out here anyway? Don't you have a crew to holiday down with and stuff?"

"Sure, if you're willing to count standing near random strangers who look like they're having fun as 'holidaying down.'"

"What about Miller?"

"Miller's not Miller, as it turns out."

"Huh?"

"Apparently Miller has a different birth name and a sister, who has informed me that he is a terrible person."

"Man, that's heavy. Do you believe her?"

"About the name, yes. I looked it up. He definitely used to go by Hunter. I don't know about him being a terrible person, though. Do you think I should trust this girl?"

"What's her name?"

"Robin Johnson. Know her?"

"Sure don't. You might want to talk to someone who does. Someone who knows them both."

Drew might. I fall back against my seat.

Harry sticks his head in the window and makes a pouty face. "I'm about to head to my ma's place to grab a bite, and then I'm going to hit it with some of my boys. You want in?"

"It's a nice offer, Harry, but I think I want to be alone today."

"You sure?"

I nod.

"Hey, I'm sorry about last night."

I cover my face as the unwarranted image returns. "Do you remember what happened?" I ask.

"Some of it. I remember falling asleep by myself in a parking lot because you kicked me out of the party."

"It was a race."

"You know what I mean."

"You party a lot, huh?"

"Eh." He shrugs.

"I think you should consider cutting back."

He pulls his head back out of the car. "What else is there to do?"

I want to let this conversation drop here. But there's a look in Harry's eyes that begs me to dig in. To speak up. I sit up straight. "Harry, if that's how you feel, you might want to find new friends. There are people in this world who do stuff other than party. Maybe hang out with Miller for like a month. That'll detox you real fast."

Harry stretches his arms out over the car and drops his head onto the top.

"You probably already know this, Harry, but you used to be, like, basically a celebrity to all the underclassmen girls in high school. You had everything going for you: looks, mad lacrosse skills, personality."

His mouth cracks into a grin. "You think I'm hot."

I roll my eyes. "What I'm trying to say is, where did that guy go?"

His scrunches up his face as if I hit him.

"I think you need to find him. I think you need to get help."

"You think it's that bad?"

"I think it's close."

He nods for a while, his mind clearly somewhere else.

I drift to Miller. Solid, slightly neurotic, adorable Miller. I want to spend my day with that boy. Too bad he doesn't really exist.

If he's not Miller, though, who is he?

"Adia." Harry smiles at me with a fragile no-teeth smile, the sincerest expression to have crossed his face since we've known each other. "You're a good friend. I'm sorry I put a move on you at the office party. You're better than that."

"Thanks, Harry. All is forgiven."

"Have a Merry Christmas."

"You too."

He jogs away with his head held high.

I'm glad someone's feeling empowered. I just feel like slop.

I pull out my phone and bring up the articles about Hunter again. They talk about some inappropriate things he did, but they don't tell me who he is. Is he an asshole?

And why did he run from his whole identity? What am I missing?

I do need to talk to someone who knows the whole story. I don't think I can trust Drew though, since he's obviously already taken a side. But one of the articles mentioned a mom. I skim it, looking for a way to track her down. Then it hits me, Maureen Johnson.

I know that name.

It was the name on the package I dropped off for Miller before the tree farm. It was the beginning of a major turning point for us. I remember everything about that package.

Including where I delivered it.

I'm staring at a bad painting. I know I should be looking at the bigger picture, but I can't help analyzing what the artist was trying to cover up.

Maureen's hair doesn't move a millimeter when she tilts her head, and her face is caked with tinted makeup. "Are you here to pick up product?" she asks.

I shake my head.

"Can I help you with something?"

"Um…" I get scanned by the piercing pale green of her eyes. It's the one thing I know is real. I fell in love with that ocean.

"I'm not interested." She goes to shut the door on me.

"I know your son."

The door stops. "What did you say?"

"Miller. Well, Hunter. He goes by Miller now."

She opens up the door and gives me a closer inspection. "Did my son say something bad about me?"

"Uh, he didn't say anything about you, actually. Your daughter mentioned that he cut ties with you both. I'm wondering what happened."

She pushes the door open. "Come inside."

From the outside, this house looks no different than all the other two-stories in this middle-class neighborhood. The inside elevates it. It's a magazine spread of balanced decor and cozy touches. Nothing falls short of perfect, not a poorly folded blanket or photo smudge. It's all on trend.

We sit down on a tufted gray settee. Maureen wrings her hands.

"Can I get you something to drink? Maybe a super-fruit shake to help sustain your youthful glow? My shakes fight free radical damage."

I wouldn't want to be responsible for so much as water in this museum. "No thanks."

"How do you know my Hunter?"

I'm here to *get* answers. I'm not sure yet how much I'm willing to give. "We work together."

"Where do you work?"

"UPS."

"Hunter's working for UPS?"

I figured she'd at least know that. "He has for years."

She takes a breath. "You have a marvelous skin tone. What products do you use?"

"Uh... Oil of Olay?"

"Oh, my. Have you ever had a beauty profile made?"

"I can't really afford fancy beauty products."

She pulls a pamphlet from between a stack of magazines on her coffee table and holds it up to my face. "Everyone can afford them if they make it a priority. It's worth it. If you start when you're young, you can really retain your vitality."

I wrinkle my nose but take the pamphlet and set it in my lap.

"My poor daughter. She doesn't quite have a bone structure like yours. Too much jaw."

"I think she's really pretty." Besides the fake hair and meddling personality. "Will you tell me what happened between her and Miller?"

Lipstick smears across Ms. Johnson's front teeth as she sucks on her lip. Between that and the baked skin, it's hard to see much of Miller in her. Except for the eyes. He's definitely there.

"I mean, I read about the things he said, about that teacher and the woman he worked with. But I don't understand why he's so cagey about it all. And why won't he talk to you? And why is Robin so mad at him? What am I missing?"

She pulls some lipstick from a drawer and replaces the lost coverage. Then she clears her throat. "The thing is— What's your name?"

"Adia."

"Adia. The thing is, my son actually didn't deserve as bad a deal as he got." She folds her hands over her crossed legs and leans in. "His sister saw an opportunity to hurt him, and she took it."

"She saw an opportunity?"

"When Hunter came home upset about his suspension at work over that dumb joke he made, she turned around and went public with the incident. She had her guy friend post it to make things less obvious. Then, they dug up the old tweet about the teacher and *bam*, Hunter was a monster. His life spun out of control. People he didn't know from Adam posted the most awful things on all of his social media accounts. Hundreds of jokes and memes were made at his expense. A wildly popular thread started: #huntthepig." She puts a manicured hand to her chest. "Someone threw a bloody pig head through our front window. Things got violent."

"Is that when he was attacked?"

"More like he was beaten within an inch of his life, in the middle of a high school party, with hundreds of kids watching. But that wasn't even the biggest part of the spectacle. While he was in the ICU, fighting for his life, all these strangers showed up at the hospital with signs and music to celebrate. They broadcast it on the news. I had cameras on me day and night. It was awful." She pats her hair.

My eyes shut as every one of Miller's scars passes through my mind. Every time he flinched at my touch. "His sister started this?"

"Robin can be problematic if you get on her bad side."

My skin crawls. I'd probably run away from that too. "What did he do to get on her bad side?"

"To be honest, I don't know. Robin is a complicated girl. Trouble follows her around."

That's it? That's all she has to say about her daughter almost getting her son killed? For the love! He pretty much *did* lose his life, the Hunter Johnson life. "Why didn't you defend Hunter if you knew what your daughter was doing?"

"I didn't know she was behind it at the time. She threw that in my face years later. And since Hunter got so defensive about the accusations, I just assumed he was guilty. I was so angry with him. It wasn't just Hunter who got hurt in all of this. Those people online called me all kinds of names. Said I was an unfit mother." Her voice cracks. "I didn't raise my kids to be crude. It was all so humiliating. I couldn't leave my house." She dabs the moisture in her eye with her thumb. "I just think if Hunter had been more apologetic, it wouldn't have escalated. We wouldn't have had to go through all that."

"But getting set up by his own family member must have been really hard for him."

"He left us, so I wouldn't know."

The acid in her tone ruffles me. I mean, what the heck? This is her son we're talking about.

"Couldn't you have at least defended him in public when you figured out the truth? Everyone still thinks he's a belligerent sexist. He changed his entire identity because of this."

She looks out the window. "I love my son, Adia. I do. But he's a big boy now. He doesn't need his mother fussing over him. I've let that all go." A black tear rolls down her cheek until she traps it.

Mothers can do that? Just let parenting go? Is *my* mom doing that?

"This isn't fair. Hunter needs someone in his corner. Robin's still going around spreading lies. When does it end?"

Ms. Johnson leans forward and rests her hands under her chin. She watches me for too long. I squirm. "Adia, are you in love with my son?"

Hunter or Miller?

"I don't know."

"Well, let me give you a little advice. Stay away. If Robin doesn't want you two together, you don't want to get wrapped up in this."

My stomach twists.

What is wrong with these people?

I want refuge. I want to hug my mom. I stand.

Before I can escape, she presses the pamphlet I left on the settee into my hand. "Text me if you're interested in any products. I get deep discounts for friends."

Lady, we are anything but.

Looking into her seductive, callous eyes, I feel the hopelessness Miller must have felt when he left. I take a deep breath. I don't want to be in this position. I *refuse* to be in it.

And I still have hope.

"You should reach out to your son. People never stop needing their moms."

I'm going home to mine.

When I get to the porch I spin back around. "Also, you could use better Christmas decorations. Yours have no personality."

FORTY-EIGHT

I weave around numerous parked cars to get out of Ms. Johnson's neighborhood. Tonight is the night, the big night, and people are preparing. What does the night before Christmas look like when you're an adult though?

No Santa. No cookies for Santa. No giddiness about presents. What else is there?

Have I blown this whole holiday out of proportion? Have I been dragging out something that was supposed to die a long time ago?

Maybe my mom *has* babied me. Maybe traditions were never meant to be an ongoing thing. And I've aged out. Maybe nothing is wrong with my parent at all, and it's me. I'm the one who's acting crazy.

My phone buzzes in my pocket. It's another text from Drew. *Okay, universe. I get the message.*

I need to stop whining. I need to stop avoiding my family. I need to grow up.

"Hey," my stepbrother says, picking up my call immediately. "You doing okay? I've been trying to get in touch with you."

"I need to talk to you about something important."

"Shoot."

"Does the name Hunter Johnson ring a bell?"

He goes silent.

"I take that as a yes. Well, Miller is Hunter."

"Oh… That's why I recognized him." He curses under his breath. "You're dating Hunter Johnson?"

I can hear the judgment in his voice, and I immediately get defensive.

"Are you going to say more bad stuff about him? Haven't you punished him enough?"

"That situation is…really complicated."

"I know you beat him up, Drew. What the heck?"

He blows out a big breath. "Look, Ads. I'm definitely not proud of what happened, but I thought I was doing the right thing. The guy was being such a jerk. My boy Eric, who was close with his sister, felt like we needed to take a stand on the crap he was saying. I thought we were just going to scare him, push him around a little, teach him a lesson. Then it got way out of control. But I didn't throw any punches, I swear."

"You realize Miller was set up, right? That his comments were manipulated and overblown? He never needed to be taught a lesson. He was just a normal, immature teenager. But his sister wanted to hurt him, and you were her pawn."

The gravity of my brother's inhale presses through the phone. "He acted so guilty."

"He acted *defensive*. Because he was being attacked."

"Damn."

I pull into my parents' apartment complex and park. How did I just get here without thinking?

Drew says, "I feel really bad for the guy."

"Well, you should. Miller can barely touch someone without flinching. You guys broke him, Drew."

"Can you tell him I'm sorry?"

I feel like this is one of those moments where Mom would say *sorry doesn't cut it* or *actions speak louder than words*.

"I think you owe him more than that. Hunter needs people to stand in his corner if he's going to get his life back. He's too powerless to rebuild on his own."

"What do you think I should do?"

I don't even need to ask myself what Mom would say. I know it in my gut.

"Speak up."

He pauses. "I'll see what I can do."

"Thanks."

"Still love me?"

"Yes, I still love you. I will always love you. Count on it."

Cal greets me at the apartment door with a smile. It's nice to see I haven't burned *everything* down. "Good to see you, Ads. Can I get you something to eat?"

"I don't have much of an appetite."

Cal sits down with his bowl of beef and vegetables and turns on the TV. The dogs are overtaking the Christmas feast in *A Christmas Story*. I don't have the energy to laugh. I don't even have the energy to miss Wizard.

"Where's Mom?" I ask.

"She's out for a bit."

"I want to see her."

"She'll be back later."

"Tell me she didn't ditch you for her friends on Christmas Eve."

"Don't talk badly about her new friendships, baby. They're really good for her right now."

"Well, they're the only people she seems to have any interest in these days. She hasn't wanted to do anything with me."

"You know your mother loves you more than anything. But she's also got to look after herself once in a while."

"She can't do both?"

My tone prompts Cal to stop the movie and turn around. His eyes fill with concern. "There are some things you don't understand."

"Well, help me understand, because what it feels like is when I went to college, I lost my mom, along with everything else familiar. It feels like Mom's done with me."

He sets down his bowl. "I can't be in the middle of this anymore.

Come on. We're going for a drive." He pauses and grimaces at my fabulous leggings paired with a peacoat—which was my only winter jacket not in storage. "Do you want to change first?"

"Nah." This is who I am right now, and I'm good with it.

We pull up to a fancy brick church.

"What are we doing here?"

What is Cal pulling? I know my attitude is sour, but church isn't warranted. Maybe a nap, sure, but religious intervention?

"Come with me," he says calmly.

I follow my stepdad through the parking lot and into a back entrance. We walk down a hall toward a room with a closed door.

This has confession written all over it. My feet hesitate.

He nods toward the room. "Have a look."

I crack the door just enough to peep. Inside, a group of ladies sit in a circle. One has a lap dog. I recognize Linda and Caroline. And…

"Mom?"

Cal grabs my arm a moment too late. Mom turns around with the tissue still situated under her nose, and her eyes widen.

"I'm sorry, Sammy," Cal says, leaning his head to the side. "I had to let her see. I can't watch you guys fight like this anymore. You need each other right now."

"I agree," says Linda. "Go talk to your daughter."

Mom grunts and gets out of her chair. She shuts the door behind us in the hall. Cal ignores her eye-daggers and excuses himself so Mom and I can "have a minute."

"Let's sit," she says, pointing to a bench.

"What's going on? Is that an AA meeting?" I ask. They always meet at churches in the movies.

"Honey, no. It's nothing like that. I've been having some health trouble." She chews her lip.

Is the room starting to spin?

Don't say you're dying. "What does that mean?"

She squeezes my knee. My eyes fill with fluid.

"Well, where do I begin?" She takes a deep breath. "After you left for school, I started feeling weird. I couldn't get out of bed some days. Kept having to call out from work. At first, I figured it was typical depression. But these other weird things were happening too. When I would try to eat, I couldn't grip my fork enough to get the food to stay on it. And do you remember that issue with my eye?"

"You mean when I put Drew's football pads on you after you kept bumping into the kitchen counter because you refused to go get your eyeglasses prescription updated?"

She makes a small laughing sound. It gives my lungs a moment of unencumbered breath. "Unfortunately, it wasn't my eyesight that was the problem. I was trying to deny that there even was a problem since I didn't have any health insurance, but after one particularly bad week on the couch, Cal forced me to go to the doctor. They sent me to a specialist, who had to run a lot of tests. We found out I have a slowly progressive neurologic condition."

I can't breathe again.

Why didn't she tell me?

"Is it life-threatening?"

"We don't know. Every case is different. It depends on how I respond to the medication. We've just started something new that we're hopeful will slow the disease down."

I drop my head into her shoulder. "Do you have that thing where people's bodies stop working, like that scientist guy has?"

"Are you talking about ALS?"

"Yes. Do you have that?"

"No. Fortunately not that. Mine's something called multiple sclerosis."

That doesn't sound good. "I don't understand why you didn't talk to me about this."

"Adia, look what happened when I broke my arm. You want to take on everyone else's burdens, and I love you for it. But I refuse to hold you back from your life, so I decided it was best not to tell you. I'm sorry, baby girl."

I wrap my arms around her and squeeze. How do I fix this? "Is money so tight because of treatment?"

She rubs my back in that perfectly soothing way. "It is. But as soon as I get another job, with benefits, things will settle back into place."

"I can help with money. I got offered a full-time job at UPS."

"Heck no! You can help by taking care of your expenses and nothing else. We have some resources, and we will be fine. The neurologist is working with us. Plus, ever since I got fired, I—"

"You got fired!" My head flies up. "You told me Dr. Spitz retired."

"I know. I didn't want to—"

"Worry me," I finish. This is becoming an ugly trend.

"Yes. It wasn't all bad, though. It was a wake-up call. I started going to counseling, and my counselor encouraged me to join the grief counseling group here. This is where I met Linda and Caroline and all the other ladies who brought us dinners. Adia, these women have changed my life. They've made me less lonely with my only daughter gone. And they are an army of support. You saw how they showed up when I broke my arm. They pick me up, and I do that for them too, however I can. This disease has led me to such special friends. I hope you'll come to love them like I do."

Jemma pops into my head. My chest clenches again. Having Jemma was like having a sail. I'm grateful—and envious—that Mom has found some people to carry her through things too. I wish Miller would. "How can *I* help, though?"

"You can help by going back to school and thriving."

I cover my face.

"Honey, what?"

I don't want to upset my mom, but keeping secrets isn't any better. "I quit school," I blurt, peeking out of my hands for her reaction.

She squeezes her eyes shut. "What does that mean, exactly?"

"I emailed my resignation to the dean. And I never finished that linguistics paper."

She nods once, twice…at least ten times. The silence slices me into little tiny bits. I would much prefer to duke it out. "I hope you didn't do this for that boy."

Or maybe silence was fine.

"Jeez, Mom! I did it because everything was all too much. Working, homework, you being weird. Plus, I don't feel like I fit in at Avery at all. And, actually, *that boy* made me feel happy for the first time in months."

And then he crushed me.

Or his sister did.

"Do you *want* to go back to school?" Mom looks up at Cal as he returns. His eyes widen and he freezes.

"I don't know. I have no idea what I want."

Mom turns my face toward her. *"That's what college is for, baby.* It's the transition from a life with no choices to a life of all choices. It's a jumping-off point. A practice round for adulthood."

"Well, I hate adulthood."

"Come on. It has its perks…eventually. You'll get to be a mom one day. That's pretty fun."

"Until your kids become teenagers and their brains stop functioning," Cal says, squeezing in with us on the bench.

They scoop me into a hug. My entire being settles into the trouble-proof sphere we form.

"I'm sorry I'm a mess, guys."

"Baby, we know being away has been hard for you," Cal says. "But you are such a strong, amazing girl. You can do anything you put your mind to."

I nod into their chests. They squeeze tighter. Maybe I'm supposed to have outgrown comforting parent hugs by now, but I can't bring myself to let go.

The doors open and the grief group walks into the hallway. Linda comes over.

"Is the meeting done?" Mom asks.

Linda nods. "We're about to go to the candlelight vigil in the sanctuary upstairs. Adia, do you and your family want to join us?"

Well, I'm wearing yoga pants and my makeup's smeared, but you know what? Not every holiday affair has to be fancified.

I link arms with Linda and my mom, and we walk together.

FORTY-NINE

The most amazing smell calls me out of my dreams.

Cherries and dough.

Not much can get me to want to climb out of my warm blankets without some snoozing first, but fresh-baked pastries will do it every time. I stretch, stuff my feet into my UGGs, and wander into the common area.

"Merry Christmas, honey!" Mom scurries over in her snowflake pajama set and envelops me in a hug. "I was going to wake you with cherry cider and a special treat, but the treat has a few more minutes in the oven."

"It smells divine."

We gather around the fireplace where my mom has creatively staged all the presents. She smiles at a Santa-covered envelope perched on the mantel with my name on it. "Kris Kringle seems to have found our new address."

I grin. I want to tear into my unexpected surprise right this instant. What will it be?

I shake, sniff, hold it up to the light.

It's thick paper. The possibilities are endless.

Cal emerges from the bedroom with his crazy hair and chuckles at my giddy clapping. "I love how excited you get before you open gifts. It may be my favorite part of this whole day."

What an old-person thing to say.

Mom tucks a reindeer mug with warm red liquid into each of our hands. She pecks Cal on the lips and sits beside me on the couch. The timer on the oven beeps before she can complete the first sip of her drink.

We hop up together.

I pull out three plates and savor the smells wafting from the oven door. Wedges of pastry with little brown flecks in them emerge.

"Those smell like heaven."

"They'll taste like it too. I got the recipe from Linda. They're cinnamon scones."

"Put one in my mouth immediately." I pretend like I'm going to eat my mom's face if she doesn't heed my demand.

She shoos me away and sets a flaky treat on each plate. "Come on, silly girl. Let's open gifts." She hands Cal his plate. "I sure wish Drew could be here."

I push an end table over near the fireplace and set a box on it. Then I look around for the iPad.

"What are you doing, Adia? Didn't you hear me say presents?"

"I'm making a spot for Drew and Claudia."

When they answer the FaceTime, the whole room fills with cheer.

"How's Florida?" I ask.

"Well, I've seen Claudia's dad completely in the buff, doing his business on the porcelain throne, so we're getting pretty well acquainted around here."

Claudia covers his mouth. "Drew! Your whole family doesn't need the details of my dad's toilet habits."

"Who's talking about my toilet habits? Is that Drew's family?" asks a voice off-screen. A bronze-skinned man with creases around his eyes pokes his head in front of the camera. "I'm educating your son on the ways of the world. A man cannot be held accountable for his actions after an entire day on a boat during a period of high wind gusts."

"Or after an entire case of Pacifico," chides a female in the background. A hand thumps the grinning dad's head, and he squeals.

I cackle. Drew is in good company with this bunch.

After they divulge the whole sea-sickness story, Drew, Claudia, and her parents join us for opening a few gifts. We showcase our items over the screen and chatter above the chaos in the background of their home. The occasional stranger pokes their face in front of the screen to shout hello.

The cinnamon scone disappears from my plate but forever embeds itself into my brain. No other Christmas will ever be complete without one.

Mom and Cal graciously dote over the ornaments I made them out of old t-shirts. There's an angel for Mom and an Eagles football fan for Cal. They prop their fabric dolls up on the mantel since there is no tree.

I guess Abies and I weren't meant to spend Christmas together.

"Your turn to pick again," says Mom, after we end the call with Drew.

My restraint jumps ship. "Give me the Santa one!"

Mom wraps her arm around Cal as they watch me open the gift.

I pull out the slip of paper and my heart stops.

A ticket to London in the spring!

"Mom." My eyes wrap themselves around her. "Mom!"

"Merry Christmas, honey."

"We can't afford this," I whisper.

"Don't worry about that. I had some things around here that were worth a pretty penny."

"But this ticket probably cost a thousand dollars. What was worth that much?"

"You know that china we only use once a year?" She gestures that it's all gone.

"You gave up your beautiful Christmas china?"

"I decluttered."

"Mom." I hug her. There aren't words for this.

She squeezes me until it hurts. "This can be something for you to look forward to. It's important to have those things. I have something else for you too." She reaches beside the couch and pulls out a short, wide box tied together with a puffy bow.

I stow it in my lap. "It's your turn."

"You go ahead. There will be time for us later."

"Okay." I snatch off the lid. A photo album sits inside some tissue paper. Oh, boy. "You're not going to make me cry, are you?"

She crinkles her nose. "Go on. Take a look."

I take a deep breath, already feeling a few tears at the rims of my eyes. My mom made me something. Everything feels right in the world.

On the first page is a picture of Moses Cone Hospital where I was born. The next page is the little dance studio near the mall where I took my first lessons. All three of my schools get a page. As does the Hayes building, where I took knitting classes. Numerous special family spots fill the book. Frequented businesses. Our favorite restaurants. Our house.

"I wanted to remind you who you are, in case you forget ever again."

I flip through more pages. It's all here. My history. "These pictures are decent, Mom. Have you been secretly pursuing photography?"

"My friend Margaret's the photographer. She took me around yesterday to gather all these photos."

"Your friend gave up time with her own family to help you make this for me?" A full-blown tear drips out.

"She loves you. They all do. They'd do anything for you."

"Wow."

The last page is a large photo of me when my parents dropped me off at my college dorm. I'm grinning ear-to-ear. Underneath is a note from my mom: *All grown up and ready to tackle the world...*

I want to tackle the world! Only, what does that mean? What do I want to get out of this world?

It isn't dentistry...but is it managing a UPS store?

All the other tears push past my barricades. Mom and I hug and rock until my eyes are dry.

We take the morning slow, sharing a few more gifts and lots of stories. We sip cider and refill our plates. We lounge. No toys or quests draw me away. I stay in the cozy land of the adults. And I enjoy myself.

When Mom excuses herself to her bedroom to rest, Cal and I clean up all the wrapping mess. He uncovers one last gift, the one Miller left when he bailed on me.

I sit down and slip my finger beneath the crease of folded newspaper, wondering what I want to find beneath. Wondering if it will change anything at all.

Miller hasn't reached out to me, and I'm still mixed-up about everything.

And sorry.

And sad. Sad for Hunter, who went into hiding. Sad for Miller, who made up his own world so he didn't have to be a part of the real one. Sad for me, who fell in love with that make-believe.

My fingers travel across a smiley Labrador keychain holding a little brass house key. Beneath the key is a leather bracelet with a heart charm. A swirly symbol is etched onto it. On a tiny slip of paper, Miller has written: *I promise this key will never lead you to some weird, hairy dude. Only me. Forever.*

Forever?

I've got a whole lot to prepare before I can throw *that* party.

"I think I've made a big mistake."

I need to talk to Miller.

FIFTY

I set the photo album at the top of my suitcase and zip it up. Cal holds the door for me as I juggle it and Miller's present.

"You sure I can't carry any of that for you?"

"I've got it."

I chuck the bag into the back of his Tahoe, then poke my head in the front window.

"Where does this boy live?" he asks.

"He's off Wendover. Follow me."

Miller's gone dark since our fight. I texted a few times but never heard anything. I set his present on the floorboard of the Honda, not having any idea if he'll be home to receive it.

By the time I pull into his driveway, my heart is pounding. I park the car in the carport and lock it. "Be right back," I yell to Cal.

My legs struggle to wade through all their previous steps. That first date. The night I nearly froze to death. Him helping me save Abies. Those were my holiday moments, and they were unforgettable.

My feet falter.

I suck air into my lungs. I can do this. He's just a boy. Not some strange animal.

He doesn't answer my knock. Or the doorbell. Or my yelling his name.

My nerves subside, but disappointment takes their place.

I guess this is the Miller goodbye.

I place the wrapped box and letter on his doorstep. In the letter, I tell him he may hate my gift, but he's not allowed to get rid of it because he should have a blanket for guests, and because it's made from repurposed clothing, and because, mainly, I sweated over it. I tell him I'm sorry for blowing him off at the race and for what happened to him when he was seventeen. I thank him for making my mess of a holiday beautiful.

In case he never sees it online, I also leave a copy of the letter that Drew posted on all his social media accounts telling Hunter Johnson's side of the sexism scandal. I hope it builds a bridge for Miller. It reinforces the bridge between my brother and me, at the very least.

I don't tell Miller goodbye. I figure that's best said in person. Or maybe goodbye didn't feel like the right fit. Either way, I think he'll get the message when he finds the car and both sets of keys that I'm leaving behind.

Gulping down the burn rising up from my chest, I turn away from an alternate version of myself.

When I get in my stepdad's car, my phone dings. I thrust it at the dashboard trying to tug it from my pocket.

It's not Miller. It's my roommate.

Adrienne: Glad you can make it on Thursday! Here's the info

The next text has a picture of a flyer for the Avery City New Year's Eve bash.

"Do you have everything you need?" Cal asks, pulling away from Miller's house.

"Yeah." I watch the quaint little brick one-story until it shrinks out of sight.

"Be sure. We can't turn back once we're on the road. I have an appointment at two."

"I've got what I need."

I don't, but I've got everything my parents can help me get. The rest is up to me.

FIFTY-ONE

If working could really make your butt come off, I'd be a size zero right now. The undergrad library houses me for three solid days. I subsist on facts about chemistry, literature, and statistics. I haven't had dessert in days. If I don't ace my exams, it will be whatever the opposite of a miracle is. A really bad movie ending? It will be Rose-not-moving-over-for-Jack-on-the-freaking-raft bad.

I put my books into my bag and stretch. This girl is going out tonight.

When my phone emerges from airplane mode, it gifts me several good tidings. Adrienne's pregaming plans. A Happy New Year's Eve meme from my mom. And an emergence of the missing man.

Miller: Can I come see you?

It's been six days since Christmas Eve. Six. If it takes Miller almost a week to come out of hiding after an argument, how would we have ever managed to live together? What would he have done when we fought, eat in the carport? Sleep in his compost bin? I stop in my tracks and click away at my screen.

Adia: I'm back at school

Miller: You decided to go back to school???
Adia: I would have told you but you ghosted me
Miller: Something came up
Adia: For six days?
Miller: Kind of. It's a long story

I'm not sure I even have a response for this. In light of this inven-
tion called the internet, who actually thinks they can get away with
completely falling off the face of the earth for a week? If he had
wanted to get in touch, he would have.

Miller: Why did you leave so soon?
Adia: Makeup exams
Miller: Are we still together?
Adia: You want to have this conversation over text?
Miller: You left, remember?
Adia: You need a real phone
Miller: …

I wait a solid five minutes for those dots to turn into something
intelligible before I give up and tuck my phone away. I have a killer
party outfit to assemble.

My phone rings at nine forty-three in the morning, waking me up
from a dead sleep. I wake up to an unrecognizable room and remember. Last night was epic! The party was a blast *and* I made a friend. We
met on the dance floor. We were both wearing blinking Happy New
Year headbands and singing off-key at the top of our lungs. Instant
besties for life.

I silence my phone and sneak down the side of my new friend's
bunk bed. Luckily, Brooke's stick-straight auburn hair is still moving
in and out of her mouth with each snore. I wouldn't want to be rude
by waking her after she let me crash at her place.

I slip out into the hallway. "Hello?"

"It's me."

"Miller?"

"I got a phone, so save this number."

"Wow." I slide down the wall, not yet ready to carry on a serious conversation while also holding myself upright.

"Are we over?"

I swallow. "I don't even know who you are."

"Yes, you do. I'm me. That stuff you found out about, that doesn't have anything to do with me anymore."

"I talked to your mom."

Silence.

"I get why you left now."

Is he still alive?

"She explained how you were setup. Robin told her everything a while back. Now she knows that she was on the wrong side, at least."

His inhale squeezes in on me. I wish I could comfort him. If he hadn't disappeared, I would have. "I'm really sorry I turned on you like everyone else did."

"It's fine."

"It's not, though. It's not going to be fine until you learn to let it go and start living a real life again."

"I don't want to go back to all that."

"I didn't want to go to college and lose everything I knew in the process. Sometimes life kicks you in the hiney, but you can't..." *Where am I going with this?* "You can't walk around with a dirty butt."

"Hiney?"

"What I mean is, you need to stop pushing everyone out of your life."

He doesn't respond for a long time. My eyes start to droop. The three hours I slept aren't cutting it.

"Can you just say you're going to be with me?"

My throat swells into a rock. Doing the right thing is hard. "I want to say yes, Miller, but you need me to say no. We both do."

"Adia...I love you."

I might die of a heart attack. His words curl around my throat. I blow out, trying to keep it from collapsing. Why does everything good in my life lately have to be linked with something horrible? I love this boy! I love him. I love him. I love him. And I can't tell him. I can't say those sweet words and then expect to spill out unpleasant words like "it's not a good time right now." Gulp. "Miller...since I met you, you've become my favorite person, but it's just... I'm not ready to deal with what that means. I'm not ready to leave school. And although I'm super awesome at being an elf, doing that full-time would ruin all the fun."

He doesn't laugh.

I guess we're going about this the hard way. The tears way.

I take the deepest breath I can without passing out. "I'm not ready for you. I'm not ready for forever."

Silence. The drizzle of water on my cheek is the only thing that meets me in the void I'm building between us.

"I feel safe with you," I say, "and I could so easily escape into that. But safety isn't what either one of us needs. We need to face our cat poop."

"Cat poop?" His voice cracks.

So, it's definitely tears then.

"What I'm saying is I need to figure out how to stand on my own two feet before I can cozy up with you. And you need to find yourself again."

A sniffle reaches through the speaker and chokes me. This is a far cry from the restrained robot boy I chased down for a package. "I'm really sorry I dragged you into my problems."

"I'm not." His voice cracks.

I want to hold him the way he held me that day by his car—as if the world depended on that embrace.

After a big breath, his tries again. "I'd let you drag me through hell and back, if it meant I got to keep even one of those days with you."

"Are you comparing being with me to hell?"

"You're the only thing in my life that hasn't felt like that."

I drop my head back against the wall and let the tears have free reign. Why am I breaking up with this guy?

"Good luck, Adia," he breathes. "I hope college becomes everything you deserve it to be."

"Adia?" Brooke says, poking her head into the hall. Her eyes widen at my soaking wet face.

"Miller," I mouth, pointing to the phone.

She nods. Brooke and I covered a lot of ground last night. We stayed up talking until six-thirty this morning, which is why I ended up sleeping on her roommate's bunk.

She sits and scoots in beside me.

"Just promise me one thing," I say into the phone. "Make a friend. Maybe a few. People deserve to know you. Some of them, anyway."

"I'll see about that." He sighs.

He's still scared. How can I fix this?

Maybe I can't. Maybe Robin has to. I wonder if I could get in touch.

When the line goes dead, I shiver. Life is immediately darker without the promise of Miller somewhere ahead of me. I want to press his number and take back everything I said.

Brooke wraps her arms around me. "That sounded like a lot."

I nod.

"You want to go to Mama Sue's and order one of everything?"

She gets me already.

And since we're both freshmen, I'll have her around for four whole years. As long as I survive this breakup. I grip my aching chest.

FIFTY-TWO

"Holy skinny hippo," I say, sitting up. My Twinkie breaks in half. The Hostess snacks are half of my downward spiral. The other half is social media stalking.

Did anyone else know how hard breakups were? The despair and self-doubt have chewed a giant hole through my rib cage and are currently infiltrating my heart muscle. Katherine Heigl never conveyed this effectively.

I continue my decline, scrolling through a few more photos on Facebook. Hunter Johnson closed all his social media accounts, so I have no choice but to stalk all of Robin Johnson's photos and posts from six years ago. I'm looking for evidence.

"I think I found something. Look at this."

Brooke looks over my shoulder at a photo of a bleach blond version of Robin standing next to a guy I don't recognize and smirking as he burns a Berkeley envelope. The photo's caption says, "Sweet dreams."

"What a witch," says Brooke. "But it's not really proof she did anything wrong. It just proves that she was happy about Miller's punishment."

I slam the computer shut. "I can't stand that she's getting away with what she did. Why isn't this kind of thing a crime?"

"Sorry, boo."

Robin's smug face clings to my thoughts. She stays with me all the way back to my own dorm for the night. I can't fall sleep with her in my head.

Finally, I get up and open my computer.

I compose a letter detailing what I think of what she did and of how she's still acting. I tell her it's all very ugly behavior. I use a few mean words. I delete those.

I add them back.

My three a.m. brain rationalizes delivering this tirade. I send Robin a private message. Then I conk out in an empowered heap.

I don't come to regret my delirious decision until a week later, when the first text comes.

Hailey: Um…is this you?

Attached is a photo of my face dressed up like a sheep with the caption: "This desperate girl is standing up for a pig."

I find the same photo on Snapchat, Instagram, and Facebook and they're all linked to the private message I sent to Robin. But she's cut out any incriminating parts and manipulated the document to look like a desperate rant.

Comments start pouring in, mostly about how I'm pathetic or brainwashed or a "poor excuse for a female." Random strangers judge me for caring about Miller when he's "a trash human being." One educates me on the likeness of my chin to a baboon's rear end, which is off-topic and frankly dilutes the overall message of my ignorance.

These people don't even know me. So much for trying to do the right thing.

I eventually get overwhelmed by the flood of hatred and shut down all of my social media accounts. Goodbye, cyber world. Goodbye, social life.

Now I can be heartbroken and pitiful all by myself, at least.

I throw my phone into the trash can, close the blinds, and pull the covers up over my weary body. Goodbye, everything.

Katherine Heigl definitely never prepared me for this.

FIFTY-THREE

A small beam of light forces itself on my face. I open my eyes to see the outline of my roommate in our doorway. She left after the New Year's Eve party to go on a ski trip, so she doesn't yet know about my exile.

"Ew. What is going on in here?" Adrienne pinches her nose and steps over the three-day-old plate of food I've left on the floor.

I don't have the energy to respond.

"I guess I'll pick this up so that I can breathe inside of my own room." She throws everything associated with the old dinner into the trash, even the reusable plate. Then she turns on the diffuser. "Can you deal with this trash bag and whatever else smells so bad? I'll be back after things have had time to air out." She starts to set down her duffel bag but decides against it and walks out.

I get out of bed and grab my keys and student ID. I don't bother changing clothes. Anyone who recognizes me has probably already formed an opinion about my character anyway. I leave the dorm room behind to rot.

Where to?

I find a bench in the middle of campus and settle in for the long haul.

Life happens around me. Part of me wants to jump in with the groups that go by laughing. A bigger part of me wants to throw pine cones at them all.

Hours into my staring, after I've entered a complete state of numbness, Brooke steps into my view.

"I was convinced I was never going to find you." She squeezes in beside me and wraps me into a hug. "Have you been on Facebook today?"

"I'm never getting on the internet again."

"That's totally valid, and I support you. But you need to see this one last thing."

I turn my whole body away when she breaks out her phone.

Miller's voice comes out of the little speaker. Brooke increases the volume.

"…but most people know me as the Cyber Hothead. I screwed up when I was seventeen. Said a dumb thing that I should have apologized for. And you can feel free to continue pointing fingers at me and using me for laughs, but please let that be where it ends. Don't use someone who took pity on me to get your next thrill. Please leave Adia out of this."

I grab the phone and peer into the face of a disheveled boy who, even talking to his phone screen, looks spooked. His eyes plead to the camera. I cling to his image.

"If you knew Adia, you would see what a big heart she has. You would see that she fights for the good in people and is quick to forgive. You would see that she's a human being with feelings, but beyond that, she's an incredible person. It's because of her compassion that I'm finally doing what I should have done a long time ago: owning up to my mistake. I am sorry to Tracy and my teacher Mrs. Randall for making crude and insensitive remarks when I was a stupid teenager. I realize I probably made you feel uncomfortable and objectified and that I propagated a sexist culture. I won't ever again stand for that behavior in myself or anyone else. I hope you can believe that.

For anyone else following this story, please stop attacking my friend Adia. You people all have hearts. Use them."

My thumb slides over Miller's gaunt face. My gut crawls with fear seeing him on here. He's so vulnerable. So exposed. I don't want people to be allowed to judge him anymore. I don't want them to attack him anymore. But I abandoned him. What have I done?

Oh, Miller.

I want to shield him with my body. I want to wall us off in his house, in our own little world where social media doesn't exist.

Brooke takes her phone back and gives me the concerned-friend smile. "Miller linked that video under every single negative comment about the message you sent Robin. It must have taken him forever. What are you going to do?"

I can't process this in broad daylight. I need darkness and tears that can summon a fairy godmother whose wand bestows wisdom instead of clothes.

Or maybe in addition. If the grease stains on my sweatpants are any indication, I'm looking less than stellar. Definitely not reunion worthy.

"What should I do?" I ask my friend.

"Call him and work it out."

When I get back to my phone, I dial Miller's number—over and over—but he never answers.

In the middle of the night, I get a single text.

Miller: I'm so sorry about all of this. Robin won't bother you again

He doesn't respond no matter how many times I text back. Maybe he was willing to defend me, but he sure doesn't want to talk to me about it.

I don't know if he gave back his phone or what, but I don't hear from him again.

It hurts in the beginning. Losing my first love.

But when his smell fades from my clothes and my body forgets exactly how blissful it felt to touch him… When closure becomes a less robust need and I've loosened my grip on the anger, I am able to see my time with Miller for what it was. A gift.

When everything I cared about felt like it was drifting away, he showed up. Picked me up. But he wasn't just a raft. He was the whole sea. He poured into me, quenched my parched soul, then carried me somewhere new.

Like a ghost of Christmas future, he gave me a sweet glimpse of how things might be if I keep on with the business of growing up. He helped me let go.

Miller was my Christmas miracle.

EPILOGUE

The only class I have to redo after my academic probation is linguistics, so I stay right on track. I enter a work-study program to cover expenses. With renewed purpose at Avery, I dive into my classes. But I can't stomach science anymore. I want to enjoy learning. I change my major to communications and connect with the PR professor who inspired me. She becomes my mentor. She encourages me to take a job with a local nonprofit that implements self-sustaining healthcare systems in African villages. They put me on the marketing team, where I plan and publicize fundraisers. I fall in love with my company. I want to be CMO one day.

Little by little, I let go of the love that kept me afloat at a time when I had lost my footholds. My life shapes into something independently buoyant, and I flow forward.

I slowly reenter the social media world, focusing first on more business-related sites like LinkedIn and Twitter. The more positivity I post, the deeper I bury the old trolls in my feed. I consider reaching out to Robin to try and reconcile, but Brooke talks me out of it. She doesn't want me to get dragged down into the muck again, and she's got a valid point. But I still wish I could change that girl's heart...hate breeds.

The first time Hunter Johnson comments on one of my publicity posts, I don't even realize who it is. After HJohn433 comments on several more, I make the connection. Hunter has rejoined the digital world. He follows me on Twitter, always apt to retweet and promote my events. And he has thirty-three followers of his own. Thirty-four once he accepts me.

I search all the socials to see where else he's spreading his wings. According to LinkedIn, he's the CEO of an up-and-coming green company called Bottled, which has sixty employees. Wow. *He went for it.* According to Facebook and Instagram, he continues to prefer some privacy.

I start promoting his business when and where I can, linking him on any environmental articles I read and boosting his LinkedIn page with commentary. We never reach out to each other personally, but he's always there in the background, cheering me on. And I him. Not quite friends, but still allies.

The Christmas of my junior year, I bring my boyfriend, Levi—whom I met at work and have been with for almost a year—home to meet my family.

"Don't expect anything big," I say. "My mom isn't able to cook much these days because her hand dexterity is declining."

"How's her new med working?"

"She thinks it's helping, but it makes her nauseous. Cal doesn't think she'll be able to stay on it. She's not eating enough. Maybe I'll try to make some cinnamon bread while we're there. It's her favorite, and I think you'll love it too."

"I don't need anything but a few hours to get to know the people my girl came from."

I reach over to the driver's seat and tuck my hand into his.

When we arrive, Levi grabs our bags and follows me to the front door. We were side-door people in our old house, but this place doesn't have one. I stare at the entrance, briefly flummoxed. Do I just...? I tap my knuckles gently against the wood.

"Adia, is that you?" Cal throws open the door. "You know you don't have to knock, baby."

"The front door thing throws me off. It's so formal."

"Get in here." By "here" he means his arms, which he wraps

around me.

After a good squeeze, I turn to my boyfriend. "This is Levi. Levi, this is my stepdad, Cal."

"You're the boy who likes the Giants." Cal frowns. "Any chance you're flexible on that?"

Levi laughs. "I'd need to hear a pretty convincing argument." Levi doesn't actually have that much time to spend watching sports, so he's not die-hard. But the Giants are a family thing, and that's enough to make him loyal.

I follow Cal inside, catching a whiff of broth and potatoes. "It smells amazing."

"Your mom's making that kale sausage soup you love."

"Mom, I hope you're not overdoing it!" I scurry to the kitchen, leaving Levi to his own devices with the bags. I'm greeted by a marvelous sight: the dining table set with heaping platters arrayed in style. Caprese skewers. A meat and cheese tray. Fresh bread with dill dip. Spinach quiche bites. Chocolate cake.

"Honey. Welcome home!" Mom shuffles toward me, one foot dragging behind. She's lost all of her curves and her cheeks look almost hollow. I hug her neck hard, trying to clear my face of any distress before she sees it again.

I turn to the spread. "This is too much."

"The girls brought most of it, and this is my only daughter's first time bringing a boy home to meet us. If that's not a cause for celebration, I don't know what is."

"Well, I'm here now, so you are off duty. Have a seat and give me orders from the chair."

"I am just fine, Adia. I want to spoil you two a little bit." She lowers her voice. "Where is he?"

"Putting our bags upstairs. He's excited to meet you."

"Sounds like a gentleman."

"A perfect one. Does the soup need anything?"

"Just a good stir. Maybe turn the burner down a touch and check the potatoes in about five minutes."

"I feel bad you did all this for us."

"Hun, I want to do this stuff as much as I'm able. It's who I am."

"I know that…" I catch sight of Levi in the hall and wave him in. "Mom, this is Levi."

She stands, and he moves in for a hug. "It's so nice to meet the lady who made Adia so fantastic."

"Oh, well, I can't take all the credit. That girl's got a mind of her own."

"I've noticed." He winks at me. "This looks amazing, Mrs. Bell."

"Help yourself. I wasn't sure if you'd eaten lunch, so I set out some appetizers to nibble on before dinner. Let me get you a plate." Mom's lagging foot catches the edge of her chair, sending it crashing to the ground. She catches herself on the table. Levi helps set her right.

"My goodness, Mom! Sit down. I'll get the plates." My mom lets Levi pick up the chair. She avoids my gaze when I come around with our dishes. "What do you want, Mom? I'll make a plate for you."

She shakes her head.

Levi turns his attention elsewhere. "Are these bacon-wrapped scallops? I love scallops."

"I'm so sorry about that," she says. "I lose my balance sometimes, but I'm fine."

"It's not a problem. Adia told me about your MS. You don't have to hide anything. I'm premed, so I find this kind of stuff interesting."

Mom looks away.

I want to shake her. She can't go around pretending that nothing's wrong again. It only drives a wedge between us, when all I want to do is be there for her.

How bad off is she if this is how it comes across when she's trying to seem okay?

"Cal," I call toward the living room, where he's watching a football game. "Why don't you take Levi with you to set out luminaries before dinner, while I help mom? He said he wouldn't mind."

Levi nods to no one in particular. Maybe to himself.

When the men leave, I turn to my mom, my hands holstered to my hips. "Are you going to wait until you have another crisis, or do you want to go ahead and tell me now what's really going on?"

～

After hearing Mom's hour long confession, I'm ready to put the neurologist on speed dial and change my major to premed.

"Adia, honey," her fingers trace my face. "I love you, but you can't fix me."

I frown. How can she be so sure?

"You know what you *can* do?"

Is my mom finally going to ask for my help? We shall forevermore celebrate this momentous day, the day my mom needed me.

"How about having some fun with me? Lend me some of your endless energy and pep."

Well, if I must. I happy dance around her and promise to be the best cheerleader she's ever known.

Mom insists we go to the Twinkle Dash. Turns out, the race participants who witnessed Harry's indiscretion adored the event too much to make any fuss. The tradition lives on.

We all roll out of bed before dawn on Christmas Eve and slip into warm athletic gear. Cal tucks a wheelchair I've never seen before into the trunk of his car. At least Mom opened up about using one so I didn't have to find out by surprise.

Having wheels at the race turns out to be rather fun. We get Mom zooming on the downhills, and then take turns riding them with her. Even Levi tries it once. The lighted balls swoosh past us in a continuous stream of neon rainbows. Mom laughs until tears flow out from the corners of her eyes.

I'm proud to see a cookie booth at the finish line. None of the cookies are as good as my mom's reindeer ones, but maybe I can remedy that next year.

In the evening, we all get sleepy early. Levi and I retire to the guest room, where he tucks in with a thick WWII novel and I tuck in with WebMD.

I read about MS until I'm cross-eyed. None of the information is straightforward or simple. Apparently, every disease course is different, though I'm gathering that my mom landed on the worse end of things. Balance issues are not a great sign.

And here she is making six-course meals and decking the halls in full force. She's overdoing it.

What if I lose her to this? Or what if I have her, but the best parts of her stop working, like her skillful hands and her sunshine smile?

These thoughts ruin any chance I have of sleeping. I lie awake, turning this new knowledge over and over in my mind, picturing weird things...me in a hospital room with a baby that my mom can't cuddle...cooking all alone in our old house's kitchen...putting on a black dress and netted fascinator...

Fancy hats aren't even a thing I would do. It's an unhealthy path that leads straight to Anxietyville, but my brain won't quit.

I get up at three a.m. and take my favorite pillow and blanket into her bedroom. I lie on the floor on her side of the bed. It's the sound of her steady breathing that finally eases me to sleep.

I awaken to the bewildering clap of a foot smacking my jaw.

"Adia, my word. I almost squished you. What are you doing in here?"

"I'm worried about you."

"Don't you start that. I told you, things are under control."

"Well, I don't care. I've got one life to spend with you, and if this MS has any say, I won't get my full share. You may not need me, but I need you. I need to be here with you for this."

"No, ma'am. We're not doing this again. I will not be responsible for torpedoing your college career. The only thing I want from you is for you to flourish. Whether I get to watch it from here or up there, I don't care, but that is all I want."

"Okay."

"Okay, you're dropping this?"

"I didn't say that." I pick up my pillow and blanket and start walking toward the door.

"Adia May."

"Samantha Ruby, I'm going to flourish right here, and there's not a thing you can do about it." I swoop out the door, Catwoman style. Boom. That's how you tell your mom what's what.

I stop and lean against the hallway wall. I think I just decided not to go back to school because I'm afraid my mom might be losing the ability to take care of herself. That's heavy.

Big, bulging tears fill up my eyelids.

I wipe them away, choosing to focus on action over reaction. What needs to be done?

The one good thing about making mistakes is knowing how to avoid them the second time around.

I'll start with a call to the dean.

I wrap the muscle stimulators around Mom's legs and tuck the sheets under her. It's hard to think about not returning to school, but, at the same time, I love being near my family again. Perhaps my path in life won't look like everyone else's, but I see this change as a blessing. I've got so many things I love about my hometown, so much I've missed. Enjoying it all again will feel like one great big holiday. I'll experience this old turf with fresh, grown-up eyes, and make a life here, in this place I adore. Maybe even share it with my own daughter someday.

"When is Levi coming back for New Year's?" Mom asks.

"Day after tomorrow."

"I'm so sorry you guys have to be apart now. It's okay to change your mind, you know."

"We have cars and smartphones. It's not a big deal."

Levi and I are very busy people. We rarely saw each other before, so I have no concerns about us being able to handle this transition.

I take my laptop into the living room and sit beside Mom's tree, which is artificial thanks to my dumb allergies. I light my pine-scented candle. It's become a nightly ritual to work here, and when the holiday ends, I might have to buy different decorations for my new friend. I've heard of people decorating their trees year-round....

I finish responding to emails and decide it's time for a little break. How can I amuse myself?

Oh, I know. I don't even wait for Brooke's response to my TikTok challenge. Grabbing all of my Christmas accessories—including my green suspenders and blinking, school-girl-style skirt—I begin choreo-graphing. I'm halfway through my dance routine when there's a knock at the door. Cal's out in his tool shed tinkering, so maybe he got locked out. I pause the Boss's "Merry Christmas Baby" and scuttle over in my reindeer slippers.

A dark-haired man with his hands in his pockets looks me up and down and shakes his head, smiling. His shag is no more, replaced by a short, gelled cut. His jeans fit great...really great.

I pull off my reindeer headband. "Miller."

"People don't really call me that anymore."

"I can't help it."

"I like that."

"What are you doing here? Like, how and...why?"

"My neighbor, Shana, came over today and told me you aren't returning to school. She keeps up with your mom at the neurology clinic. She's a nurse there." He tilts his head. "Did your mom not tell you that?"

What else has she been hiding from me? And *why*?

"Did you really move back?"

I nod.

"For how long?"

"Depends. However long my mom—" I choke on the rest of the words.

"Is she not doing so hot?"

"She claims she's fine." I roll my watery eyes.

He strokes my arm and my breathing catches. "I'm so sorry, Adia. I really, really am. I know how much you care about her."

I try to smile, but my emotions twist my face into something that I'm certain looks reptilian.

"Hey, you want to go somewhere with me?" he asks.

I can't deny the excitement these few words bring. It's a welcome reprieve. I look up and let his sea-greens flood through me. My heart swirls in the tidal wave. "Maybe?"

"I'm getting together at the beach with a couple friends for New Year's Eve. We went last year, and we're kind of making it a tradition. Harry will be there."

"A tradition?"

"Yeah, well, Harry's been sober for a while, and we wanted to keep him away from all the New Year's partying and whatnot. So last winter we drove to the coast and made a bonfire on the beach and watched the fireworks over the water. We all crashed at this beach house and stayed up too late doing stupid stuff."

"You do stupid stuff?"

"I guess so." He smiles a wistful smile. "I think you'd really like the crew. They're good people."

A crew? Who is this man standing in front of me?

He looks at his feet. "We're going to stay a few nights, but I can bring you back early if you need to be here."

"Can I... Let me think about it, okay?"

Miller nods. Then he snaps his fingers. "Oh, I got you something." He runs back to his same old futuristic car and returns with a cloth grocery bag.

He hands me a six-pack of ginger beer. "It's not homemade, but it's from Fresh Market."

"Aw."

"It's actually supposed to help with nausea too. I saw your post that your mom was having trouble with that."

"Have you been cyberstalking me?"

"I mean, I check-in from time to time." He looks back down. I miss the way his hair used to fall into his face when he dropped his eyes. "I brought you this too." He swaps out the headband I'm holding for my long-lost Christmas tree tumbler. "I think of you every time I see it, so..."

We watch each other. I start to miss him all over again. He steps closer and slides the antlers over my head.

My eyes flutter closed, and I soak in the familiar buzz of his proximity. This is kissing distance. Does he kiss any different than he used to? Has he been practicing?

"Wait." My eyes open. "I have a boyfriend."

"Okay," Miller says, looking around. "Does he want to come to the New Year's thing too?"

"Uh...I don't know." Frankly, I don't know what's going on right now. What is this? Where is it coming from?

"You want to let me know tomorrow?"

I nod, blankly.

He steps off the porch, and I instantly want him back up here. He gets closer and closer to his car. The last time I let him walk away, I didn't see him again for two years.

"Miller?"

"Yeah?"

I rush to him and cling, like if I hold tight enough I'll absorb some part of him that I'll get to keep forever. He tucks his fingers into my hair and around my waist. We fall against his car. It's the kind of hug that you would expect after two years of waiting. The kind of hug that promises much more. His woodsy smell mingles with my long-forgotten desires.

"Thanks for coming," I whisper.

"I couldn't wait any longer. I need you in my life, Adia Bell."

His arms scoop me in tighter, like he might never let me go.

The knots twisting inside my heart are proof that things officially just got complicated. I know there's going to be stuff I need to work out, but right now, I let myself soak him in.

Because nothing lasts. This I know for sure. Not a single thing in this world is permanent. Sometimes there are even better things to come, but good things will go too. And the only way I can cope is to treasure exactly what I have while I have it in my grasp.

WANT MORE OF THE STORY?

If you enjoyed celebrating the holiday with Adia and Miller, there's more! See what happens next in the sequel, *My Totally Sparked New Year*, set to release in early 2021.

Can't wait? I have two bonus chapters from this story. Get access to them by visiting my website at audreyfurnas.com and joining my reader newsletter.

NOTE FROM THE AUTHOR

Have you ever dipped your toe into something only to become instantly certain you could not go on without that thing as a part of your life? That is how writing fiction happened for me. I got a story idea one day, wrote a few sentences, and lost my former self. Honestly, it was insane. I wasn't an English major. I wasn't even, by some standards, an avid reader. I was just a girl with a newborn and a medical degree.

For a while, I hid my hobby. I wrote stories for a reader I knew I would probably never have. I studied the craft, feeling a little silly. I took secret classes. When I started coming out to people about my writing, I treated it like an unhealthy habit I'd picked up. Something I needed to break. I didn't dare call myself a writer, even after having three stories under my belt. I didn't consider calling myself that until my sister gave me a book titled *You Are a Writer*, but I only said it in my head. Saying it out loud felt weird. It still does.

But I was an addict from the first toe dip.

Thank goodness.

Because, I couldn't quit. Even when I felt like I should. Even when I started to think that having dreams might be too selfish, too debilitating. Even when everything was against me. *I could not let it go.* And I think that is what transforms people into what they really want to be. A heart clinging to a desire so hard it cannot beat independently.

So here we are, me and my heart, having done our work. Our book is out in the world. And even if it fails miserably, we will be okay. Because to have gotten here, to have been swallowed whole by this ocean and paddled long enough to find treasure, is enough. That makes the risk worth it. The struggle worth it. The sacrifice worth it.

I hope you too, lovely reader, have something worth that much. If you don't, keep looking. But not outward. Look deep within. If there is something in your heart that looks crazy or seems unreasonable, lean in. It might turn out to be the sanest thing you've ever done. It might be your happily ever after.

Thank you for being a part of mine.

Audrey

ABOUT THE AUTHOR

My Totally Elfed Christmas is Audrey Furnas's debut novel. She writes New Adult romance because she thinks romance is the best part of life, well, that and singing in the shower. When she isn't busy dreaming up more college romances, she loves to take long walks with her family or get sucked into a good tv show or book series. She lives in Apex, NC with her husband and their two young kids. She and her husband work together to independently publish her books, and they have lots more to come.

Connect with Audrey!

ACKNOWLEDGMENTS

I have to start by giving a huge thanks to my husband. My complement. The guy who fills in all my gaps. He embraced my passion and helped me give it life. He is my first reader and my sounding board. He read the story *three different times*. The one thing he complained about during this grueling writing and publishing process wasn't the dirty dishes or the extra parenting duties or my lack of showering but the fact that he missed hanging out with me when I was working. He went on a rollercoaster ride with me, and we managed to hold on long enough to see this project through. This book would be in a much different state if not for his help. Thank you, Jay, for believing in me. Thank you for listening to me drone on and on about writing. Thank you for making me lots of smoothies. And thank you for doing all the extra household tasks. You are my favorite person to ride rollercoasters with, even when you get sick.

I would like to thank my children for sharing me with my characters and for keeping me stocked up with lots of hugs and office wall decorations. Life would be nothing without you two.

A huge thank you to my beta readers Nancy, Christy, Sara, Karli, Tori, Courtney, Channah, and Sharon. Thank you for telling me when I was being out of touch or boring or far-fetched. Thank you for rooting for Miller and Adia. Thank you for rooting for me.

For my first experience with a copyeditor, I feel very lucky. Caroline Knecht, you put the wind in my sails. I am so proud of the final product, and it is thanks to your keen eye, enthusiasm for my characters, and mad grammar skills. Thanks a ton for your hard work.

Thank you, Sarah Hansen, for a killer cover. Your talent astounds me, and I am honored to have your work be the face of my story.

I thanked my mom in the dedication (to reiterate, you are wonderful and the best cheerleader a carbon copy of you could ever have). I am also lucky enough to have two dads to thank for their enthusiasm and encouragement. Thanks, Pop, for making me a killer website, for cheering me on, and for reading all my stuff, even the awkward parts. Thanks, Dad, for sending me the link for that discounted online writing class all those years ago. That lit the fire. So basically, I blame you for all of this madness.

To my Instagram community, where would I be without you guys? You make me feel understood and supported, and I love being a part of this little corner of the internet. Thank you for keeping this dream-chasing fun and for having my back. And, if you made it this far with me on my author journey, you will just have to deal with me loving you forever.

As I write these last lines of my first completed book, I want to say to you, lovely reader, that you have made my day—my life—by making it through all these words. Thank you for being here to let my story serve its purpose. This may be more emotional for me than anything I could ever put on a page. I am so grateful.

Made in the USA
Monee, IL
07 October 2020